M.D. LAKE'S
PEGGY O'NEILL

"GREAT FUN"
Publishers Weekly

"AN INTELLIGENT FEMALE SLEUTH
WHO GETS RESULTS . . .
A WELCOME ADDITION TO THE GROWING
CORPS OF FEMALE MYSTERY SOLVERS."
Macon Telegraph and News

"PEGGY IS THE MOST LIKABLE CHARACTER
I'VE MET IN A LONG TIME."
Joan Hess, author of the *Maggody* series

"STARTLING, CHALLENGING, MEMORABLE"
Drood Review of Mystery

"A REAL TREAT"
Minneapolis Star-Tribune

"A WINNER!"
Armchair Detective

Flirting with Death

M. D. LAKE

AVON BOOKS  NEW YORK

VISIT OUR WEBSITE AT
http://AvonBooks.com

FLIRTING WITH DEATH is an original publication of Avon Books. This work has never before appeared in book form. This work is a novel. Any similarity to actual persons or events is purely coincidental.

AVON BOOKS
A division of
The Hearst Corporation
1350 Avenue of the Americas
New York, New York 10019

Copyright © 1996 by Allen Simpson
Published by arrangement with the author
Library of Congress Catalog Card Number: 96-96022
ISBN: 0-380-77522-0

First Avon Books Printing: August 1996

AVON TRADEMARK REG. U.S. PAT. OFF. AND IN OTHER COUNTRIES, MARCA REGISTRADA, HECHO EN U.S.A.

Printed in the U.S.A.

RA 10 9 8 7 6 5 4 3 2 1

For Max and Roger Linehan
and the memory of Hawkeye

Acknowledgments

My thanks to Dr. Ralph Weichselbaum, D. V. M.—
justly adored by his patients—and to Polonia Novack
Schroth, for taking the time to answer my questions
about veterinary medicine and the *good* things that
take place in veterinary hospitals.

One

I had time to kill. I was sitting on a bench on the shore of the small lake below the University's veterinary hospital, my hands in the pockets of my windbreaker, my legs stretched out in front of me, my mind idling in neutral, the warmth of the March afternoon sun on my face. Ducks paddled aimlessly in the still-icy water. They seemed to be killing time too.

A man came strolling along the path from my left, tearing pieces of bread from a loaf and tossing them to the ducks. The sun glittered in his long blond hair and beard. I watched him approach out of the corner of one eye, hoping he wouldn't stop to talk. Nobody else was on the shore; it was just us and the ducks.

As he reached my bench, I pulled in my legs so he could pass by, but he paused instead and smiled down at me. I smiled back, my minimum-polite smile, no teeth, the one that says I'm a friendly person but you've caught me at a busy moment, please go away. I also took the opportunity to size him up quickly before turning my attention back to the lake.

He was about five-ten, lean, and young but not student-young: he looked as though he'd lived too much to be a student. His beard needed trimming, and he wore his hair in a ponytail held by a leather thong. He was also wearing sunglasses, the reflecting kind. People who want to conceal their eyes make me nervous.

"The sunlight's beautiful in your hair," he said. "Or maybe it's your hair that's beautiful in the sunlight."

I gave the line the thin smile it was worth and went on looking at the lake. Something told me he wouldn't have said that to me if I'd been a man with beautiful hair, or an old woman, but I didn't know that for a fact, so I was willing to give him the benefit of the doubt.

"You mind if I sit down?"

It was a public bench. I moved over.

"Thanks. You want to talk?"

"I'd rather just sit here, lapping up the sun."

"Oh. Okay, sorry."

One of the male ducks was fussing at a female, flapping his wings and generally making a pest of himself. The female moved away, the male rushed after her. I wondered why she didn't fly across the lake to get away from him. Maybe she was making a minimum of fuss, hoping he'd go away.

The man laughed suddenly. "It's not just humans who commit rape, you know that? I read somewhere that ducks do it too, except it's not called 'rape,' it's called 'forced copulation.' It's supposed to serve some purpose, but I forget what it is. Just that it's natural."

I glanced around, couldn't see anybody else on the path. I gave him another quick glance to see if I'd missed anything important the first time and reconfirmed my initial impression that I could deal with it in the event he decided we were ducks. I don't like strange men discussing rape with me; it puts me on edge.

"I wasn't arguing in favor of rape," he said, his

voice rising a little, as though my silence was getting on his nerves. "I hope you don't think I was."

"No," I assured him, fighting to keep the annoyance out of my voice, "I don't."

"I mean," he went on, "just because it's natural doesn't mean it's good. For example, the praying mantis doesn't even wait until copulation's over before she starts eating her mate. That's supposed to serve some natural purpose too."

Gives her extra protein, I thought, and shuts him up when she just wants to be alone with her thoughts.

"You got a pet up there for treatment?" he asked, gesturing behind us at the hospital on the hill.

I wondered what made him think that but figured he must have seen me coming out of the hospital or down the steps from it to the lake. "No, a friend's," I answered.

"Dog or cat?"

"Dog."

"I guess it's the best small animal clinic in the country," he went on, stretching his legs out in front of him the way mine had been before he arrived. His jeans were well worn and dirty, his work boots scuffed and run-down in the heel. The windbreaker looked as though he'd been sleeping in it and seemed too light for the weather. "Is Doctor J your friend's vet?"

"Who?"

"Doctor J. You know—Doctor Atwood, the television vet."

"Oh. No."

"She's the best—or was, at least. I suppose she's too busy doing research and all that to take care of individual animals anymore. She's working for the good of all animals now, no longer has time for one," he intoned with mock solemnity. "That's kind of funny, don't you think?" He cocked his head and smiled at me, a strangely vulnerable smile—or it may have been a trick of the afternoon light.

I returned the smile in spite of myself. I'm a sucker for a vulnerable smile.

"Of course," he went on, "working for the betterment of all animals through science probably pays a lot more than treating individual dogs and cats. And the working conditions are better too. You don't have weeping pet owners begging you, 'Please, doctor—save my kitty!'" He clasped his hands together beseechingly. I noticed that his fingernails were chewed to the quick and his hands were dirty.

I twitched a small smile, suspecting that if I did anything less he'd get mad and anything more and I'd have a friend for life I didn't want. I wondered if he was drunk or on drugs.

He got up suddenly and looked down at me—his glasses did, at least. I tensed my legs, ready to jump up if I needed to. Just then a young man and woman came strolling along the lake, holding hands and laughing and talking. He glanced over at them, and I took the opportunity to slide off the bench and stand up too.

He turned his attention back to me. I told him I had to get back to the hospital, gave him a smile, and headed for the steps, getting there just after the young couple started to climb them.

"Nice talkin' to you," he called after me from the path. "Sorry you have to run. I can't get over how beautiful your hair looks in this light, you know that?"

The woman glanced over her shoulder, first at me, then at him, then back at me. I rolled my eyes and she gave me a smile of commiseration.

A day in the life.

*   *   *

My friend Lillian Przynski, with Rufus in his carrier at her feet, was waiting for me when I got to the Small Animal Clinic, which was on the veterinary hospital's second floor. She'd noticed a lump in Rufus's mouth a few days earlier and made an appointment at the clinic for that afternoon at four-thirty. I'd driven them to the hospital because Lillian, who's bent nearly double with osteoporosis, doesn't drive anymore.

I stooped and peered into the carrier at Rufus and asked him how he was doing. The aged beast lifted his head from his forepaws and bathed me in bad breath, one of his specialties.

"Jim took blood and is going to do some tests," Lillian said. "He'll call me tomorrow when he knows what the problem is."

Jim Gates had been Lillian's vet for years, until he'd decided to return to the U's School of Veterinary Medicine and get a doctorate in radiology. Now he worked part time in the Small Animal Clinic to support himself while completing his studies.

I wanted to speak the meaningless, comforting clichés to assure Lillian that Rufus would be fine, but I couldn't because I didn't know anything about it. Instead, I told her I'd keep my fingers crossed, picked up the carrier, and took Rufus out to my car.

Two

I'm a campus cop and—no pun intended—I take the dog watch whenever I can, which goes from eleven P.M. to seven A.M. I like working at night because there are rarely any administrators around, and fewer people in general making unreasonable demands. If the weather's nice, I bike home when my patrol's over at seven, arriving after other people have just left for work. If the weather's bad, I drive.

I sleep until about two in the afternoon and then I'm ready to start the day: run errands, clean house when absolutely necessary, walk or ride my bike, read. I also play racquetball a couple of times a week with friends at the U, and ski, skate, and work in my garden in season. I spend my evenings alone or with friends or with my lover, Gary Mallory, who's a feature writer for the local paper. Gary lived with me for a while, but he moved out when I could no longer stand having him underfoot. Now he lives with Lillian and Rufus, helping Lillian take care of her old house, which is much too big for her. She mothers him, does his laundry, irons his clothes. He cooks and fixes things that break. He's good at that.

As soon as I'd got up the next afternoon and made coffee, I called Lillian to find out what Rufus's tests had shown. She said Doctor Gates had diagnosed the problem as something with a long Latin name that translated as a benign tumor with a fairly high cure rate.

"He won't need an operation, thank goodness," she said, "but he's going to need radiation treatments five times a week for three weeks. I asked Jim if that means three painful weeks for Rufus followed by a short, miserable life. He said he didn't think so. He said Rufus is healthy for his age and there's no reason on earth why he shouldn't be his old self again if he gets through the radiation all right. Jim wouldn't say that if he didn't believe it, Peggy, so I said, let's go for it!"

"That's great, Lil," I said.

"Yes, it is. And Jim has agreed to treat Rufus free if we come after hours—isn't that sweet? Can you imagine how much radiation treatment costs?"

It was sweet, since Lillian is as poor as a church mouse. "And maybe he can do something about Rufus's breath too," I said.

"Oh, I don't think so, Peggy—Jim's not a miracle worker. My neighbor, Buzz Colby, has offered to drive me, but he can't this afternoon, so I wonder if I could prevail upon you again . . ."

I said I'd be glad to, which explains how I happened to be sitting on the same bench on the lake below the veterinary hospital that afternoon, watching the same ducks or some of their kin, when lightning struck again. This time he came straight to me, his hands in his pockets, the sun sparkling on his blond hair and beard.

"Well," he said, "here we are again."

I barely cracked a smile, just nodded and turned back to the lake, ready to spring up quickly if necessary.

"Your friend up at the clinic with her dog again today?"

"Yes," I said, pleasantly but firmly, "and I'd like to just sit here and stare out at the lake and not have to talk to anybody."

"The reason I was so nervous yesterday," he said, ignoring my words or perhaps not even hearing them, "is that I was working up to ask you if you'd have coffee with me or something. At that little espresso place over on Singleton—it's only a few minutes from here. Not now, of course," he added quickly, seeing the expression on my face, "on account of your friend'll be waiting for you. But tonight? It's always packed with students, so you'd be safe. I mean, it wouldn't be just the two of us there; we'd be in a crowd."

"No," I said.

"Is it the way I look or something?" he asked. He looked down at himself. He was wearing the same clothes he'd had on the day before. They looked a little worse today, as though he'd slept in them. "Some places I been, this'd be fancy dress."

I smiled, since what he'd said was mildly funny and I hoped it was meant that way, but I didn't answer his question.

"Okay," he said, "it was just a thought. I wasn't hitting on you or anything like that, but see, I'm an author. I'm writing a novel and I've got a female character in it who's driving me nuts. I just can't seem to breathe life into her, you know what I mean? You're not an author yourself by any chance, are you?"

"No."

"No." He laughed. "Of course not. I spend so much time around authors and wannabe authors, I think everybody's one. But you'd be doing me a real favor if you'd just let me ask you a few questions. Just a few," he went on quickly, so he couldn't hear my no, "and then I'll leave you alone forever." He raised his right hand and said, "I promise."

I looked at him, but there wasn't really much to see on account of the sunglasses and the beard.

All my instincts and experience told me to say no again. But I really wasn't busy, was I? I was just killing time. And a woman sitting alone doing nothing isn't much prized in our world except by male artists. If I told him no and he went away, I'd feel guilty and mad—at him, at myself—and he'd be there anyway, inside of me instead of on the path in front of me, for a while at least. And if I told him no and he got angry, he'd ruin the moment for me anyway.

Besides, I rationalized furiously, what harm would it do? He's probably down on his luck, homeless. "All right," I said. "But I only have a few minutes. What kind of novel are you writing?"

"Hey, I'm askin' the questions, right? Besides, I haven't quite made up my mind yet. Maybe a kind of Kerouac thing, you know? Sort of like *On the Road* for the nineties. Or maybe a mystery. I dunno."

I'd read *On the Road*—my brother left it behind when he disappeared—and hated it.

He smiled, reached into a pocket, and pulled out something metallic that glittered in the sunlight: a small tape recorder. He nudged a switch with his thumb, pointed the recorder at me, and asked, "What's your name?"

"Peggy." If I'd known he was going to record my answers, I might have had the guts to say no. This was something like posing for pictures for a stranger.

"Do you have a last name?" he asked.

"Next question?"

His laugh had a slight edge to it. "My name's Jason," he said, "and my last name's a secret too. What do you do for a living?"

"I'm a campus cop."

"Oh." He sounded momentarily taken aback but recovered quickly. "Really? I'll have to think about

making this woman in my novel a campus cop—
that's if I make it a mystery. If I do, maybe I could
talk to you sometime about what you do. I'll bet you
have some stories to tell!"

He waited for me to say something to that, but I
gave him my minimalist smile, the one that feels like
a paper cut and probably looks like one too. "If I
decide to make use of you," he went on, "I suppose
I can always call the campus police department and
ask for Peggy." It wasn't a question.

Make use of me! "You're running out of time," I
said.

"Okay, okay! The trouble with being a guy and
trying to create a woman character is that guys don't
know all the words for women's things," he said.
"For example, how would you describe the color of
your hair?"

"Red," I said, delving into the arcane vocabulary
of women's mysteries.

He frowned. "What shade of red is it?"

"It depends on the light," I replied, "and on
who's looking. It's mostly men who try to define it."

He stared at me as if weighing the possibility that
I was putting him down. The low afternoon sun
glinted on the reflective lenses of his glasses. I
would have thought an author would appreciate "It
depends on the light, and on who's looking," if not
the rest of it.

He nodded finally and brought the recorder up to
his face again. "Your eyes are green," he went on.
"And you've got a kind of pointy nose. Your skin's
sort of white, isn't it? Could I call it milky, with a
light scattering of freckles?"

"That's fine with me," I said, my milky skin now
starting to prickle. I'd made a mistake agreeing to
this, but I wondered how I could have got out of it
without creating a scene. I knew now that very soon

I was going to create one anyway. I decided to make it sooner, get it over with.

"I have to go now," I said, glancing at my watch and getting up. "It's about time to pick up my friend and her dog." I turned and started toward the steps that led up to the hospital.

"Okay," he said, getting up too and coming after me. "I'll follow you up and ask a few more questions, if that's okay."

I didn't say anything, just muttered something to myself—speaking in tongues.

"I'm sorry," he said, hurrying to catch up. "You said that too softly even for my tape recorder, which is pretty sensitive. What'd you say?"

"Nothing."

"Are you married?"

I shrugged the question off.

He was right behind me on the steps. "You're not wearing a wedding band, so I'll take that shrug as a no. But I suppose you've got a boyfriend?"

"Yes."

"Living together?"

I stopped, turned, and looked down at him. "You're getting obnoxious," I said, trying to keep the disgust out of my voice, at myself mostly for having agreed to answer the creep's questions when I hadn't wanted to and in that way creating a situation I might not be able to control in a peaceful way. "You don't need personal information about me to write a novel." Not that I believed he was writing a novel, but I decided to keep up the pretense in the hope it would cause less fuss. "You can make up your characters' lives."

"Okay, okay," he said. "Sorry!" I saw the white anger spots blossom on his cheeks as I turned and started back up the steps.

"This isn't a personal question," he went on

behind me. "It really isn't: what do women in your age group—not *you*, just women you know—think of the various forms of contraception? Condoms, the pill, the diaphragm, the female condom for example. Not from personal experience or anything, Peggy, but could you rank them on a scale . . ."

I climbed faster, wondering why I hadn't noticed before how many steps there were or how the still-leafless shrubbery on both sides seemed to overgrow them and reach out and try to snag me.

"Hey, you don't have to run!" he called after me. He wasn't even panting, although it was a steep climb, which meant he must have been in pretty good shape. "I told you, that wasn't a personal question. The woman in my novel—her name's Peggy too, isn't that odd?—is young, modern, and sexually active, so I need information like that. How else can I get it if I don't ask somebody like you, since I don't know any sexually active women right now?"

When I still didn't say anything, just kept my head down and kept climbing, he shouted, "All right, if that's how you're going to be, let me ask you this: do redheads have freckles all over their bodies? I haven't made love to a redheaded woman—not yet, anyway—so I don't know. It's a research question, okay?"

Now I was at the top of the steps, the hospital about a hundred feet in front of me, separated from me by a lawn. I turned and stared back at him and, my voice trembling, said, "Stay where you are or I'll kick you back down the steps. I mean it."

He froze, one foot on the top step, his face turned up to me, apparently trying to decide if I really did mean it.

"Hey, police brutality," he said, throwing the hand with the tape recorder up in front of his face as if to protect it from my attack and then peering at me around it, trying to look vulnerable and appealing. "It's just that I've never seen a redheaded woman with her clothes off," he went on, "and I'd hate to get it wrong. You know how picky some readers are about the details."

"I'm going to walk from here to the hospital," I said, struggling to keep my voice steady. "I don't want you to come after me. If you do, I'll arrest you for disorderly conduct—for engaging in offensive, obscene, and abusive behavior," I added, reciting from the law. "Stay here until I'm in the building. Do you understand?"

"Arrest me?" he exclaimed. "What is it with women today? Not every guy's a sex fiend, you know! Don't you think you're denying yourself some interesting experiences by being so paranoid about everything? You looked so—so *pretty* yesterday, sitting there by the lake with the sunlight in your hair. I wanted to get to know you a little—and not just for my novel. I *liked* you! And you're going to arrest me for that?"

I wanted to grab him and shake him like a rag, throw him down the steps, and watch him tumble into the lake like a character in a cartoon. Sitting there by the lake, minding my own business, he'd made me the caretaker of his needs and his mood, a fate I had no right to want to escape since, after all, he *liked* me!

For a moment, I considered arresting him or at least making him show me some identification. I'd recently finished a refresher course in defensive tactics, and over the years I've been a cop, I've learned ways to restrain men and women of all sizes, so I probably could have handled him. I could have done it, even though I wasn't in uniform or on duty, because he'd crossed the line into the area of disorderly conduct—hadn't he? Or was I just being too sensitive?

But what would I do then? Then I'd have to get him up to the veterinary hospital somehow and call the campus police station and request a squad car to come and get him. And then I—and Lillian and Rufus, her groggy, just-radiated poodle—and Jason would have to wait there until one of my colleagues arrived in a squad car. And then I'd have to go along to the station and write up the complaint.

I decided it wasn't worth the trouble. I wasn't a cop at that moment; I was just a woman going about her business.

I told him again to stay where he was until I was in the hospital.

He started to climb the last step, but something he saw on my face must have made him change his mind. He glared at me instead and whispered, "Yes, *ma'am.* Yes, Officer Peggy, *ma'am.*"

I turned and crossed the lawn to the hospital, looking back twice to make sure he wasn't coming after me. When I got to the entrance, I glanced back one last time. As I did, he raised a hand and waved, the little tape recorder glittering in the sunlight in front of his face.

"It's not 'Good-bye,' Peggy," he shouted. "It's 'So long for now.'"

Three

Since it was after five when I got up to the Small Animal Clinic, the waiting room was deserted. I pushed through the door that led back into the hospital and walked down to the radiation therapy waiting room where Doctor Gates had taken Lillian and Rufus.

They were all three in there when I arrived. I stooped down and peered into the carrier, and Rufus, still groggy, opened one eye and looked at me and then closed it again. Not a happy poodle.

I stood up and asked how the treatment had gone.

"Very well," Gates replied. "Rufus is a model patient. As I told Lillian, his chances of recovery are excellent, but it'll be a while before we know for sure." Jim Gates was a man of about forty, well over six feet tall and skinny, with curly dark hair, close-set eyes behind wire-rimmed glasses, and a ready smile. He looked like a basketball player.

"What's the matter, Peggy?" Lillian asked me, peering up at me closely. "When you came marching down the hall, you looked like you wanted to murder somebody."

"I did," I told her. "Want to, I mean." I asked Gates if he'd heard any complaints recently about a man harassing women around the lake or hospital.

"Somebody harassed you, Peggy?" Lillian asked.

I described what had happened.

"You should've shot the nasty little SOB," she flared angrily, and then put a hand up to her mouth, appalled either at her violent thought or profanity. "Or given his beard a good yank," she added, because she's basically a gentle woman. She explained to Gates that I was a campus cop. Lillian's very proud of me.

"I haven't heard anything like that recently," Gates said, "although women do get accosted around here occasionally, of course. The lake attracts all kinds of weirdos who've been holed up all winter, so I suppose they're starting to come out now that the weather's getting nicer."

I asked him if there was anybody around I could ask about it. Now that I'd decided not to take any action against the man, and it was too late to do anything anyway, I was having second thoughts. I wanted to know if any other women had encountered him.

"Most of the clerical staff have gone home for the night," he said, "but there are always people working late in the Atwood Lab. It's just down that hall. I'll take you, if you want."

I asked Lillian if she minded waiting a few minutes, and she said of course not. She settled herself into a chair with Rufus at her feet and picked up a magazine on pet care and began reading.

Gates led me through double doors that had ATWOOD LABORATORY: AUTHORIZED PERSONNEL ONLY stencilled on them in black paint. "It's named after Julia Atwood, of course," he told me. He took for granted that I knew who Doctor Atwood was, just as the man I'd encountered on the lake had: "the television vet."

I did know who she was, of course, even though I'm not an animal person. Years ago, Doctor Atwood had had her own program on pet care on public television, and she still made news occasionally, although I couldn't tell you for what, exactly.

"If anybody's been accosted by this fellow in the hospital," Gates said, "the lab's secretary, Lorraine Cullin, will know about it. Nothing goes on around here that she doesn't know about."

Scary, I thought.

The secretary's office was the first door on the right off the lab's corridor. It was a large room with several desks, only one of which, in a glassed-in area at the back, was occupied.

"That's Lorraine," Gates said. "That's Professor Pyles with her."

The secretary was sitting with her hands in her lap and staring up at a plump man perched on one corner of her desk, one leg crossed over the other, the tassles of his brown loafers flipping up and down with each waggle of his foot. It wasn't a pleasant sight.

"I'll try, Millard," she was saying with exaggerated patience as we approached. "That's all I can do. But if you and Charlie had got me the data I requested earlier—"

"I know, Lorraine, I know," he interrupted her, "and I'm sorry. But what could I do? You know as well as I do that Julia has no time to collect data—she's much too busy and important for that!" he added sarcastically. Catching sight of us, he said, "Yes, what is it?"

"Excuse me, Professor Pyles," Jim Gates said, "I didn't mean to interrupt."

"That's all right," the man said, sliding off the desk, "Lorraine and I were finished anyway." He gave me a curious look, then dropped his eyes to my feet and ran them quickly back up to my face professionally. I would have done the same thing to him except that I already had.

He was about fifty, a couple of inches shorter than I but a lot heavier, and he looked pretty much the way you'd expect a man named Millard Pyles would: expensively cut brown hair with a metallic sheen to it that isn't found in nature, button eyes in a perfectly round face, and a thin mouth he unsuccessfully tried to hide with a thick mustache.

When Gates had introduced me to them, I described my encounter with the bearded man down by the lake. "He said his name was Jason," I added, suddenly feeling foolish and self-conscious and wishing I'd forgotten the whole thing.

"Over the years," Pyles said, "we've had complaints from women about men harassing them, but this is the first case I've heard about this year. I've never heard of a bearded man with a tape recorder, though. Have you, Lorraine?"

"No," she said sourly. "But it's just luck that none of us who have to work in the building late because the faculty doesn't meet its deadlines have been raped or murdered yet. The hospital's a maze, and anybody can get in who wants to, since nobody takes even the most elementary precautions to keep strangers out at night. On more than one occasion when I've been working late, I've felt eyes on me, looked up, and found strange men standing in the doorway, staring at me."

"I'll bet you turned them to stone with one of your patented basilisk glares, Lorraine," Pyles said, winking at me.

She apparently didn't find that funny. She fixed him with what I supposed was one of her patented basilisk glares, which elicited from him a high-pitched nervous laugh.

Lorraine Cullin didn't look much like a basilisk. She was a small woman who could have been anywhere from fifty to seventy, with papery skin and gray hair pulled back in a bun. The only thing striking about her were her glasses—the frames glittered with sequins, the temples were curved— that only emphasized the plainness of her face.

Pyles, now with his fat rear end perched on a side table stacked with computer printouts, chuckled and said, "I remember in high school, some of the guys used to pretend they were journalists and they'd go around interviewing the good-looking girls about their love lives—silly stuff like that." He grinned and shook his head, as though wondering where the time had flown.

"You say you're a campus cop," Lorraine said to me, breaking into Pyles's reverie. "Why didn't you arrest the man if he's worrying you so much now?"

"He didn't do anything I thought was quite bad enough," I replied. "And I had to get back here to pick up my friend and her dog," I added, feeling suddenly defensive.

"But you're worried about it now?" Millard Pyles pointed out.

I shrugged and started to say something when a young woman in a lab coat came into the office. She walked over to us and handed Lorraine a folder. "Doctor Charlie asked me to give you this, Lorraine," she said. "It's for the grant proposal."

"I wanted it yesterday," Lorraine snapped as she took it.

Professor Pyles said, "Thank you, Dana," as if to make up for Lorraine's rudeness.

The woman didn't look particularly fazed by Lorraine's tone of voice. She nodded to Pyles, smiled at Jim Gates, and gave me a curious glance as she started to leave the room. Her eyes were a striking green behind no-nonsense glasses.

"Oh, Dana," Pyles called after her, "just a moment."

The woman turned and gave him a questioning look. She was in her late twenties, with short reddish-brown hair, and about my height—I'm five-nine—but heavier.

He nodded to me. I described my encounter with Jason again. When I'd finished, she shook her head and said, "No, I've never met a jerk like that. But I'll ask around and keep an eye out for him. What should I do if he's bothered other women in the lab?"

"Have them lodge a complaint with the campus police," I said, "so we'll at least have a record of what he's doing."

"Okay," she said. She gave me a smile and left the room.

"If I'd been you," Lorraine said, "I would have arrested him on the spot."

"At the very least," Pyles stuck in, "you should have got his full name, don't you think? Made him show some identification."

"I hope you plan to report this to your superiors," Lorraine said.

Feeling a little battered, I told them I intended to mention it that night at roll call, in case anybody had reported Jason that day. I knew that nobody could have complained about him up until I'd gone off duty that morning or I would have heard about it.

"I suppose I'll have to be more careful than usual tonight when I leave the building," Lorraine said with a noisy sigh. She gave Pyles a frosty look through her sequined glasses.

He rolled his eyes. "I'm sure you're careful every night, Lorraine," he assured her. "It's a dangerous world out there—especially when cops are too busy looking after their friends' dogs to arrest potential rapists.''

I started to say something to that but bit my tongue.

As I followed Jim Gates back to the radiation waiting room, he said softly, "Pyles's a nasty character at the best of times, and these aren't the best of times, I guess, for the Atwood Lab.''

"Why?''

"Investigators from the National Science Foundation in Washington are coming in tomorrow. They're going to look over the facilities and talk to the faculty, to see if they want to continue pumping taxpayer dollars into the lab. So everybody's burning the midnight oil putting together a report to show they're still on the cutting edge in veterinary medical research. Lorraine, I suspect, has to do most of the work.''

I nodded. Because some of the people I play racquetball with are secretaries, I know that a faculty member's place in the pecking order is determined by how late he or she can be in meeting deadlines, thus forcing the secretaries to miss lunch or work late or both.

"What's Pyles do for a living?" I asked. "I noticed you called him 'professor,' not 'doctor.'"

"He's the lab's director—a kind of office manager. There's a rumor going around that he never even went to college, but he needs a title to impress people, so Doctor Atwood had him made a professor.''

I said I supposed there were still people out there who were impressed with that title.

Neither Lillian nor I spoke much on the way home, since it would be a while before she'd know if the radiation treatment she was subjecting Rufus to would work. He was curled up in the bottom of his carrier in the backseat of the car, asleep and snoring quietly, unaware of the fuss he was causing because somebody loved him.

Four

My beat that night was the Old Campus. It's my favorite part of the University. The buildings are mostly ivy-covered and reflect a gentler world than the one we live in now. Of course, that world was laying the groundwork for this one—but the people who lived here then probably didn't realize it. The streetlights are a bit brighter now, but there are still a lot of large oak trees and shrubbery and shadow. It's possible that, someday, the trees and shrubbery will all be cleared away and the lighting increased for safety reasons. I don't want to be here then.

Walking around in the night has never bothered me because I wear a pistol I know how to use. I also have a portable radio on my belt that keeps up a constant tinny chatter from the dispatcher and other cops. Maybe all women should carry guns and portable radios.

None of those things replaces judgment when you see a figure coming toward you in the night, though. There's no curfew on a university campus, and you meet all kinds of people out and about at all hours. You can't walk around with your pistol in your hand, and pride doesn't allow you to give someone coming toward you a wide berth. Instead, you smile and say "Good evening," sometimes feel the hair rise on your neck as he passes, and you strain your ears to hear his footsteps fading away, and you wonder why only strong men can walk

around alone in the night unarmed and uncon-
cerned.

It was raining very lightly, just a fine mist.
Around one, as I was walking up the Mall from the
old Student Union, a man came around the corner
of the bell tower and started toward me. He was
walking slowly and with his head down and wearing a poncho with a hood.

"Good evening," I said before he reached me,
because I wasn't sure he'd seen me and didn't want
to startle him as we passed. Professors lose themselves sometimes in their own minds.

He raised his head slowly and turned his reflective glasses on me, silvery black now in the night. It
took me a moment to be sure, on account of the
hood and the darkness, but it was the man who'd
harassed me on the lake that afternoon. Jason, he'd
called himself. He kept walking.

"Stop," I said.

He stopped and looked over his shoulder. "Yes,
what is it?" he asked, sounding puzzled.

I went back to him. "You're stalking me, aren't
you?" I said. "Why?"

He shook his head. "What're you talking about,
Officer? We're just two people passing in the night.
Besides, I wasn't following you, I was coming
towards you! How does that add up to 'stalking'?"

"What're you doing on campus this late?"

He laughed. "What any diligent student would be
doing," he said. "Going home after a couple of
beers at Harold's. Cutting through campus. I live
over there." He nodded to the west side of the
campus. "It's not against the law, is it? I'm over
eighteen and there's no curfew that I know of."

The fact that he'd been walking toward me meant
nothing—he could have been following me since I
left the police station, then run around one of the

buildings that lined the Mall to approach me from the front.

"Could I see some identification?" I said.

"Why? I haven't done anything wrong. You ask everybody you meet for ID?"

"How about showing me some," I said, keeping my voice level, "as a sign of good faith?"

"Good faith?" His laugh had an edge of bitterness. "That's funny, coming from you, Peggy — Officer, I mean. What if I say no?"

"I'll take you in," I said.

"For what?"

"Your disorderly conduct this afternoon."

"It's a little late for that, ain't it?"

"We'll let a judge decide."

He stood there, stray light from somewhere glittering in his glasses, his teeth bared in a smile behind his thin blond beard.

Then his shoulders slumped. "Oh, all right," he said. "Why not?"

He reached under his poncho, groped in his back pocket. I tensed, wondering what he'd come out with. His forehead wrinkled in concern. "I must've left my wallet in my other—wait!" His face seemed to light up. "Hold on a sec before you start clubbing me. Here it is."

He sighed noisily as he opened his wallet, pulled out a student ID, and handed it to me. "This damned poncho leaks, but take your time. I don't mind being cold and wet."

I compared the picture on the ID with him. It showed a man without a beard and shorter hair, but it could have been Jason. Brown hair. Twenty-six years old.

"This says your name's Robert Hill. You told me it was Jason."

He shrugged, looked rueful. "What can I say? You

wouldn't give me your last name this afternoon, why should I give you my first? No law says I have to tell everybody I stop to chat with my real name, is there? Besides, I'm thinking of using a pen name as a writer. 'Jason Hill' sounds better than just plain Bob, don't you think? By the way, I'm sorry I teased you the way I did this afternoon. I guess I really did cross the line."

I couldn't tell if he was being sincere or not and didn't really care. "Do you mind taking off your glasses?"

He sighed noisily as he did as I asked. "Next, I suppose it'll be a strip search. I hope."

His eyes were brown too, matching the ID.

I pressed the button on my portable radio and called the dispatcher and read him the name and student ID number. He called back a moment later and said it hadn't been reported stolen. I asked him if anybody had called and asked for me earlier. Nobody had, he said, at least not on his watch.

I told him thanks, then handed Jason—Bob— his ID.

"I don't believe our meeting like this was an accident," I said. "What do you want?"

"Nothing!" He shrugged again, helplessly. "I told you—I was just crossing campus. I live over on the other side of the river, behind the New Campus. Bumping into you like this was a pure accident. And I'm getting wet and cold."

"If there's another 'pure accident' like this," I said, "I'm going to arrest you. Do you understand?"

I thought I saw anger on his face. "Yes, I do," he said. "May I go now?"

When I nodded, he looked me up and down quickly, then turned and strolled off down the Mall. I stood and watched him.

Some distance away, he looked back over his

shoulder and called after me, "You're sure you wouldn't like to meet me for coffee somewhere, Peggy? I think you'd like me, once you got to know me. We just got off on the wrong foot, that's all."

"No."

He made an elaborate shrugging gesture with his shoulders and hands, like a clown. "You're too cautious," he said, "too afraid of adventure. That can't be good in a cop—especially one who walks around all alone late at night." He stared at me a moment longer. Then he turned away and continued on his way toward the bridge that leads over to the New Campus, and I continued my patrol.

Fortunately, I thought, I had the next three nights off—we work a six-on, three-off schedule—so Jason, or Bob, would have three days to put me behind him and move on to something that wouldn't involve bothering me or, I very much hoped, other women.

Five

I usually try to stay up most of the day at the start of my three days off so I can get into the rhythms of "normal" people—if people with day jobs can be called normal. There's no point in being awake all night if you're not working and all your friends are asleep.

That morning, after showering, eating breakfast, and reading a while, I took a two-hour nap, then went back to the U to play racquetball with a friend on her lunch break. When I got home again, there was a message on my answering machine asking me to call Pam, the midwatch dispatcher. I'd planned to call her anyway to find out if Jason—Robert Hill, that is—had called the evening before to ask for me. That would have been the only way he could have known I'd been on the dog watch.

"You remember the guy you had Ron check the student ID on last night?" she asked as soon as I'd told her who I was.

Could I ever forget him? "It was stolen, right?" I said.

"Yeah. The guy—Robert Hill—reported it a couple hours ago. Whoever stole it didn't take anything else out of his wallet, just the ID, which is why he didn't notice it missing until he went to the library to check out a book."

"Who is he?"

"A grad student in social work—married, two kids."

Jason had gone to a lot of trouble for me last night, I thought. Even to the point of planning his escape by stealing the ID of somebody with his general characteristics.

I asked Pam if somebody had called asking for me last night on her watch. "Yeah. Said his name was Jason. Newman, I think, or Neeman—something like that. Said he'd tried to get you at home but you didn't answer. I said you wouldn't be in until ten-thirty or so, and he said he'd try then."

"Did he ask for me by name—Peggy O'Neill?"

"Just Peggy. He asked how you spelled your last name. I told him. Why?"

When I told her why, she apologized for not realizing he was pumping her for my name and schedule, but I assured her it was okay. Jason had conned me too, and more than once.

I asked to talk to the duty officer that afternoon and told him the story. There wasn't much he could say and nothing he could do except pass the word to the other cops to be on the lookout for the guy with the ponytail and beard with Robert Hill's student ID, who might really be a creep named Jason.

I spent the evening with my friend Ginny Raines, watching an old movie on my VCR. Ginny's a detective, short, dark and plump, with curly brown hair that always looks uncombed. She doesn't wear makeup either, or earrings. The dimples in her cheeks when she smiles give her a deceptively cute appearance, which makes her a highly effective interrogator.

She's a fan of the musicals of the '40s and '50s, but I'd grown tired of their endless good cheer and had insisted that we alternate them with old thrillers. Tonight it was *Gaslight,* with delivery pizza first and then popcorn. I love the old thrillers: the passage of time and the decline of civilization have turned their noir almost cozy. It was even cozier that night because I had a fire going in the fireplace, and around eight it started to rain, with even a little lightning and thunder, unusual for that early in the spring.

When the movie was over, we sat and talked about it, as we always do. We're not film buffs or anything, but we have strong opinions. I said I thought Ingrid Bergman was miscast.

"Oh, yeah?" Ginny mumbled through a mouthful of popcorn. "She won her first Oscar for the part."

"She deserved it," I said. "It must've been a real stretch for her, playing a cute little ingenue who falls in love with a loser like the character Charles Boyer plays, and then lets him turn her into a pathetic, confused child."

I'd found it hard to sit through the psychological torment Boyer puts Bergman through.

"I suppose people thought women's brains were mushier back then," Ginny said.

"Leslie Caron should've had Bergman's role," I said. "Somebody wide-eyed and not too bright. Bergman just can't look pathetic convincingly, or confused either."

"Caron was probably only about ten years old when *Gaslight* was made," said Ginny, who knows things like that.

"Yeah, that's about right for the part."

When the film had rewound, I aimed the remote at the VCR and fast-forwarded to a scene near the beginning, where Bergman is in a train compartment with an old lady named Miss Thwaites.

"Now watch this," I said.

Miss Thwaites is reading a cheap thriller. Suddenly she turns to Bergman and, wide-eyed, exclaims that the killer in the book has six wives buried in the cellar! "Seems a lot," Bergman replies, trying to suppress a grin.

"See that?" I said, pressing the Pause button. "Bergman's toying with her." I rewound it again and played the scene over. "See the mockery in her eyes? I'm surprised the director didn't cut it out, since it makes her look too worldly. She'd see through a man like Charles Boyer in a flash. She might have an affair with him, but she'd never marry a loser like that."

"That's because you think mockery is a defense against anything, Peggy," Ginny retorted. "Maybe it is for you, but for a lot of people it's just a thin attempt to hide the fact that they don't have a clue. *Gaslight*," she pronounced, "shows just how frail a reed mockery can be."

Ginny wanted to discuss the police work in the movie. She'd groaned all through the last few minutes, when Bergman asks the police detective, played by Joseph Cotten, to leave her alone with Boyer after he's been captured and tied to a chair, and Cotten agrees.

"Dumb," Ginny pronounced.

"Yeah," I agreed, yawning. I'd only had two hours of sleep in the past forty, and since I was through dissecting the film to my satisfaction, I wanted to go to bed. A few minutes later, I stood in my doorway to watch Ginny dash through the rain to her car and drive off. Then I locked up and went to bed.

The ringing of a phone cut into my dream. I reached for it, an old-fashioned French telephone, but a gloved hand came out of the darkness to stop me, a pale bearded face . . .

I sat up, peered over at the bedside clock. It was a little before two. The phone went on ringing. I picked it up, ready to shower a careless, or more likely drunk, misdialler with outrage. I wanted it to be that because the only other thing it could be at that time of the morning was bad news.

It was bad news, in the voice of Buck Hansen, a homicide cop friend of mine.

"We've found a body on the Ag Campus, Peggy," he said without preliminaries. "A woman. We think she's been murdered. We think you might know something about it."

"Why?"

"Would you mind coming over here," he said instead of answering the question.

I didn't ask it again, just said okay. The shadows of the nightmare flickered at the edges of my consciousness, mixed with the darkness of the black-and-white film Ginny and I had watched a few hours earlier.

"Where are you?" I asked, and I think I knew the answer before Buck gave it.

"At the steps that go down to the lake below the veterinary hospital," he said. "A cop'll show you the way."

"Okay," I said again, because now I knew what this was going to be about.

It was still raining, a steady, cold spring downpour, when I ran out my back door to the garage in the alley my landlady, Mrs. Hammer, lets me share with her. The lights in front of the garage sprang on, activated by motion detectors, as I crossed the backyard. I'd used the remote from inside my apartment to open the garage door.

As I drove down the alley to the street, I muttered

a prayer, a selfish prayer to a God I don't believe in but pray to anyway when I'm in trouble, that if a woman had to be murdered, it had nothing to do with me and the man who'd called himself Jason, and that Buck's calling me out in the middle of a cold and rainy night was just a horrible mistake.

I parked in the hospital lot, flipped up the hood on my raincoat, and walked to the yellow police tape that barred access to the steps down to the lake. I told the cop huddled in the rain-slicked poncho next to the steps that Lieutenant Hansen had asked me to come down. He nodded, let me pass.

About two-thirds of the way down, a tarp had been stretched across the steps on the shrubbery on each side to protect what was underneath from the rain. Figures illuminated by harsh light from porta-ble lamps knelt under it in a circle but not, I was sure, in prayer.

Buck was standing just outside the tarp, the rain running off his rain hat, his hands shoved in his pockets. He nodded when he saw me and said something to the others, who moved aside to let me into the circle under the makeshift tent. I walked down slowly, staring straight ahead because I wanted to put off the moment as long as I could. At the bottom of the steps, on the path by the lake, I recognized Jesse Porter, standing with one of Buck's detectives. Jesse had probably been patrolling the Ag Campus that night, must have found the body. Then I stooped and peered under the tarp. A woman lay sprawled facedown on the steps. Her head, turned to one side, was bloody, her green eyes were open, her hair soaked with rain or blood—I couldn't tell which—and plastered to her head. Her arms were thrown out in front of her, as though she'd tried to catch herself as she pitched headfirst down the steps. One of the crime scene specialists

shined his flashlight on her face as I stooped down
to take a closer look.

"Did you find her glasses?" I asked, just to say
something.

"In the bushes down the steps a way," said
Bonnie Winkler, an assistant medical examiner I'd
met before, who was squatting next to me.

I stayed there a while longer, staring at the
woman's body. I didn't know her; I'd only spoken a
few words to her in the Atwood Lab the day before,
when she'd come in to deliver some papers to the
secretary. But even as I realized that, I also realized
that before this was over, I was going to know a lot
more about this woman and that she would be as
much a part of me for the rest of my life as the sister
I'd never had.

I backed out into the rain, straightened up, and
turned to Buck. "Her name's Dana," I said. "I don't
know her last name. She works in the Atwood Lab."
I pointed up the hill to the hospital looming above
us in the night.

"What do you know about this?" he asked. He
held up a plasticine envelope that contained a small
tape recorder with burnished metallic sides. "We
found it in her jacket pocket."

Selfish prayers are never granted.

"What is it?"

I jumped and turned, startled. It was Lieutenant
Bixler, the duty officer that night, peering over my
shoulder to see what was in the envelope. Rain was
dripping down in front of his face from the black
beak of his uniform cap, not veiling enough of his
ugly face.

Buck filled him in, then turned back to me. I told
him the story of my three encounters with the man
by the lake, adding that he'd told me his name was

Jason and that he'd given the dispatcher a last name that sounded like Newman or Neeman.

"He accosted you three times," Bixler said when I'd finished, his voice choked with incredulity. "He showed you an ID he'd stolen with a name different from the one he'd given you earlier. And you didn't arrest him?"

"No," I replied. One-word replies are always best with Bixler. I didn't tell him my first encounter with Jason didn't count as "accosting" or harassment and neither did the last.

"But he threatened you."

"No," I said again.

"He was threatening, though, wasn't he? Offensive and obscene?"

I didn't know how to explain it to him or to Buck—or to anybody. Offensive and obscene are in the eye of the beholder.

"Didn't you *look* at the picture on the ID, O'Neill?" Bixler roared.

"It was dark," I said. "I thought he'd grown the beard since the picture was taken. People do, sometimes. There's no law against it."

"You had a duty to arrest him for disorderly conduct. He might have a record as a sex offender. If you'd done your job, O'Neill, he might be in jail now where he couldn't have done—that." He pointed to the body under the makeshift canvas shelter. "Or at least we'd know who to look for now."

"You think Jason's his real name?" Buck asked me, breaking into Bixler's tirade.

I shrugged. Didn't feel much like talking to Buck either.

"You should've made him show some ID when you had him down here," Bixler blustered. "Then he couldn't have fooled you with a fake ID up there." He pointed a fat finger in the general direction of the Old Campus.

"I don't suppose his name's on the recorder," I said to Buck. It's sometimes just that easy.

He shook his head. "No, but in addition to his interview with you, there are three others. We think the last one's with the victim. She knew what Jason was up to from you. As they climbed the steps, she toyed with him. Then she got mad and, it seems, took the tape recorder away from him."

"The way you should've done, O'Neill," Bixler said. "He probably killed her tryin' to get it back."

I looked at Buck, whose face was expressionless. He doesn't like getting between Bixler and me. I asked the obvious question: "Then why didn't he take the tape recorder after he'd killed her?"

"It was in her jacket pocket," he said. "Under her body. Maybe he couldn't lift her, or got frightened away by something before he could."

Partially to tune Bixler out, I asked Bonnie, who'd come out of the tent, if she thought Dana had been raped. Jason had talked about rape the first time we'd met.

Shaking her curly blond hair, she said, "There aren't any obvious signs of it, but I won't know for sure until I've done the autopsy." It took me a while to get used to a medical examiner named Bonnie Winkler, especially when she also looks like Shirley Temple.

"And she didn't just trip on the steps and fall?" We wouldn't all be there if she had, I knew, but I had to ask anyway.

"She did that too," Bonnie answered dryly. "But no, this was no accident, Peggy. She was hit once for sure with something blunt, and it looks to me as though she was hit at least once more." She stepped out of the way to let crime lab technicians back under the tent.

I spent another half hour telling Buck everything I knew or guessed about Jason. I told him I didn't think he was a homeless man—at least not over a long period of time: he wasn't filthy or unkempt enough and he didn't smell. I was quite sure he wasn't drunk, and I didn't think he was high on drugs, although he looked like he might have done his share of them in his time—but how he talked, dressed, and wore his hair could have influenced me about that.

"To tell you the truth, Buck," I concluded, "he looked to me like a throwback to the sixties." I know a little about that.

Buck smiled grimly. "I'll check to see if there are still any communes around." He told me he'd have an artist downtown at nine to work with me to create a picture of Jason.

Bixler jumped in: "And how 'bout you go back to the station right now and look through the mug shots of the perverts, O'Neill. Maybe you'll recognize your friend Jason among 'em."

I nodded, too numb for once to feel offended by Bixler's words, and went back up the steps. Newspaper reporters and television people were milling around behind the yellow tape, but they didn't know who I was or what part I played in the tragedy, so they didn't pursue me when I walked through them with my hood covering my head and my head down.

Six

I drank the bitter dregs of the squad room coffee as I went through the photographs of known sexual offenders who'd been caught on or around campus. I'd gone through them recently, as we all do periodically, but it was possible Jason's beard, which I was sure was real, was of recent origin, so I studied each face carefully, trying to imagine how it would look with a beard like his. We also have a log, which goes back a long time, of complaints by women against men who have harassed them on campus, but none matched Jason's description or my experience with him.

When I'd finished, I put my head down on my arms on the table. I wasn't crying; I was just tired and depressed, disgusted with myself, but I wasn't crying.

Sergeant Heller, who's one of the nice guys, found me like that, and he sat and talked to me for a while. He said he'd treated annoying people the same way I had when he was off duty. "It's always a temptation for a cop to throw his or her weight around," he said. "Flash your shield at 'em and tell 'em to shut up or they're under arrest. It seems to me you tried to deal with him in a civilized manner. He didn't have fangs, did he?"

I shook my head.

"Then how could you know he'd be the kind to

do a thing like that?'' he asked, gesturing out the window at the night.

He followed me to my car in the station parking lot, leaned in, and said, ''Be careful, Peggy. It sounds like he's got some kind of thing for you, going to all that trouble stealing the ID, finding out your last name and when you work.''

As I drove home I thought about what Buck had told me. The tape in Jason's recorder apparently indicated that thanks to me Dana had known about him, and when he'd accosted her she'd toyed with him. Was that why he'd killed her? What would have happened if I hadn't gone to the Atwood Lab to ask about him? Maybe Dana would have answered his questions innocently, as I'd done at first, until she'd reached the hospital and safety. If she hadn't known that he'd also accosted me, would she have taken his tape recorder?

But why didn't Jason retrieve the tape recorder after he killed her? Maybe he hadn't meant to kill her and panicked when he realized he had. Or maybe somebody had come along on the path below and scared him away.

It was five-thirty when I got home, still dark but with a thin line of blue showing under the clouds in the east. I parked in front of the house—I didn't want to drive down the alley—locked the car, and ran to the house. I'd left the porch light on and could see the porch was empty.

Safely inside my apartment, I undressed, fell into bed, buried my face in a pillow, and tried to get some sleep. Although I'd had only about five hours of sleep in the last forty, I lay awake for a long time, going over everything that had happened since I'd first met Jason: the crude way he'd started talking about rape, then the way he'd stood over me just before the couple had come strolling along the lake.

What would have happened if they hadn't come by when they did? At the time, I'd thought he was just a nuisance, socially inept, a nerd.

And then the way he'd used the fiction of being a writer to try to get me to talk about my personal life and grown nastier when I tried to get away from him.

I saw Dana the way she'd been in the Atwood Lab, listening to me describe my encounter with Jason intently, the way nearsighted people sometimes listen. She said she'd keep an eye out for him. There should be lightning and thunder, stark lighting and odd camera angles at moments like that. Instead, there'd just been the pompous Millard Pyles, the drab Lorraine Cullin, Lillian's nice radiologist, Jim Gates, and me.

My alarm jarred me awake at eight. I stood a long time under a cold shower and drank a pot of coffee while staring out my front window at the rain falling, then drove downtown to the police station.

First I gave the artist, an Asian woman whose name I didn't catch, Jason's approximate age, height, and build, and without letting me watch, she put together a portrait from transparencies of individual features, predetermined for people who fit that general description. She showed me the result and asked what I'd most like to change. I went through transparencies of noses, mouths and hairlines—trying first one and then another—in search of Jason, and when I'd finished, we discussed what she could add freehand to make the likeness even closer. She made the cheekbones a little more prominent, the eyes narrower and a little closer together.

It wasn't very satisfactory, of course; it captured very little of the man I'd met three times and dreamed about once.

"Why the frown?" she asked.

"It's missing something," I said. "A kind of indifference, or passionlessness—but with some self-mockery too, as though he knew he was behaving like a spoiled child. I don't know if that was really there or if it came from the way he talked—from his personality."

She laughed and said she thought one of the German expressionists or Edvard Munch might have been able to capture that quality in a face, but she wasn't up to it. "Besides," she went on, "this is only a police sketch, more to exclude suspects than pinpoint the guy you're after!"

I went down to Buck's office after that and knocked on his door. "You look like hell," he greeted me as I walked in.

I slumped into the old overstuffed chair he keeps in a corner. He couldn't have gotten much sleep last night either, but he didn't look like hell at all; he looked very nice.

Buck Hansen's about forty, five-ten but looks taller because he's thin and moves with such grace. His hair is so blond it looks silver. The lines at the corners of his ice-blue eyes—laugh lines, my Aunt Tess calls them—give him the look of a benign lizard.

As he poured me a cup of coffee, I asked him if he'd heard anything from Bonnie Winkler. He said she'd called to confirm that Dana hadn't been raped and that what had killed her had been blows to the head: one to the back, the others—at least two—to the temple. The first blow had knocked her down the steps, Bonnie thought, the others had been delivered after she was down, stunned, and probably unconscious.

I nodded, thinking about that: Jason striking her from behind and then crouching beside her to do it again and again. I closed my eyes and didn't want to open them again right away.

"Who was she?" I asked after a moment. I had to ask the question twice to get it out.

"Her full name was Dana Louise Michaels," he said, reciting from a card. "Twenty-seven. Unmarried. A doctor of veterinary medicine. She got her D.V.M. at the University of California at Davis—that's near Sacramento. She stayed on at Davis to get a Ph.D., then accepted a postdoctoral position here to work with Doctor Atwood. She arrived in September, about six months ago."

I knew what a postdoc was: somebody doing advanced research, either while waiting for a permanent position to open up somewhere or because they want to work under the supervision of a distinguished person in their field. Doctor Atwood was certainly distinguished enough, I thought.

"How'd she end up on the steps going down to the lake?"

"She was on her way home," Buck said. "She was subletting a town house in the faculty housing complex on the other side of the lake—it's just a fifteen-minute walk from the hospital."

A walk unarmed women shouldn't do alone after dark. "And she met Jason," I said. "She took his tape recorder, and he killed her to get it back."

"That's what it looks like," he said, "except not all at one time."

I gave him a questioning look.

"She met Jason twice," he went on. "The first time, she was on her way to the lab from her house—that was around five o'clock, about the same time you met him the day before. He gave her his line about writing a novel and wanting to interview her for it. She knew he was a phony from having heard your story, so she started teasing him. But when he began making up a nasty story about you—"

"Me!"

"You can listen to it, if you want," Buck said. "She told him to shut up. He didn't, so she took the tape recorder from him. The tape ends there, but she told her office mate what happened afterward."

Buck rustled through papers. "Her office mate's name is Barry Russell, an assistant professor in the Atwood Lab. He happened to be going into the hospital just as she and Jason arrived at the top of the steps from the lake. I guess he's what kept Jason from attacking her right there. He heard her tell Jason she was going to give the recorder to the campus police and file a complaint against him. She also told Russell she thought she knew Jason from somewhere."

"From where?"

Buck made a face. "She didn't tell him."

"Did Russell hear anything Jason said to her?"

"He says he shouted that she'd be sorry she'd ever set eyes on him—he was going to kill her. She was out of breath, but she called back something about how he'd be a lot sorrier than she was before she was through with him."

"So when did Jason kill her?"

"Sometime after eight, when she left the building. According to Russell, she told him she was going home before it started raining, and that's the last he saw of her."

Assuming Dana had done what she said she was going to do, try to beat the rain home, she and Jason must have been the last to use the steps until Jesse Porter had found her body at a little before midnight. Well, probably not too many people of either sex used those steps late at night, and last night it had been raining heavily too.

I remembered hearing the sounds of the approaching storm as Ginny and I sat watching *Gaslight* and eating popcorn, an empty pizza box on the coffee table in front of us, a fire in my fireplace. Several miles to the east of us, Dana must have heard it approach too and decided to go home before it reached her.

"And she thought she knew who Jason was," I said. "That's something, anyway. He could be a student in the veterinary school or somebody who works there."

"If that's the case," Buck said grimly, "it shouldn't take us long to find him."

"How about fingerprints?"

He shook his head. "We found some on the cassette. We're waiting to hear from the FBI if they're on file."

I told him Jason seemed to know something about Doctor Atwood. "At least he knows her name and that she gave up being a practicing vet to devote herself to research. He doesn't seem to approve."

"A lot of people know about Doctor J," Buck said, "especially pet owners. You wouldn't know anything about that, of course, Peggy," he added with a smile. When I didn't return it—I didn't feel like smiling—he went on more seriously, "You don't look like you're taking this very well."

"I didn't kill Dana Michaels," I replied.

"I know you didn't. So don't blame yourself."

"I should have told him no when he asked if he could interview me," I went on, "but I just wanted to avoid causing a fuss. Why didn't I have the guts—

or the integrity or whatever it is—to tell him to just go away? He would have gotten angry, probably, and maybe he would have crossed the line with me right then. I could have handled that, might have arrested him—"

I broke off, choking on "shoulds" and "woulds" and "maybes," and put my head down on Buck's desk and started bawling, which was something new in our relationship.

He came around his desk, stood next to my chair, put his hands on my shoulders, and most important of all, didn't say anything.

I wasn't crying only for Dana Michaels; I was crying for myself—and maybe more for myself than for her. So I made it brief.

"The thing is," I said, wiping my eyes with the Kleenex he handed me and then blowing my nose, "trying to avoid causing a fuss is what I did best growing up with an alcoholic dad. I thought I'd pretty much gotten over it. But I haven't—and maybe that's why Dana Michaels is dead!"

I put my head down again, bawled some more. It felt good.

He stayed where he was, waited for me to get it out of my system, then said, "You could have arrested him and charged him with disorderly conduct. Of course, you might have had to chase him down the steps and tackle him and use what you know about subduing people to make him do what you wanted. And then you would have had to frog-march him back up to the hospital and call for backup and he'd have been charged and jailed, and the charges would have been—what?"

He went back behind his desk and sat down.

"That he'd asked you some personal questions for a novel he was writing," he went on, answering his own question. "And for that you'd used force and maybe got both of you scratched up. Imagine what the meathead Bixler would have said to that when you finally dragged Jason in, hollering about police brutality! And he would've been back out on the streets as soon as he made bail—and how high do you think bail would have been set, Peggy? And he would still have been out there waiting for Dana Michaels or some other woman to come along."

I nodded, took some deep breaths.

"So after she snatched his recorder and went into the veterinary hospital," I said, "Jason must have stayed in the bushes by the steps and waited for her to come back. He must have known she'd come back that way sooner or later. Maybe he even knew where she lived. But after he'd killed her, why didn't he take the tape recorder?"

"We think we know the answer to that one now too," Buck said. "Her purse is missing. According to her office mate, she was carrying one—a shoulder bag—when he last saw her."

"Then the stupid loser killed her for nothing!" I almost shouted. "You'd think he would've made sure the tape recorder was in it before he ran off."

"From your description of the man," Buck reminded me, "Jason's not a cool, professional killer."

No, I didn't think he was either. What was he? A nerd who'd hit Dana on the back of the head as she went down the steps—ignoring him, contemptuous of him? And then, when he realized what he'd done, he'd panicked and hit her again and maybe again to keep her from reporting him, since she apparently knew who he was. Or did he do it because he was enraged at how she'd teased him, taunted him, didn't take him seriously?

It was a scene I didn't want in my head, but I

wouldn't get it out of there until I knew everything there was to know about what had happened and until Jason was safely behind bars.

I asked Buck if I could listen to the tape.

"There's a copy of it in that machine over there," he said. "Help yourself."

Seven

"What's your name?"

"Sarah Ann Gillespie. With an h."

"Gillespie with an h?"

"Sarah!" She laughed. She sounded a little self-conscious.

As he'd done with me, he began with innocuous questions about the color of her hair and eyes. "*How would you describe the way your hair's cut?*"

"I dunno. It's just short—kind of a bob, I guess. I didn't want something that would, like, take me all day to make it look nice, you know?"

"I don't," Jason replied. "*That's the trouble with being a guy who wants to create a woman from the inside out. I don't know how you think—or all the words, anyway.*" He chuckled. "*I should really be conducting these interviews in June or July, when it's warmer. I don't know what you've got on under your jacket, so I can't ask you about it.*"

"Well, you can—but I might not answer!"

"Why not?"

"C'mon!"

"Hey, it's for a good cause—literature."

"Well . . . So what'd you want to know?"

"What feels more comfortable, a bra or no bra?"

"That's easy! It depends on what kind of blouse you're wearing—the material, you know. And what you're doing. I always wear a bra when I'm doing aerobics, for example."

"Why?"

"Because . . . Well, can't you figure that out for yourself?"

"I'm pretty slow, I guess."

"I guess you are! Well, because of the rubbing, you know?"

"But doesn't that feel sexy?"

"You'd better watch it, Mister Author!"

"I'd like to."

"I'm warning you!"

"Okay, okay. How many men have you had sex with?"

"That's rude!"

"You gonna tell me?"

"Hundreds! That's why I'm an accounting major—so I can keep track!"

"Accounting's your major?"

"Business administration and accounting."

"Wow, that sounds exciting! What do you intend to do when you graduate?"

"I dunno. Get a job working for a company that wants an accountant, I guess. How about you? Do you, like, write full time, or are you just starting out?"

"Listen, Sarah Ann, thanks a lot for your cooperation—and good luck with your courses. I gotta go now."

"Already? What's the—?"

The recorder clicked off. I put the tape player on Pause and said, "Once he realized she'd answer any question he asked her, he lost interest—or else he doesn't like business majors. He also didn't like the fact that she seemed interested in him."

Buck looked up at me from the report he was reading at his desk and nodded. "Listen to the next one."

The woman in the second "interview" also gave her full name, Lynn Hunter, and answered some innocent questions without any hesitation, as though she had plenty of time and took his story of writing a novel at face value. She was an English major, she said.

When he asked the question about her bra size, she said: *"That's an odd question, isn't it? I mean, most male authors just describe a woman as being 'stacked' or 'big busted,' or showing lots of cleavage. If they're middle-aged and fantasizing about their daughters' friends—or worse, about their daughters—they say their breasts are 'heartrendingly small.' But they don't actually give cup size. Is this something new in literature?"*

He sounded flustered when he told her yes, the novel he was writing was going to be different. He wasn't going to use adjectives, just numbers and nouns, to avoid feelings, subjectivity.

"Fifty-five D," she said.

"Really?"

"Trust me."

Then he asked her how many men she'd had sex with, and she said she thought an author with any talent could give his female character as many men as he thought were necessary for the purpose of the story. *"But I'll answer the question if you really want me to. I've had nineteen lovers—twenty if you count Jeremy, which I don't."*

From her tone of voice, I couldn't tell if she was pulling his leg. He clearly didn't know either.

Every question he asked from then on she found fault with and if she answered it, made it clear—to me, at least—that she was lying. Pretty soon I found myself laughing, in spite of myself.

"That's a really boring question," she replied to one of the last. *"What're you writing, soft-core porn or a hard-boiled mystery?"*

The tape ended in midsentence, just as the first one had.

I looked up at Buck. "Have you talked to these women?" I asked him.

"I worried about those abrupt endings too," he said. "But both Sarah Ann Gillespie and Lynn Hunter are alive and well. They're coming in later this morning to tell me about their encounter with the man and critique your portrait of him."

"Lynn Hunter made him sound like a complete moron," I said.

"She had more time to waste on him than you did, Peggy," he reminded me. "You could have turned him inside out too, if you'd wanted to spend time on it, but you had better things to do than toy with him—and you're not a naive undergraduate flirt, like Sarah-with-an-h Ann Gillespie."

I pressed the button again. After a few moments, Jason said, *"What's your name?"*

"Peggy."

I listened to the entire interview, comparing my way of dealing with Jason with Lynn Hunter's and finding mine woefully lacking and worse— ineffectual. She'd had a natural-born way of dealing with him, whereas I'd started out taking him seriously and ended up getting emotional, angry. Having listened to two of his other "interviews," I could see how I'd played right into his hands—or his need to upset women with personal questions.

"My, what a nice tape recorder you have! Is it yours?" I recognized Dana Michaels's voice, heavy with sarcasm.

"What's your name?" he asked, sounding a little uncertain, perhaps on account of the mockery in her voice.

"You'll never guess—but I'll bet I can guess your name."

"What?"

"Jason."

"How'd you know that?"

"One of the other characters in your novel told me."

He didn't miss a beat. *"Oh, sure—Peggy."* He made a tsking noise. *"Sad case—really sad! I thought the interview was going great—until she started to come on to me."*

"I'll bet she did!"

"She did! Surprised the hell out of me. I mean, she doesn't look the type, does she? I was just asking her these questions, you know, and she's givin' me answers I didn't want to hear!" He whistled. *"I mean, I don't need stuff like that for my novel—I'm not writing porn or anything like that. If I was, I could make it up myself."*

"Uh-huh."

"She's got red hair and freckles, you know? So she asked me if I could guess how far down her freckles went!"

"That's enough, Jason," she said coldly.

He laughed, ignoring her. *"Then she asked me if I'd ever made love to a redheaded woman—except she didn't say 'make love to,' I just cleaned it up for you. I said, look, I'm not interested in anything personal, okay? But no matter what I asked her, she said something filthy."*

"I said—"

"You know what she offered to do—right here on the steps? Hey, slow up, will ya?"

"Get away from me, damn it, you little creep! Get back!"

"Hey, I'm not bothering you. What—?"

"Okay—if that's the way you want it, give me that!"

"Hey—!"

The tape ended abruptly.

I sat there a long time, frowning at the machine, feeling Buck's eyes on me.

Dana Michaels had been upset with Jason on my behalf, not just her own. Maybe the things he said about me were the last straw for her; maybe she wouldn't have taken the tape recorder if not for that.

"Why didn't she call the police when she got back to her office with the recorder?" I asked.

Buck shook his head. "I have no idea. She might have remembered who he was and decided to confront him herself, rather than bring in the police."

I got up wearily, thanked him, and headed for the door.

He followed me, put his arm around me. He's one of the few men who can do that and not lose the offending limb.

"You free for dinner one of these nights?" he asked. "We haven't been seeing much of each other lately. I think it's my turn."

It's usually Buck's turn because I'm a rotten cook. "I'll check my calendar, give you a call," I said listlessly, and waved without turning around and kept going.

Eight

It was nearly noon when I got home. I ate a bowl of cereal and afterward undressed and crawled into bed. It took me a long time to get to sleep, as the events of the last few days kept floating in and out of my mind, and for a while I kept waking up to the sounds of the creaking old house.

Somebody was kissing me, and I turned my head away as I tried to hit him. "Sorry!" he said.

I woke with a start and a half-scream. Gary was sitting on the edge of my bed.

"What're you doing here?"

"That's what I like about you," he said, "that look of radiant happiness on your face at the sight of me. We had a date tonight, remember—a play and dinner afterward?"

"What time is it?"

"Almost seven. You don't look ready. You okay?"

"No," I said, and reached for him.

"We'll miss the play!"

We did.

We've tried living together, Gary and I, but in addition to working for our largest metropolitan newspaper, he's also a writer, and I didn't like his notes, papers, and books scattered all over my apartment. I didn't like having him at such close quarters either, but I wasn't prepared to move into something bigger with him yet, including marriage, which he'd hinted at. So he lives with Lillian and

Rufus and is slowly gentrifying her old house in lieu of paying rent. It's good for both of them, and for me too. We spend most of the nights I'm off duty together either at my place or his.

We sent out for Chinese, and while we waited for it to arrive, I told him what had happened. When I'd finished, he lay there staring at me for a while, and then he said, "You think you're responsible for her death, don't you? You're probably right. But explain it to me anyway, will you? Slowly."

"I should have been more assertive with him," I said. "I should have done what she did—Dana Michaels did. At the very least, I should've snatched the tape recorder away from him and made him eat it."

"Uh-uh, Peggy. You're not God. You couldn't know he was a disaster waiting to happen. He was also nastier to Dana Michaels than he was to you, and she had the benefit of knowing he'd accosted you. If he'd gone after her first, and you knew about it, you would've treated him just the way she did." He brushed the hair out of my eyes. "No, Peggy, you behaved the way any normal woman would've under the circumstances—"

"I'm not a normal woman!" I protested.

He laughed, tried to kiss me. I shoved him away. "Of course not!" he said. "But when you're not on duty, you have a right to behave like one. You don't have to arrest everybody who annoys you, if you don't want to."

The doorbell rang then, and Gary threw on a robe and went to get the food we'd ordered.

We ate in bed. After a while, he said, "Jason didn't kill Dana because he's a sex pervert, did he? He killed her because she took his tape recorder and that made him mad." He pointed a chopstick at me. "Or because she let him know she recognized him.

Maybe he couldn't afford to be exposed as a social flatliner. Maybe it would ruin his career plans."

"Social flatliners don't have career plans," I said.

"Your take on this character was that he was just a nerd, right?"

I thought about it as I dipped a steamed dumpling in soy sauce. "I guess 'nerd' is the right word," I said, when I'd swallowed a bite. "At least until I discovered he'd stolen somebody's ID just in case I made him show me some. Now I don't know what to call him. But there's something awfully immature about him—unformed, as if he'd been brought out of the oven too soon. He didn't seem to know what he wanted, somehow. He lost interest in the first woman he interviewed on the tape when she turned out to be a flirt who'd probably be too easy for him. But the second woman was too much for him. She didn't get mad, just treated him with contempt, so he stalked off in a huff. That's what I should have done. Instead, I lost my temper."

"But you didn't see any signs of violence in him, did you?"

"There's violence in everybody," I said. "All it takes is the right trigger. What are you getting at?"

"How sure is Buck that Jason killed this woman?"

"Pretty sure, I guess."

"But it's possible that Jason just shrugged and went away after Dana took his tape recorder away from him, right? And somebody else murdered her—a jealous lover, say, or a rival in the School of Veterinary Medicine. There've been scandals over there before, you know."

He was right, of course. It was still early in Buck's investigation, and he didn't know much about Dana Michaels yet. She could have been killed by an enemy in the department or an ex-husband or lover, and Jason just happened to be in the wrong place at the wrong time. I didn't think it was likely, though; I'm not a strong believer in coincidences, especially when it comes to murder.

"It won't do Dana Marshall any good," I said, mostly to myself, "but I'd like her killer to be somebody other than Jason. I'd sleep better at night. That makes me pretty selfish, doesn't it?"

"Just human," Gary said.

"What did you mean, there've been scandals in the School of Veterinary Medicine? I've never heard of any."

"Not the school," he said. "In Doctor Atwood's lab."

"Oh?"

"Max Weinstock—you've met her—used to be the University reporter. She was talking about it this morning when I came in—on account of the murder."

"So tell me about it," I said.

"According to Max, five or six years ago somebody in the Atwood Lab blew the whistle on Doctor Charlie—accused him of some serious research violations."

"Doctor Charlie?" I remembered hearing the name when I was in the Atwood Lab asking the secretary about Jason. Dana Michaels had come into the room to deliver a report she said came from him.

"That's right, Doctor Charlie. In the eighties, when Doctor Atwood—Julia Atwood—had her television program on pet care, she was called Doctor J, so people started calling her son, who appeared with her occasionally—handing her animals and other cute things like that—Doctor C. He didn't like it apparently, so once he actually became a vet himself, people started calling him Doctor Charlie."

"Not a great improvement, is it?"

"He must've thought so or the people who work

in his mother's lab wouldn't do it anymore. Anyway, this whistle-blower couldn't get anybody at the U to listen to him, naturally, so he came to us and told his story. Max was assigned to look into it."

"What happened?"

"What usually happens when somebody's accused of skulduggery at the U," he replied. "Nothing."

"End of story?"

"Well, the University fired the whistle-blower, of course. They always do."

"Huh?"

Gary opened his fortune cookie. "Don't pretend you're surprised, Peggy. You've been around the U a long time. Anybody who criticizes the U from within gets clobbered. It's just the way it is."

"I know the medical school has enough clout to shrug off charges of misconduct," I said, "but it never occurred to me that the veterinary medicine school did."

"Well, it does. This is an agricultural state, after all, in case you hadn't noticed. And a population heavy with dog and cat lovers too. So the School of Veterinary Medicine attracts a lot of money from agribusiness, the pet food companies, the pharmaceutical companies—even the federal government. And the Atwood Lab's one of the biggest attractions."

"So they fired the whistle-blower and the story just died?"

"Yep. Then, in addition to the University president standing up and saying that an attack on Doctor J was an attack on all small creatures wearing fins, fur, and feathers, one of Doctor Atwood's sons died. The editorial page, according to Max, was suddenly inundated with letters to the editor from the bereaved mother's pet-loving fans, attacking the paper for trying to smear a modern-day Saint Francis at this time of personal sorrow. Max was told to turn her brilliant investigatory skills to less controversial stories, such as students going up the down staircase, bike and computer theft, and purse snatchings. 'You will be awarded some great honor.'"

"What?"

"My fortune cookie. Means I'm going to get the Pulitzer. What's yours?"

"I dunno," I said, suddenly exhausted. "I think I ate it with the cookie."

There were always a lot of rumors of scandals at the U, I reflected drowsily, and most of them vanished into the sand. Under the guise of academic freedom, the U can get away with almost anything—probably even murder, although there are so many less risky ways of destroying the people who annoy it than that. Usually when anything threatens the U, the thugs who run the place bring out the president, Hightower, and make him do that twinkly thing he does with his blue eyes that always charms the taxpayers.

I heard Gary fussing around in the kitchen, heard the refrigerator door open and close, then something that could have been the microwave oven. By the time he returned to the bedroom with hot fudge sundaes, I was sound asleep. I only knew about them from the empty bowls I found on the nightstand the next morning. I was pretty sure I hadn't eaten any of it. I would have remembered.

Nine

I hitched a ride downtown with Gary the next morning to do some shopping and stopped in at Buck's office to find out how the investigation was going.

He gestured to the coffeepot, and while I poured myself a cup he said, "We haven't caught Jason yet, but we have found somebody who's sure he saw him at the crime scene at the time Dana Michaels was probably killed. We've also found where Jason's been staying."

"Where?"

"In one of those storage buildings on the Ag Campus's experimental farm—about half a mile from the vet hospital. They're unused this time of year."

"How do you know he was living there?"

"A lot of fast-food wrappers, a comfortable and not-too-dirty bed of straw. Even a couple of pairs of dirty socks with holes in them—"

"Could be any homeless person," I interrupted him. "We find them in those buildings sometimes in the winter."

"—and Robert Hill's student ID," he went on as though I hadn't spoken.

"Oh. Well, Mr. Hill'll be glad to get it back, won't he? Who saw Jason at the crime scene?"

"Somebody who doesn't let a thunderstorm interfere with his jogging. He lives in the same neighborhood as Dana Michaels and jogs around the lake every night at about the same time. As he came past the steps, a man who looked like your description of Jason came running down them. The jogger thought he looked so strange that he stopped and asked if he wás okay, but Jason just shook his head and ran off. The jogger said he thought Jason looked like he'd seen a ghost."

"Did the jogger know Dana?"

"He says not, but we're checking that too."

"What else do you have?"

"Not much. One possibility, and one confession by a nutcase whose story doesn't check out and neither does his description."

"Who's the possibility?"

"Dana Michaels's office mate, Barry Russell. He dated her a few times shortly after she arrived here. They'd known each other in California when they were both students at the veterinary school at Davis. Then one day, Russell went to the Atwood Lab's secretary and asked to be given a different office, but there weren't any available. The secretary later heard him call Michaels a 'calculating, two-faced ass-kisser.'" Buck read that off a piece of paper.

"A vivid image," I muttered, shaking my head. "Just think how many homicide cops, medical examiners, and prisons we could do away with if it weren't for love!"

"Oh, love might not have had anything to do with it," Buck said with a short laugh. "Russell's a visiting assistant professor, and the Atwood Lab's got a vacancy coming up next year, a permanent position. I guess he thought he was a shoo-in for it—until Michaels arrived. The vet school needs to hire more women, and she apparently had a lot more going for her than just her sex."

I thought about that a moment, then said, "It was this Barry Russell who met Dana having the shouting match with Jason, right?"

"So he claims."

"And she told Russell she thought she knew Jason from somewhere."

"That's right."

"She also told him she was leaving to go home on account of the rain at around eight."

"Well, we do have another witness to that, at least," Buck said. "The lab's executive secretary, Lorraine Cullin, was there when Michaels announced she was going home. She even offered her a ride if she could wait a few more minutes, but Michaels told her she'd rather walk."

"That's too bad," I said. "I assume you're going over Barry Russell's whereabouts at the time of the murder carefully."

"Of course. We haven't found anybody who saw him prowling around the steps yet, though. We're also looking into his relationship with Michaels when they were both at Davis. He claims there was nothing between them back then—says he hardly knew who she was and didn't get to know her until she arrived here and moved into the office with him. We'll see. We're waiting to hear what the detectives come up with in Davis."

"You don't sound like you think this Doctor Russell's a very reliable customer," I said.

"He's not a very pleasant one, but that doesn't make him a killer."

"What about Dana's life since she arrived here?" I asked. "The news report says this is where she grew up."

"That's right. She and her mother and stepfather moved here when she was just starting high school. She went away to college as soon as she graduated.

She doesn't seem to have made any close friends since coming back, as far as we've been able to find out so far. Some of her colleagues say they thought she was standoffish and they don't know much about her life outside the lab. Apparently she just did her work and went home. Doctor Atwood and her son thought highly of her, though, and everybody agrees her work was excellent."

"And do you have any idea where the Atwoods and the other faculty were at the time of the murder?"

He smiled as though he could read my mind. "Forty-two people, counting part-time students, lab technicians, and faculty, work in the lab. We're interviewing all of them, although I have only one serious suspect, your friend Jason."

"He's not my friend," I snapped.

"Sorry," he said, giving me a surprised look. I'd never snapped at him before like that. "Doctor Atwood claims she was at home," he went on, shuffling papers. "But since she lives alone, it might be hard for her to prove, if we ever had any reason to think she wanted Dana Michaels dead. Her son, Charles—"

"Charlie," I said. "Doctor Charlie."

"Yes, right. Doctor Charlie was in his office most of the evening. So was the lab's director, a man named Millard Pyles."

"I've met Pyles," I said. "He has the personality of something that lives under a moist rock. And the secretary was there too, huh? They're all busy little beavers, aren't they? Somebody told me they were working overtime to get ready for some visitors from the federal government. Was that why Dana was there that night too?"

"No, she was there studying radioactive dog poop."

"I'm sorry, Buck," I said, "I didn't sleep very well last night. I could have sworn you said Dana was working late that night studying radioactive dog poop."

"Do you want me to explain?"

"Yes, please."

"She was working on a project for a dog food company that involved, among other things, determining how much of a given nutrient a dog absorbed in his chow and how much passed through."

He rummaged through some papers. "To do this," he went on, "she incorporated radioactive isotopes into the nutrient, stirred it into the dog food, and waited to see how much of the nutrient ended up in the dog's stool—which would tell her how much the dog had absorbed."

The thrill of discovery.

I told Buck I was glad he was looking into other possibilities besides Jason.

"We're not overlooking other possibilities," he said. "Who knows? Maybe, when he sees your description of him, Jason'll turn himself in and give us a solid alibi for the time of the murder."

"Yeah, including a believable explanation for why a jogger saw him at the crime scene at the time of the murder, looking as though he'd just stared into the mouth of hell. He's a fair liar. I'd like to be there to hear that story!"

Buck also said he'd had Dana's house checked to see if her killer had used the keys in Dana's missing purse to get in, but there'd been no indications that anybody had gone in after Dana was killed.

"Of course," he added, "if somebody did go in, they had all the time in the world to go through the house and take whatever they wanted."

"Wouldn't her mother know if anything of value had been taken?"

He shook his head. "No. She hadn't seen that much of her daughter since she moved back here—they weren't particularly close—and she didn't think Dana owned much of value either. Dana wasn't very interested in acquiring worldly goods, she said."

That night I was sitting in my easy chair by the window that looks out onto a corner of Lake Eleanor, reading a novel by Ann Patchett called *Taft*, when the phone rang.

"I'm sorry," Jason said quietly.

I didn't know what to say, so I didn't say anything.

"You still there?"

"Turn yourself in, Jason," I said. I had to clear my throat before I could get those four words out.

He whispered a laugh. "I'm not that sorry—not yet, anyway."

"Then what do you want?"

"I hope you don't mind my calling you at home, but this isn't a business call, really. I only wanted to tell you I didn't mean to kill her and I'm not a sex fiend or a serial killer or anything like that—I just wanted my tape recorder back and she wouldn't give it to me. I guess I just lost my head, you know?"

As though it were something that could happen to anybody.

"Dana, her name was," he went on. "Funny—I had to learn that from a newspaper I picked up off the street. You'd think a guy would know the people he killed better than that, wouldn't you? But as I say, I really didn't mean to kill her. She made me mad and I guess I hit her harder than I meant to. First she made fun of me. I hate that. That was on account of you warned her against me, Peggy—so she was ready for me. And then she scratched me when she grabbed the tape recorder. She probably didn't mean to, but on top of everything else—"

He paused, perhaps waiting for me to say something.

"Hello, hello? You still there, Peggy?"

"I'm still here, Jason."

"I had to stand out there in the cold and wait for her to come back. I wasn't dressed for it. I almost gave up when I saw it was about to start raining— but then there she came, out the hospital door. Hurrying, probably to get home before the rain started."

Silence for a moment and then he went on, his voice rising, "I waited until she got mostly down the steps and then I jumped out at her. I just meant to scare her, so she'd give me the recorder. But she wouldn't: she just shoved me out of her way, into the bushes, and tried to go on down the steps like I was nothing—*nobody!* I didn't mean to hit her that hard, but you can understand I was provoked."

"What did you hit her with?"

"You mean," he asked with exaggerated amazement, "the cops didn't drag the lake for the rock? It was kind of gray and rough and about the size of a baseball. Haven't they found it yet? It's in there somewhere."

"Turn yourself in," I said again. "It'll save a lot of trouble for everybody."

"Trouble's my middle name, Peggy, and I've never taken the easy way. Besides, would turning myself in bring Dana back to life? Or do you think it would bring some kind of *goodness* back to the world if I went to prison? Shit, Peggy! I could introduce you to some people—friends of mine, some of 'em—who've killed people just for a few bucks or a bottle of wine or a bag of dope. They're not losing any sleep over it—and they *meant* to do it! Why should I go to jail for something that was almost an accident?''

"It doesn't sound to me as though you're like those people," I said. "Why are you telling me all this?''

"I don't know. Maybe 'cause I wanted to tell you about it—since we're kind of in on it together. And you're right, I'm not like those guys I was telling you about. Goddamn! I was just passing through here. Why'd I have to stop?''

He fell silent again.

"I'm not 'in on it' with you, Jason," I said.

"Yeah, you are, Peggy—a little. But it doesn't matter.''

"You said you were just passing through? You seem pretty familiar with the University. And you know quite a lot about Doctor Atwood and her lab too. You knew that she used to be called Doctor J and had a television program.''

"You're quite the Nancy Drew, aren't you?" he jeered. "I know about her because I used to live here when I was a kid, and anybody who had a pet knew Doctor J. I had a *dog*, for Chrissakes, a German shepherd, so I listened to the ol' doc's program religiously, sitting right up there next to the TV screen, legs crossed Indian-style, Heinrich's cute little head in my lap. Heinrich was my dog's name.

"I have family here," he went on. "My dad, the big-time law—oops! Well, I was gonna say 'big-time lawyer,' but I decided I'd better not, it might give me away—but it's too late now; you probably figured it out, you're pretty sharp. Anyway, after my dad, the brain surgeon, kicked me, my mom, and my li'l sister out and married the first in a long string of aerobics instructors—his rewards for getting through business school and becoming a CEO— after that, Mom took me and Louise—that's my li'l sister—and we moved somewhere else, and I'll bet you'd like to know where, wouldn't you? Let's just say that enchiladas are a big food item there, and let it go at that, *sí, señorita*? Anyway, I came back here and stopped in to say hello to the old lecher and check out his latest wife."

"What else?" I asked, when he seemed to have run down.

"Isn't that enough? Aren't you ever satisfied, Peggy?"

"You're pretty funny, Jason. I'll bet you laughed your head off when you saw Dana lying there on the steps. You must've laughed even harder when you discovered the recorder you'd killed her for wasn't in her purse and that you'd killed her for nothing."

"I didn't kill her for nothing, Peggy," he said, his voice suddenly hard, cold. "She shouldn't've made fun of me. She was asking for it—flirting with death. I could've gone back and got the tape recorder, but I got scared—I admit it. Like I told you, I didn't mean to kill her. I was only having fun with you—with all of you. I was just killing time."

"I thought you were gathering material for a novel," I said. "You wanted to know something about being a woman. I'd like to know how it feels to be a murderer, Jason. Tell me."

After a long pause, he said quietly, "It doesn't feel very good, Peggy."

"You're going to have to pay for killing her, one way or another," I said, drawing on an old tradition. "It might feel better if you turned yourself in."

"I'll give it some thought," he said. "Thanks for being so concerned about my mental health. Well, the cops won't get me, anyway. I told you, I don't live here anymore and I haven't in a long time. I'm just passin' through to say hello to some people I once knew."

He laughed tonelessly, but whether it was real or put on, I couldn't say. "Oh yeah, I'll pay for killing her, Peggy—but in my own way. My conscience'll eat away at me until someday I say, Oh what the heck, I'll come clean! And you'll be the first person I call—won't that be nice of me? I'll tell 'em my conscience came to me in the guise of a redheaded campus cop named Peggy O'Neill, and you'll be a hero: Jiminy Cricket O'Neill."

"What about your dad?" I asked. "Your picture's in the paper now. He'll see it."

"Gimme a break, Peggy! Dear ol' Dad would never turn me in, not even if he recognized that dumb picture you did of me—but I forgive you for it; you were never at your best when we were together, were you? Shit!"—he laughed bitterly—"I could go to Daddy now and point to that picture and tell him 'Hey, Dad—see! I'm famous! That's me.' And after he was through pissing in his pants, he'd give me every penny he has to get out of town. You think the pastor of the biggest church in town would want the world to know his son's a killer?"

"Do you ever tell the truth, Jason?"

"I am tellin' you the truth, Peggy," he said. "You just don't know how to listen. I had a friend once, a guy named Tolliver. I'll tell you about him sometime. I owe him a lot." He laughed. "In fact, I owe him everything. You know what he told me once?"

"No, what?"

"Reality's what people end up with when their lies stop workin'."

"I've heard that one before," I said. "I had a brother who must've been a little like your friend Tolliver. He disappeared in the sixties. Sounds like they might have known each other. Sounds like you might have known him too."

"Maybe I did—we'll have to talk about that

sometime too," he said. "But nobody knew Tolliver. Look, Peggy, it's been nice, but I gotta go, okay? Gotta catch that ol' Greyhoun—oops! There I go again! Airplane, I mean; I gotta catch that ol' airplane outta here. I'm sorry we didn't get to know each other better. Maybe we can get together and talk sometime—about your brother and Tolliver. How about it, Peggy?"

"Name the place, Jason."

He laughed uneasily. "I'll give it some thought. And I'm real sorry I didn't get the answer to my questions—especially the one about your freckles, remember? You wouldn't tell me now, would you? As a going-away present?"

"No, Jason."

"If I promised to turn myself in?"

"No."

"The fate worse than death, huh? Well, we'll see about that, maybe. Bye, Peggy."

I called Buck at home. When I'd described Jason's call, he asked me what I made of it.

"I don't know yet, except that he seems to hate his father."

Buck sighed. "Do you suppose Dana Michaels reminded him of his father?"

"He also had a friend named Tolliver. You might want to run that by the FBI and see what they come up with."

"You think anything he says is the truth, Peggy?"

"Something in all that was," I said. "I just don't have the key yet. I also think he's more upset over killing Dana than he realizes—he's being flippant about it as a way of not feeling the pain, but it's not working very well."

"You think he's going to turn himself in?"

"I don't know. Maybe. But he also hinted that he

was planning to leave town—at the same time that he implied he wasn't finished with me yet."

"Look, Peggy. You can't be out on patrol at night until we catch this man or he turns himself in. Explain the situation to your chief, ask for an inside job—or at least a day watch."

"I'm not going to let him scare me, Buck," I said. "Besides, I don't have to go back out on patrol until tomorrow night. You'll probably have him by then."

Ten

But he didn't. After finding the storage building on the experimental farm where Jason had apparently lived for a time, Buck and his detectives turned up no further signs of him anywhere, in spite of the fact that the picture of him was plastered all over campus and ran in the newspaper and was shown on television daily, and the doctors Atwood announced a fair-sized reward for information leading to his capture. The FBI had no fingerprints on file that matched Jason's either.

Something about Jason and his real or fictitious friend Tolliver made me think of my brother Kenny—my stepbrother, actually. He was the result of my mother's first and only night of sex with her high school sweetheart, just before he left to get killed in Korea. When he was sixteen and I was nine, Kenny ran away from home. I saw him occasionally after that—he wore a ponytail, of course, and a peace symbol, and there was hair on his face that he hoped, if he left it alone long enough, would someday be a beard, and he did all the drugs that were available then. He also preached a philosophy of "Do it!" that he justified by ideas he'd lifted from neo-Jungian therapists, Indian gurus, pop musicians, and anybody else trying to turn a buck off the Age of Aquarius.

Kenny would be in his forties now, if he's still alive, but the last time I'd seen him, he'd had the same look about him of passionless cynicism hiding a little lost boy that I'd glimpsed in Jason. I didn't think Jason had been high on anything when I met him or talked to him on the phone. I see people who are high on drugs fairly often in my line of work, so I have some experience with that subject.

I went out on patrol again Saturday night but didn't enjoy it. The campus is more deserted than usual on weekends in the middle of the night, so I didn't meet many people, but I approached those I did with my heart in my throat and my hand close to my pistol, and when my watch finally ended I was exhausted.

Sunday around midnight I was strolling down the darkened corridors of Watts Hall when an office door behind me opened. I spun around.

"Professor Pomeroy!"

"Sorry if I startled you, Officer Clancy," he said. "I suppose I should have knocked before bolting from my office like that."

With Professor Pomeroy, you couldn't always be sure when he was being serious. It's possible he no longer knew himself.

He was an elderly professor of philosophy I'd often seen in the building late at night, working on a book on the place of God in Plato's *Republic*. He'd invited me into his office a few times and over tea tried to explain what his book was about. I gathered it was no closer to being finished now than when he'd first embarked on it over forty years ago. It's a difficult question, he'd assured me. For one thing, what did God mean to Plato and his contemporaries?

I asked him if he wanted company back to his car.

He screwed up his faded eyes under the great skeins of yarn that constituted his eyebrows. "I shouldn't think that would be necessary," he said. He looked down at his threadbare suit. "As any thug with eyes can see, I'm not carrying enough money to make it worth his while to bop me on the head. It's yet another reason I'm pleased with my decision to take a vow of poverty and become a philosophy professor." His face darkened. "Nor am I likely to attract the sexual predator, like that poor woman over on the Agriculture Campus on Wednesday."

We said good-night and I continued on through the building as he went out into the night, armed only with his shabby suit and aged maleness, which would probably be enough to get him safely home.

I didn't attend the memorial service for Dana Michaels Monday evening because I agreed with Jason that I was in on her murder with him; I attended it because I wanted to try to create a kind of closure, put her behind me so I could get on with my life. Because of Jason, our paths had crossed briefly—for only a few minutes, in fact—but those minutes might have been decisive for her: when she'd encountered Jason, she'd known what to expect, and that had determined how she behaved toward him.

On the other hand, she'd told her office mate that she thought she'd seen Jason somewhere before. If Russell was telling the truth, it was possible Jason killed her to keep her from exposing him—for whatever reason he might have had for that.

The parking lot was about a quarter full when I arrived, with people, singly and in groups, dashing through the rain to the church. As I got out of my car I glanced up and saw a man coming toward me, his head down against the rain, his raincoat open

and flapping behind him. He was wearing a clerical
collar and a cross on a chain that glittered dully
against his dark suit coat in the light from the
church. He had on a hat that matched his suit, and a
dark, well-trimmed mustache.

He glanced up as he approached me, hesitated,
then smiled, lowered his head again, and went on
toward the church. I assumed he thought he recognized me from his congregation, and when he
didn't, consigned me to limbo.

I flipped up my raincoat's hood and joined a
group of people walking quickly to the church.
Once inside, I stood in the aisle a moment looking
around. I spotted Buck sitting alone in the gloom
beneath a softly glowing stained-glass window that
depicted people doing obscurely religious things.
He saw me coming, raised an eyebrow, and indicated the place beside him.

"Who's here?" I whispered, as I slid down the
pew to his side.

"A lot of faculty from the School of Veterinary
Medicine," he replied. "Some of Dana Michaels's
old high school friends. Her mother, stepfather, and
brother are in that alcove over there, along with
other family members. Some ghouls too, probably."

The obituary had said Dana's father was "the late
Lieutenant Commander Gordon Michaels, USN."
Her stepfather, Thomas Wallace, was listed as a
retired naval chief warrant officer. Wallace looked
sullen but sat erect—his navy training, no doubt.

Dana's mother was small, with curly light-brown
hair. Her eyes were red, but she wasn't crying now
that she was on parade—her training too, no doubt,
as the wife of two career navy men.

Dana's brother was small like his mother. The
obituary had said that he lived in Norfolk, Virginia,

but didn't say what he did. Since he wasn't in uniform, I guessed he probably wasn't in the navy.

I'd spent four years in the navy myself, two of them in Norfolk.

A stout middle-aged woman in a dark dress, her gray hair crisply permed, came through the church doorway and marched down the aisle at the head of a small group of people. They all found seats in the front pews.

"That's Doctor Julia Atwood," Buck whispered, "and the rest of the Atwood Lab people. The gangly fellow bringing up the rear is her son, Doctor Charlie."

"They all have the surly looks of kids on a grade school field trip," I said. "Which one's Barry Russell?"

"Why?"

"I guess because if Jason hadn't confessed, he'd be my first choice for Dana's killer."

He smiled, shook his head. "He's the fellow with the thinning blond hair and the glasses who's sitting behind Doctor Atwood."

"He's looking especially solemn and uncomfortable, isn't he?" I said. "I guess I don't blame him. It must feel a bit awkward, attending a memorial service for a woman you've tried to evict from your office and called names."

I recognized the people I'd met the afternoon I'd been in the Atwood Lab when I'd met Dana Michaels: Millard Pyles, the porcine man who'd been perched on Lorraine Cullin's desk, and Lorraine herself, looking small and tidy and gray, sitting next to him.

"Isn't that someone you know?" Buck said, nodding over to another part of the church.

It was Al, an old boyfriend, a veterinarian with a

private practice of his own. During the time we'd been together he was also an adjunct professor in the School of Veterinary Medicine, teaching courses to veterinary students on how to run a private practice. I used to joke that he taught Advanced Bedside Manner, since he was so good with sick animals.

After we'd broken up, he'd married a woman named Dierdre or Deirdre—however she spelled it. I'd stolen Al from her originally, so she doesn't enjoy the sight of me, and as a result Al and I had lost touch. I looked to see if she was with him, but she wasn't. Probably home with the kids, twins.

The doors closed then, the lights dimmed, and a pastor—not the one I'd encountered in the parking lot—entered from a small door off to one side and stepped to the pulpit and led us in prayer. He then spoke at some length, but without going into detail, about the mysterious ways in which God works.

The service lasted an hour and included brief talks by Dana Michaels's brother, Doctor Julia Atwood, and one of Dana's old high school friends.

Her brother admitted apologetically that he hadn't known his sister well, since she was a girl and he was a boy eight years her senior. But he recalled her as shy and sweet, and a strong and loving support for their mother after their father's tragic death. She'd had to be the man of the house during that period, he said, since he was in his first year of college and living far from home.

He also spoke of her love for animals: she brought every kind of stray animal home, he said with a laugh that ended abruptly in a sob.

Then Doctor Atwood strode to the pulpit. She was heavy and wide, like a modern tank. She gripped the sides of the pulpit with plump hands and stared out at us from slightly bulging gray eyes,

her large head just barely rising above the pulpit like
a moon.

"I was Doctor Michaels's colleague in the Atwood
Lab," she said brusquely and without introducing
herself. "I was pleased when she accepted our offer
of a postdoctoral fellowship, for I knew she had
offers from other fine institutions too. Until her life
was cut so short by a senseless act of violence, I
expected to spend many years with her as a valued
and productive member of my research team."

That must have sat well with Barry Russell, I
thought, Dana's office mate and rival for a position
in the lab. I tried to see how he was reacting to that
but couldn't see anything from the back except his
bowed blond head.

Doctor Atwood went on to say that Dana had
transformed the love she felt for individual animals,
about which her brother had spoken so movingly,
into a desire to improve the lives of all animals
through research. Had she lived, Dana would certainly have made many important contributions in
the field of veterinary medicine.

She turned to Dana Michaels's family. "I know
what it's like to lose a promising child," she said.
She seemed to want to say more, then changed her
mind and concluded with, "You have my deepest
sympathy," and sat down.

An old friend from high school got up and spoke
self-consciously of some of her memories of Dana.
She'd protested against the use of animals in biology classes. She believed it was an unnecessary waste
of life that only taught students that animals were
objects to be used and then thrown away. Stray dogs
were known to follow Dana to school, the friend
said with a smile, although the other students
suspected she encouraged them by dropping pieces

of her lunch behind her as she walked. That elicited a ripple of hushed laughter through the church.

"And not only stray animals," she went on. "Some of Dana's friends were strays too. She seemed to have a special affinity for outsiders—people like me," she added, blushing.

After the service, Buck and I followed the crowd to the reception hall in the church basement. I got a cup of coffee and went over to Al, who was talking to Jim Gates, Lillian's radiologist—or Rufus's, I should say. Doctor Atwood and some of her colleagues were talking to Dana's family.

I nudged Al in the ribs with an elbow, just like old times—I couldn't help it. He jumped, sloshing coffee into his saucer. He's ticklish.

"Peggy!" He looked flustered. "What're you doing here?"

"What are you?"

"I knew Dana Michaels," he said. "Did you?"

"I met her briefly," I said, and left it at that.

Suddenly Doctor Atwood turned and looked at me. Then she came over and, standing closer than I like, said, "I'm told you're the campus policewoman who was accosted by this man Jason the day before he killed Doctor Michaels."

Her round face was curiously flat, with a small nose that made it seem even flatter, and her prominent gray eyes glittered as though she were enjoying herself, or about to.

"Yes," I said.

"You didn't arrest him because he hadn't bothered you enough, and you also had a friend waiting for you up at the Small Animal Clinic with a dog."

"That's true too," I said, feeling my face burning.

"He accosted you again that night when you were on duty, in uniform, and armed, and you let him walk away then too." She used language like a dull ax, spoke in bursts of words, like a machine gun.

"Yes. He didn't do anything I could arrest him for then."

"But he did the afternoon before?" she demanded.

"I don't know," I said. "It was a judgment call."

"Do you think it was a good judgment call now?"

"I can't answer that," I said, trying not to revert to my Catholic girlhood, when the sisters Mary Margaret Hitler and Mary Elizabeth Stalin—they'd earned their names on account of their mustaches—could carry on an inquisition that would reduce me to a sniveling child in moments.

A little behind Doctor Atwood, like a shadow, stood Lorraine Cullin, her thin lips compressed righteously as she watched us through her sequined glasses. She was the only woman I'd seen in the church who was wearing a hat, a little black thing with a scrap of veil that partially covered her small forehead.

The man with the name so ugly it had to be psychologically corroding, Millard Pyles, was standing beside her. He said, "Perhaps the university police are unaccustomed to arresting people, Julia. It might disturb the serenity of the campus."

I wanted to tell him that loafers with tassels weren't appropriate footwear at a memorial service.

"You're a cop, and you had the opportunity to arrest the pervert who killed my stepdaughter? And you didn't because he wasn't offensive enough to you? That was your 'judgment call'?"

It was Dana Michaels's stepfather who spoke. He was shorter than I. In my experience, that's always a danger sign in a man, especially a military man. He was in his fifties, bald on top, his hair grizzled on the sides, standing at attention and rocking back and forth angrily.

His wife, Dana's mother, was standing beside him but somehow contriving to look as though she were one step behind.

"Take it easy now, Tom," she said, giving him a concerned look.

He liked the sound of his own voice too much to take it easy. He stared at her and then at me, as though the story he'd just heard were incomprehensible, surreal. It was becoming that for me now too. "Why didn't you arrest him?" he demanded, his voice rising. "Aren't you a policeman—policewoman, I mean? Is that what you're trained to do, let sex fiends go?"

"I didn't think his behavior justified my trying to arrest him," I said, struggling to keep my voice under control, angry because I could hear it trembling. I'd known people who translate grief into rage because rage is easier to deal with: you just dump it on somebody else. I'd also known people who express rage instead of grief because they don't feel grief. I didn't know which kind I was dealing with here.

"A judgment call," he repeated sarcastically. "What the hell kind of cop are you anyway? A police*man* would've arrested him for that! He would've got his name, at least, and maybe put the fear of God in him."

"A man wouldn't have accosted another man like that in the first place," Al interjected suddenly.

Tom Wallace swung around to see who'd said that and then looked up—Al's a tall man who tends to loom. Wallace closed his mouth.

The secretary, Lorraine Cullin, surprised me by saying, somewhat hesitantly, "She *was* able to give the police a description of the man, at least, and a name."

"Of course she was, Lorraine," Millard Pyles said condescendingly. "But some of the other women he accosted could have done as much."

I wondered how Pyles and Doctor Atwood would handle diamond-backed rattlesnakes in their mailboxes.

The man Buck had told me was Doctor Atwood's son, Doctor Charlie, hadn't said anything yet, just hovered in the back of the Atwood Lab group and watched us with the slightly protruding gray eyes he'd inherited from his mother. Now he added his two cents worth: "In my opinion," he drawled, "this fellow Jason was at the hospital the night he killed Dana to try to talk to you again, Officer. He seemed to have a thing for you, didn't he? But he met Dana instead. It was at about the same time you'd been there the afternoon before, wasn't it? Maybe, frustrated because it wasn't you . . ." He let his voice trail off, shrugging helplessly.

I hadn't thought of it that way. And as far as I knew, neither had Buck. Or maybe he had, but he wanted to spare me the knowledge, unlike these good folk.

"Dana's hair did have a lot of red in it," Pyles added, nodding thoughtfully. "It's possible this Jason even mistook Dana for you until he got up close to her—it was a dark afternoon, wasn't it? Then, when he realized you weren't going to be coming that afternoon, he settled on her instead. Hence the ensuing tragedy."

"You're probably lucky you didn't appear that night," Doctor Charlie added. He resembled a huge rabbit, with soft, heavy features and a sleepy, good-natured face. He didn't look as if he meant any harm.

I felt an arm going around me and turned to see who it belonged to: Al. It had been a long time since we'd stood together like that. He'd always been great with animals; I remembered that he had a great bedside manner for people too, in moments of crisis. I seemed to be needing a lot of that sort of thing lately.

I relaxed and let the awfulness of what these people were saying wash over me. I'd felt I was drowning, but it was better now.

I turned to Dana's mother. "I wish he'd attacked me," I said. "I could have handled that."

She nodded, tried to smile encouragingly at me, and started to cry instead.

"Could you?" her husband asked sarcastically. He put his arm around his wife, patting her shoulder awkwardly. "Why in God's name did Dana want to come here anyway? She had her pick of the best veterinary colleges in the country—and she chose this place! She didn't even think that highly of Doctor Atwood."

Doctor Atwood turned and looked at him with a frown she quickly turned into a sympathetic smile.

"Tom," Mrs. Wallace said, "please."

"Really!" Lorraine Cullin exclaimed. "I don't think—"

"It's all right, Lorraine," Doctor Atwood said.

"I'm only repeating what Dana herself said about it, Barb," Mr. Wallace blustered.

"She wanted to be near us, dear," Mrs. Wallace said, and started crying. "That's why she decided to come here. And of course she thought very highly of Doctor Atwood—of all the people in the lab," she added as something of an afterthought.

Her husband started to speak again, then thought better of it. "Of course she did, Barb," he said, as though speaking to a child.

Buck came up then and whispered to me, "Could I talk to you for a moment, Peggy?"

I smiled up at Al, whispered "Thanks!" and followed Buck out into the hall.

"Look at this," he said, nodding down at the opened guest book on a small table next to the door.

Near the bottom of the page, next to Buck's finger, in a bold, clear hand, was "The Reverend Jason Niemand."

I stared at it a long time, feeling the anger knotting in my stomach. I'd taken enough German to know that *niemand* means "no one." And I knew what "Jason" meant too.

Eleven

"You mean my stepdaughter's killer was *here?*" Mr. Wallace roared, his eyes wide with indignation.

"It looks like it," Buck answered grimly.

The man's eyes jumped from Buck to me and back to Buck. "Then why didn't you catch him, dammit? The two of you just come here for the *food?*"

"Tom!" his wife said. "The man was wearing a disguise. We both spoke to him too, and he seemed to be exactly what he claimed to be. We've both seen the pictures of the man—we know them by heart—and we didn't see through his disguise. Why should they?"

I could sympathize with her point. Jason had recognized me in the parking lot, done enough of a double take that I noticed it, then passed almost within touching distance, and I hadn't recognized him either.

"Because they're police—or *he* is, at any rate," he added, glaring at Buck.

He hadn't approached Dana's mother and step-father himself. Her mother had made a point of going over to him to ask him how he'd known her daughter.

"He seemed a little taken aback at first," she said. "I suppose we—I—should have been suspicious because of that. I mean, we're told that murderers sometimes attend the funerals of their victims, but you don't really expect it, do you? Especially dressed as men of the cloth."

Jason had told her he was the University's Episcopal chaplain and that he'd met Dana when she'd attended a service at his church with a friend who was a member. Later, he'd met with her several times in his office in the church. He claimed she'd shown an interest in becoming an Episcopalian.

"I wondered about that," Mrs. Wallace said. "Dana wasn't very religious, as far as we knew. And I thought it was strange that she hadn't mentioned it—"

"The creep was toying with us!" her husband broke in. "He'd murdered Dana, and he was *toying* with us—in a church! At her memorial service! What the hell kind of world is this anyway, with people like that in it?"

Afterward, Buck and I ran through the rain to his car and sat a while in the dark and talked. It was a little after nine, still plenty of time for me to get to work.

"Jason toyed with me too," Buck said, "but I decided not to tell Mr. Wallace that. He was holding a napkin with a brownie on it in one hand and a cup of coffee in the other, and told me he'd seen me on television discussing the progress we were making in locating Jason—locating *him*," Buck added viciously.

"He's being incredibly reckless," I said. "Almost as though he doesn't care if he's caught."

"Maybe, but he didn't try to chat with you in a brightly lit room."

I asked him what he'd learned about Dana Michaels since I'd last talked to him about the case. He shook his head. "Nothing that suggests her killer was anybody but Jason," he said, "if that's what you mean. If she had a social life, she didn't talk about it to anybody we've interviewed. Barry Russell's the only man she dated, as far as we know—and he denies they were dates."

"A very mysterious woman," I said, listening to the rain pattering on the roof of Buck's car.

"Not really. Just one who didn't make friends easily. I also get the impression that none of the junior people in the Atwood Lab are very close: they're in competition with each other for the few jobs available these days. It's a cutthroat business." After a moment he went on with a smile: "There is one little thing, though. Doctor Michaels under-cooked salmon."

I raised an eyebrow, waiting for him to explain.

"Shortly after she arrived here, her next-door neighbors invited her over to dinner. She had them back, but they said her cooking was terrible: she undercooked the salmon."

In Buck's eyes, I knew, that didn't necessarily mean Dana was a terrible cook. He'd once served me undercooked salmon, claiming it was all the rage in northern California. Dana had come here from California too.

I can sympathize with a lousy cook. Buck says I'm the only woman he knows over thirty who doesn't own a rubber spatula: he looked in vain for one once in my kitchen when he was making some kind of exotic dessert to try to offset the taste of my lasagna. I sometimes wonder how he knows so much about what other women have in their kitchens.

"That's all they had to say about her?"

"Not quite. They told us they thought she had a man staying with her sometime in mid-December. They heard them talking loudly late one night—it sounded like an argument to them, although they couldn't make out what it was about. The man sounded as though he'd been drinking."

"How about Dana?" I asked. The image I'd formed of her didn't include being drunk or having a loud quarrel with a drunk in her home either.

"They weren't sure about her. They thought she was trying to reason with him."

"Did they get a look at him?"

Buck shook his head. "The wife only saw him from her kitchen window one morning as he and Michaels were walking to her car. She never saw him again after that."

"I'll bet it was her office mate, Barry Russell. Weren't they dating around then?"

Buck smiled, shrugged, stared through his rain-streaked windshield. "Well, of course, he denies they were dating. He also claims he was never even in her house. They were just two single people who spent some time together, that's all."

"Sure! I'll have to see Barry Russell before I form an opinion about that," I said, which made Buck laugh.

"The California detectives haven't turned up anything that connects Russell and Dana Michaels either, Peggy. Apparently he's telling the truth about that. He barely knew who she was when they were at Davis together. As far as the guy in her house goes, well—she was an adult woman living in the late nineties, after all."

Right. If the man really wasn't Barry Russell—a big if—then he could have been anybody—even, as far as I knew, somebody she'd met in a bar. She could have had too much to drink and taken him home with her. It still happens. I know because as a campus cop, I've occasionally seen the results.

Or he could have been somebody she met anywhere on campus, faculty or student or staff. And most likely, whoever he was, he probably had nothing at all to do with Dana Michaels's murder, which was just the unpremeditated killing of a drifter, a loser, a creep named Jason.

Buck started his car, switched on his lights, and drove me across the parking lot to my car, which he'd never seen before. It was only a few months old, a liquid black Volkswagen Golf I'd bought to replace my trusty old Rabbit, which had met with a fatal accident on Lake Eleanor at Christmas.

"Nice," he said, and asked me the kinds of questions about it that people ask, mileage and such. I told him my first car had been an ancient Volkswagen Bug that I'd driven when I was in the navy, and I'd been partial to VWs ever since, even though the Golf was a far cry from the Bug. Then I gave his arm a squeeze and slid out and got quickly behind the wheel of my car before I got soaked.

He followed me out of the lot, honking once as he turned left and I turned right. His comments on my car made me savor the new-car smell and that lightened my mood a bit, made me almost forget the defeats I'd suffered that afternoon at the hands of the Atwood crowd and Dana's stepfather—and from Jason too, who'd passed within a yard or two of me going into the chapel without my recognizing him.

Something cold and sharp touched my neck. "Forgive us our trespasses," Jason hissed, and then, "Steady, Peggy! Think of your car as the Pope-mobile. Drive carefully."

Terrified and angry, I started to brake, crying "Ow!" when the knife jabbed into my flesh.

"Don't stop! I only want a ride home—it's raining out, in case you hadn't noticed. Okay?"

I nodded.

"And don't speed up. It's too dangerous on these city streets. Besides, I used to see that trick on TV all the time when I was a kid: you know, where the hero floors it so if the bad guy kills him, he'll die in the crash too. I always thought, if I was the bad guy, I'd kill the good guy and take my chances on getting out alive. Who says you can't get a useful education watching television?"

"I thought you were leaving town, Jason."

"Still have a few things to do—people to see—first. I'll give you a call when I leave, though, so you can wave good-bye. Turn left at the stop sign. You're bleeding," he went on, more softly. "I'm sorry." He wiped the knife blade on my raincoat. "Your blood's on it anyway, so a little more won't matter. I don't want to ruin the upholstery on your new car."

I glanced into the rearview mirror. I'd been right about how close-set his eyes were. They were brown, with heavy lids that gave him a sleepy, disinterested look. I'd got the high cheekbones right too. Other than that, there wasn't much striking about his features: he had a small, almost feminine mouth with muscles bunched lightly around it, and a pointy chin. The mustache was real, I could see that, but he'd darkened it with something. He had to have darkened his hair too, and cut it short. Close up he looked older than I'd thought—close to thirty, I guessed.

He was still wearing the clerical collar inside the open raincoat, and the cross on the chain hung down and lay on the back of my seat.

"Memorizing my face, are you?" he asked, catching my eyes in the mirror. "Good, maybe you'll get it right next time. I didn't think you really captured my *soul*, you know, in the last one. It missed the essential Jason."

"What's the essential Jason?" I asked. "A man

who torments women, then gets mad and kills them when they take offense?"

His eyes left the mirror, and I felt the point of the knife sketch a light line across my neck. I tried to pull my head back, out of the way, but the knife followed.

"'The essential Jason,'" he repeated thoughtfully, his eyes suddenly shadowed. "What a crock!"

"Is that all you can say?"

"Dana's stepdad's a real asshole, isn't he?" he went on, changing the subject. "I overheard him trashin' you." He sighed. "The things you've had to put up with on my account—and from ol' Doc J too. Vicious tongue on that woman." He made a disapproving noise. "Who'd believe it! I remember when she used to dandle kittens on her knee on TV, talk baby talk to puppies, her little boy—Doctor C, I think—standing by, ready to hand her more warm and fuzzy things. Now he's become a kind of big fluffy thing himself, hasn't he?"

He laughed suddenly, revealing the slightly crooked teeth I remembered from the lake below the veterinary hospital. They needed cleaning. "And can you believe the police we have today?" he went on, shaking his head. "Here you have a savage murderer loose at a gathering of mourners for one of his victims—*one* of his victims, please note!—and they didn't check the cars in the parking lot! No wonder there's so much crime in the world these days. You know what I think it is, Peggy?"

I didn't say anything. He prodded my neck with the knife, not too hard. "Peggy?"

"What do you think it is, Jason?"

"Turn at the next light. I think it's the fault of civil service! You can't fire civil servants, you know that? Once they pass probation, you're stuck with 'em. A guy shows up on time for a couple of years and passes probation, then he's got a job for life, no matter how lazy or fucked up he gets. It's kind of like mailmen or professors with tenure: you can't fire 'em no matter what they do or don't do. That's why so many of 'em get weird, you know, and buy rifles and shoot up the place—mailmen, I mean. Professors haven't started doing that yet, I guess, though it's only a matter of time."

"Sounds like you know what you're talking about," I said, thinking this was a crazy conversation.

"Me?" He laughed again. "Not from personal experience—*I* couldn't pass probation for dogcatcher!" I felt the knife prod me again, felt something warm running slowly down my neck. "Sorry, but I did tell you to drive slowly, didn't I? Here, let me get that." He produced a handkerchief and dabbed at the blood on my neck.

"Ow!" I said.

"Sorry," he said again. "You know how to get to the Ag Campus from here without using the freeway? Good, take me there, please, and don't attract attention with your driving."

I turned down a one-way street that went east to the Ag Campus.

"So tell me about your brother, Peggy," he said.

"My—? Oh. There's not much to tell," I said. "He tuned in, turned on, and dropped out in the sixties. I don't know if he's alive or dead. What about your friend Tolliver?"

He laughed. "Not much to tell there either."

"You said you owe him a lot."

He grinned at me in the rearview mirror. "I owe Tolliver everything," he said solemnly, "including my life. And it was Tolliver who taught me not to care about anything. Maybe I'll tell you all about it when we get to the Ag Campus."

He laughed suddenly, a laugh filled with relief, as though he'd just realized he'd accomplished something tremendous. "God! Can you imagine, strolling right into the chapel, talking to the homicide cop who's in charge of trying to find me? He's a friend of yours, huh? What's he got that I don't? Never mind—and then hitching a ride with you!"

"What do you want with me, Jason?" I asked.

"Just to talk, really—about life and stuff. And I thought maybe, if I promised to turn myself in afterward, you'd let me—oh, never mind! We'll talk about it when we get where we're goin'. It's one of those farm buildings on the Ag Campus—the last place the cops'd think of looking for me now, right?"

"And afterwards, you'll turn yourself in?"

"I promise."

I didn't believe him, of course, and I had no intention of driving someplace where we'd be alone: I'd never really approved of what Judith did to kill Holofernes. There's got to be a better way. I glanced up at him in the mirror again, caught the look of amusement in his eyes, and the emptiness, the passionlessness behind that, or whatever it was that I hadn't been able to get into the artist's sketch of him.

"All right," I said.

He laughed.

"Are you high on something?" I asked.

"No! I'm just naturally high these days. Who needs drugs when life's such a blast?"

"I don't think killing—and this—comes naturally to you," I said. "I think you need help."

"You wouldn't be the first," he said with sudden bitterness in his voice. "I told you already. I didn't mean to kill Dana," he added.

"Where'd you know her from?"

"Who?" His eyes in the mirror looked puzzled.

"You knew Dana from before you met her that afternoon."

"Where'd you get that idea?"

"She told somebody she thought she recognized you."

"She must've been mistaken," he said flatly. "I never saw her before in my life. She just came along the path—like Little Red Riding Hood, you know? And I was in the bushes like the big bad wolf, hoping you'd come along again. But when you didn't, and she did, I figured, hey, you know what they say about a bird in the hand bein' worth two in the bush."

I flicked my eyes up at him, trying to see if he was telling the truth, but couldn't decide. He returned my stare, unblinking.

"Maybe you were lucky, Peggy," he went on. "That memorial service could have been for you instead of Dana. If we wanted to be mean about it, we could say she died for your sins!" He flashed his grin again above the clerical collar and the cross.

I felt the blood drain out of my face, and my knuckles turned white on the steering wheel. I slammed on the brakes, flinched away from the knife as the seat belt caught my body, and turned as Jason's head and shoulders came forward over the back of the seat. I grabbed the chain holding the cross dangling from his neck and yanked.

He grunted and swore. The chain broke and he let go of the knife. The car, skidding out of control on the rain-slicked street, slammed sideways into something, knocking me against the door. Jason threw open the passenger door, scrambled out, and started running.

I grabbed the knife off the seat, unlatched my seat belt, and squeezed out the door between my car and the pickup truck it had hit. I started across the street after Jason, then flinched back as the headlights of a car flashed in my face, momentarily blinding me. The driver braked, started to lose control, regained traction, and sped away, honking.

Jason darted through a chain-link fence on the other side of the street and ran across a playground, his black raincoat flapping behind him like ravens' wings. I raced after him, splashing through puddles on the asphalt. He disappeared around the corner of an old brick school building about thirty yards in front of me.

As I swung around the corner, the knife in my right hand ready to use if he was waiting to ambush me, I saw him standing in the middle of the street in front of the school, caught in the headlights of a police car, frantically waving it to a stop. The driver rolled down the window and Jason leaned in, pointing back at me and gesturing wildly.

The passenger door opened and a cop got out and started around the car, loosening the pistol in his holster as the driver turned on the spotlight and shined it at me, blinding me. Then I realized I was still holding Jason's knife in one hand, the crucifix on its chain in the other.

"Hold on!" I cried. "I'm a cop!"

I dropped the knife and groped under my raincoat for my shield in the pocket of the dark blazer I'd worn to the memorial service.

"Freeze!" the cop standing by the car yelled, and I squinted up and saw him pointing his pistol at me— it seemed huge, even at that distance—and suddenly I saw myself for what I was: a crazed woman, her hair matted to her head, swinging a cross in one hand while chasing a man of the cloth with a knife in the other, and now reaching for a concealed weapon.

I froze, staring into the mouth of the cop's pistol, terrified he wouldn't wait for me to bring my hand out empty before shooting. The cop at the wheel slid out of the squad car and pointed his pistol at me too.

"Okay," I cried. "I'm bringing my hand out. It's empty." Why don't cops have some kind of secret code word they can use on occasions like this?

With elaborate slowness I brought my hand out of my coat and spread both hands out to my sides, open, letting the cross fall at my feet.

"Down on your face!" the first cop ordered. "Now!" He was still behind the squad car, the driver using his open door as a shield. Jason was standing at the rear of the car, watching us.

I knelt in a puddle of water on the asphalt and said, "Okay, but—"

"*Now!*"

I went down on my hands, then face, then laid my hands out in front of me. The two cops approached slowly, one on each side, their pistols never leaving me. People had pointed guns at me before, but this was worse somehow. I remembered Jason's words about civil service and cops and competency. I hoped he was wrong about these two.

I lifted my face as far up from the rough wet sidewalk as my neck would allow and hollered, "I'm a cop, dammit! And that phony pastor is driving off with your car. Look behind you!"

But like Jason, they'd watched a lot of television as kids and could see through my simple ruse. They knew I wanted them to turn around so I could somehow draw my weapon and pop them both. They didn't look back, just kept their eyes and pistols on me—until the sound of their squad car peeling rubber as it took off made both of them turn and look.

"Shit!" one of them screamed, and took a couple of running steps after it.

"Cal, no!" the other cop hollered. Cal had assumed a shooter's position and was about to fire off a couple of rounds at the car disappearing down a street of nice middle-class family homes. Reluctantly, he lowered his pistol, and they stood together and watched helplessly as their car turned a corner and disappeared.

"Can I get up now?" I asked.

They turned and looked at me, murder in their eyes.

"Slowly," the cop who wasn't Cal said.

Twelve

It was almost midnight, and Buck and I were sitting together in an all-night coffee house near City Hall. Other cops were sitting at tables around us, huddled over coffee, talking quietly.

"Why didn't I check your car before I let you drive off?" Buck said bitterly.

"Why didn't I?" I snapped, because Buck sometimes treats me like a daughter. "It wasn't your car. But who would've thought he'd hide in a car instead of getting out of there as soon as he'd signed the guest book?"

I'd left the driver's door unlocked because you have to use the key to lock it and I sometimes forget.

I contemplated the coffee in my cup with distaste: late-night cop coffee always tastes the same, no matter where you get it. "Jason could have bought the suit he was wearing anywhere," I said, "and you can get crosses like the one he was wearing in any biker or head shop. But the clerical shirt and collar looked real."

"We'll check the costume shops," Buck said dispiritedly, "and the stores that sell clerical garb. Maybe Jason wrote a check, or used a credit card, or a clerk'll remember him from your description. I take it you don't believe he's the son of the pastor of the biggest church in town?"

"No more than I believe he's the son of a lawyer or CEO," I said sourly. "But whatever he is, he can't be living on the street anymore. He's too well-groomed for that now."

He asked me if I thought Jason was a sociopath or psychopath, and I said I didn't know what he was.

"Sometimes I think he really feels bad about killing Dana, but at other times he seems to take it as a joke. I can't think of anything that explains him, except that he's got the sense of humor of somebody who's read too many comic books or watched too much television as a kid. He doesn't sound as though he thinks life's very real, or much fun. It's like he's in a time warp: somebody left over from the sixties who never grew older, just wearier."

"He's managed to avoid capture for five days now," Buck said, his voice rising in anger. "Where's he living? Who's hiding him?" He came as close to tearing his hair as I'd ever seen him. "He's making me look like a fool," he added.

"How do you think I looked," I said, "charging a police car with a knife and a cross?"

His eyes widened as he visualized it. Then he laughed. He tried to stop himself but managed only to turn it into a kind of fizzing noise, which made me start laughing too.

We stopped abruptly just before we turned hysterical as other cops in the café threw us curious glances.

"How's your car?" Buck asked, when he'd recovered his dignity.

"It still smells new," I said grumpily. "Needs some body work, but it drives okay." It had slid into the side of an old pickup truck parked at the curb, whose owner hadn't been able to see whatever damage I'd done for the dents and rust already on it.

I told Buck that Jason had said some things that made me think he knew something about universities from the inside. He'd mentioned he thought tenured professors were like civil servants: they put in a few good years, get tenure, then don't ever have to do much again. "When I was a student," I added, "I didn't even know what tenure was."

"Well, kids today know a lot more than they did when you were a student," he said. "That's why they're so cynical. You think he could be a disgruntled professor?"

I shrugged. It wasn't entirely out of the question. I'd had some run-ins with a comparative literature professor who looked and talked like Jason.

"Jason looked puzzled when I told him Dana thought she'd seen him somewhere before," I said. "He said he'd never seen her before. I believe him."

"She could've been mistaken," Buck said.

"Or her office mate could have lied about it," I retorted.

He glanced up at me. "After tonight, you'd still prefer that Russell be the killer, not Jason?"

"Of course," I said. "It would let me off the hook."

He gave me a pitying smile, then went back to doodling on his place mat: a sailboat being tossed around in a stormy sea on a napkin. I wondered if the figure in it, hanging on for dear life, was supposed to be him or me.

"Jason told me he thinks I have to share the blame for Dana's murder, since he was waiting for me when she came along."

"Losers are usually very generous when it comes to sharing the guilt," Buck said with an indifferent shrug.

"But if I hadn't told her about him, she might have fallen for his act, or at least not realized he'd harassed me with it too. She might not have snatched the tape recorder." I remembered something from the memorial service. "And both Doctor Charlie and Millard Pyles agree with him," I added.

"Which doesn't exactly make him correct," Buck said, sounding impatient with me. He'd never heard me whine before. It wasn't something I did a lot.

"And, of course," I went on, whining, "everybody blames me for not arresting Jason, or at least demanding he show me some ID the first time he annoyed me."

"I don't blame you, Peggy," Buck said.

I hate being coddled!

We talked a while longer and then I got up, weary and, like my new car, a little battered. The cut on my neck throbbed too.

Buck followed me back to my car in the police garage under City Hall. Even though there was no way Jason could have got to it in there, he made a great show of checking the backseat and trunk anyway, and then I drove up the lighted ramp and out into the night. I drove to Gary's place at Lillian's—he was expecting me. I let myself in with my key and climbed the stairs to the second floor, took a long hot shower, and then slid into bed, quietly so as not to wake him. But he was already awake.

Before roll call the next night, I told Lawrence Fitzpatrick about how Jason had tried to kidnap me. He listened wide-eyed and, to his credit, didn't laugh when I described how Jason had made his escape.

"You should ask for an indoor assignment, Peggy," he said when I'd finished, "or at least switch to a day watch." Buck had told me the same thing, and I'd had to use all my persuasive powers, which are considerable, to keep him from calling

Captain DiPrima and asking him to take me off the dog watch.

"I'm allergic to the molds growing in the walls of this old building," I said, "and sunlight can give you skin cancer." My sleeping schedule had been seriously disrupted, and I was feeling grouchy.

"But he's after you!"

"I know it."

Lawrence is our handsomest cop. Because of this, I didn't trust him the first year I was on the campus cops, although he was hard to dislike. But gradually I realized that his curly blond hair, clear complexion, and chiselled, symmetrical features—sort of like Dudley Do-Right—were as much a curse to him as if he'd been short, squat, and ugly with a complexion like old stucco.

Then he fell in love with one of my best friends, Paula Henderson and—miracle of miracles—she returned the favor, and all my reservations about him fell away. If Paula thought there was some substance behind such a dazzlingly Hollywood facade, then it must really be there. Whether it was there before Paula or not, I don't know, but it's there now.

The rain that had been falling since Monday stopped sometime around one on Wednesday morning, leaving a fine, cold mist that hung over the campus like gauze. I treated every shadow that moved as though it were Jason, tried to anticipate him anticipating me. If a spy satellite had been watching me, I would have looked like a dog trying to find its way home.

Lawrence must have tattled because the dispatcher kept finding excuses to call me, and once when I came out of a building, I saw a figure silhouetted against the light of one of the Old Campus's street lamps, the hood of his raincoat over his head, his shadow thrown across a patch of dim, mist-blurred light. It gave me a jolt, but I recognized him quickly enough: Jesse Porter, keeping an eye on me. I thought of shooting him, just to teach him a lesson, but he'd done that himself once, practicing quick draws in a mirror in one of the men's rooms in the middle of the night, so I decided not to.

"What're you doing here?" I demanded.

"How about coffee?" he countered.

"Sure," I snarled, and we slouched off together to the Adamson Hall dining room. I was glad to have his company but didn't feel like telling him so, although I wouldn't have sat alone in Adamson's dining room that night for anything—I'd once witnessed a murder in there.

We got coffee out of a machine and sat in a corner, and I asked him how he'd happened to find Dana Michaels's body.

"I almost didn't," he said, stirring the weak coffee with a finger. "When I have the squad car, which I did that night, I always drive along the lakeshore on the Ag Campus—on the path, you know—and flash the spotlight into the bushes. You can catch people doing all kinds of things in there like that," he said, shaking his head in disapproval.

"There wasn't much point in doing it that night," he went on, "on account of the rain and the cold— that kind of activity doesn't really get started until June. But I drove along the path anyway, just to watch the rain on the lake. When I got to the steps up to the hospital, I flashed my spot on 'em—and there she was."

He looked at me with his sad monkey's face. "You should've seen her, Peggy—it was terrible. Lyin' there, eyes open and being rained on, like a big doll some kid had left out. Why would anybody do something like that? And how could they just walk away and leave her there and go on about their business?"

He looked up at me with haunted eyes. "What do murderers do, when they get home afterward?"

Thirteen

I didn't sleep well that day, woke up early, and lay in bed with a cup of coffee balanced on my stomach to help me think. With Jason on the loose, I couldn't stay on the dog watch. For that matter, with him on the loose I couldn't have even the little sense of security our civilization gives us these days no matter what watch I took. And I'd be damned if I was going to ask to be allowed to work inside.

What could I do? Wait for Jason's arrest? That didn't sound very appealing, considering how little success Buck was having, with all the resources he had at his disposal.

Dana Michaels had told her office mate, Barry Russell, that she thought she'd seen Jason somewhere before—assuming we could believe Russell, that is. Where? Buck's detectives hadn't found anybody who admitted to knowing him. I wondered if maybe I could trail along in their wake and see if they'd stirred anything up.

While doing that, I could also satisfy my curiosity about Dana Michaels. I'd met her briefly and told her something that a lot of people—even Jason—claimed had led to her death. The least I could do would be to try to get to know her a little better.

My friend Ginny once called me a psychological coroner. Maybe she was right. In which case, it was time for me to go to work.

I decided to begin with Dana's mother and stepfather, who lived in a high-rise condominium on the edge of downtown, a couple of miles northwest of the University. I rode over, chained my bike to a lamppost, and went into the entry hall. I ran my eyes down the list of tenants next to a telephone until I found "Chief Warrant Officer (USN, Ret.) and Mrs. Thomas A. Wallace."

I'd known a lot of warrant officers in the navy. Maybe because they're promoted from the enlisted ranks, they tend more to extremes than other officers: the shiny metal on their shoulder tabs is either no big deal to them or else they expect you to jump from your sickbed to salute them. From what I'd seen of Dana Michaels's stepfather at the memorial service, I assumed he belonged in the latter group.

I'd known wives of career navy men too, an incomprehensible lot whose lives combined the worst of the life of a single parent with that of a 1950s-style homemaker. I imagined Dana Michaels's mother had owned a lot of rubber spatulas in her time.

I dialed the number and Mrs. Wallace answered. She sounded more curious than surprised when I told her who I was. "Yes, of course I remember you. What do you want?"

"I'd like to talk to you about your daughter," I said.

She asked me why and I decided to be honest with her. "For personal reasons," I said. "I want to know who your daughter was. Besides, Dana told her office mate that she thought she knew Jason from somewhere. I know the University campus better than the city cops do, so maybe I can help them figure out where."

She didn't say anything for a minute. Then she sighed. "Oh, I suppose so. My husband wouldn't approve, but he's not home, although he's due anytime."

She met me at the door. She looked better than she had at the service, more at ease, but still with the weary air about her of a woman who's always lived for others and now there's not that much left to do. She was dressed in apple-green slacks and a white blouse. Her short brown hair was turning gray and she wasn't doing anything to disguise the fact.

She offered me coffee and while she got it I drifted around the apartment. It was bright and cheerful, in a characterless sort of way. A ship under full sail plowed through a stormy sea in a painting above the gas fireplace, and several model ships, one in a bottle, were displayed in a glass case.

One wall was covered with framed family photographs: Dana and her brother at various ages, sometimes singly and sometimes together, a few with their mother and stepfather. Tom Wallace seemed always to stand a little outside the group, when he was there at all.

Dana's high school graduation picture was on a little white spinet piano. Her auburn hair had been shoulder length and straight back then instead of short and curly, as I'd seen it. Her face was thinner, and she was staring off into the distance, chin up, the future outside the frame. Retouching had softened what I'd glimpsed in her in the Atwood Lab just one week earlier—her intelligence and seriousness of purpose.

I realized I was sounding like a yearbook editor, trying to think of what to put under her portrait in the yearbook. Her dark green eyes were the only striking thing about her, in the picture as well as in person. Here they had the unfocused look of someone who isn't wearing her glasses. I'd seen them like that once too.

On a table in front of the large picture window that looked out over the city was a partially built model sailing ship, loose pieces scattered around it.

"That's Tom's," his wife said, handing me my coffee. "Dana gave it to him as a birthday present, just a few weeks ago," she added with a catch in her voice. "He's very good at putting them together," she went on quickly. "Unfortunately, we don't have room to display all he's done." She must have caught the expression on my face, for she went on: "He's not taking retirement very well."

"I suppose he's underfoot a lot," I said, perching on an uncomfortable chair.

She sat on the matching sofa. "He was only fifty when he retired—they have to retire after thirty years, you know. It's really so unfair."

"I know," I said. "I was in the navy for four years. Enlisted."

She smiled again, a rueful one this time. "That would be another strike against you with Tom, I'm afraid. He doesn't approve of women in the military. He's written letters to the president of the United States against allowing women on ships."

I smiled stiffly. I'd joined the navy in the naive belief that I could go to sea; I'd spent the next four years making the officers I worked for wish I had. I thought of her husband now, living in this land-locked state, making model sailing ships, and felt an emotion that of course was unworthy of me.

"Military men usually do something else after they retire," I said.

"Oh, Tom does! He went in with his brother on a bar—that's why we moved here after he retired, you see, because his brother lives here. But Tom only works there in the evenings, which means he usually just mopes around the house during the day or goes for long walks along the river. That's where he is now."

"And you've never worked outside the home," I said.

She grimaced, shook her head. "No. When Gordon was still alive—that's Dana and Gordy's father—we moved too often for that, and then there were the children to consider too. Gordon wanted me home for them. Tom wouldn't care if I got a job now," she added, a touch of sarcasm in her voice, "but unfortunately, my typing skills are rusty—assuming there's still a need for typists."

I contemplated the life she'd described for as long as I could stand it, then asked, "Your husband seemed awfully angry at the service. Even before he met me and decided I was to blame for Dana's death, he looked angry. They must have been very close."

She gave me her wistful smile—she had it down pat—and shook her head. "That's just it," she said. "Dana never warmed to him, and that's what he's angry about. She was only ten when her father died. He was a flyer, a war hero, and she adored him. Poor Tom couldn't compete—and Dana let him know it too. Children can be so cruel, can't they? She ignored him for the most part, refused to call him anything but Tom. I suppose it was a mistake for me to marry again. . . ."

In spite of myself, I felt sorry for Tom Wallace, who'd been in a rivalry with a dead man for a child's affections. I felt sorry for Dana too: I imagined her eagerly awaiting her father's returns—returns that were shadowed with her knowledge of his inevitable departures. I thought about how easy it must be to be a loving and attentive parent when you're there only part time.

Mrs. Wallace stared out the picture window at the bright blue March sky, sunlight falling on the unfinished model on the table, and sighed. We were probably thinking the same things.

"Dana took her father's death hard," she said, "much harder than Gordy did. He was so much older, just starting college. Now that she's dead, Tom can never earn her love. He's a man who doesn't like to fail."

"Well," I said, exploring, "Dana didn't see much of him either while she was growing up, did she?"

"Oh, she saw a lot of Tom. We didn't marry until a couple of years before he retired. She was twelve."

We live in an age of barbarity—or so it seems; maybe it's just an age of greater knowledge. So I thought of Thomas Wallace and the twelve-year-old girl who'd become his stepdaughter, and looked again at Mrs. Wallace and wondered if incest could have gone on under her roof without her knowing, or wanting to know, about it. I realized I didn't know these people at all, and even wondering about it was unfair to them all.

I asked her how old Dana was when they moved here.

"Fifteen." She sighed again. "She had to leave her Norfolk friends behind, and that was another loss. She'd been shy as a child even before her father died. She became even more withdrawn after that. She'd always had animals. Her father loved them, and he even gave her a horse of her own. After he died, she became completely wrapped up in her animals."

"And then you moved here."

"Yes, and that was another thing that was hard on her. She never made friends easily, so it was difficult for her to leave the few she had in Norfolk. She wasn't really able to break into any of the cliques here—you know how teenagers are. So she was thrown back even more on animals."

She laughed, remembering. "Dana was always bringing home strays and wounded animals—you heard what someone said at the service—and I always had to find homes for them, since we couldn't keep them all." She glanced at the entryway as somebody walked past in the hall. "Is this really useful to you?" she asked. "My just rattling on?"

I nodded, smiling encouragingly.

"The detectives who interviewed us asked about Dana's personal life too, of course. But it's like looking for a needle in a haystack, isn't it? This Jason could have been somebody she met anywhere, on campus or off."

After graduating from high school, Dana went to the University of Iowa on a scholarship. She earned her B.A. in biology, then got a scholarship to the University of California at Davis, one of the best veterinary medicine schools in the country, where she earned her D.V.M. Then she got a Ph.D. in radiology. She wanted to become a consulting radiologist with her own practice.

I recalled that that's what Lillian's vet, Jim Gates, was planning to do when he got his Ph.D., and wondered if he'd been in competition with Dana for anything.

"Instead of going into private practice," Mrs. Wallace went on, "she surprised us by moving back here in September to do postdoctoral research at the Atwood Lab. She'd decided she wanted a career as a university professor, a scientist."

"You must have seen something of her after that," I said.

"Of course we did!" she said defensively. "But she was always so busy. They work the postdocs so hard over there, you know. But we had her here for dinner a few times and she was with us at Christmas."

She sighed again; she'd had a lot of practice in her life. "We were supposed to have lunch on Friday— she invited me, for once. She said she wanted to talk to me about her plans—her plans for the future." At the thought of Dana's future, she started to cry softly.

A key suddenly turned in the entrance door. Mrs. Wallace reached quickly for a Kleenex as the door opened and Tom Wallace walked in. He stopped when he saw me and looked from me to his wife and back to me.

"Who's this?" he said. "What's the matter, Barb?"

"You remember Peggy O'Neill, Tom," she said.

His eyes widened as he recognized me. "By God! It's the 'campus cop' who lets sexual psychopaths go because she doesn't want to keep a dog waiting." He forced a theatrical laugh, like a bad actor playing a Gestapo captain. "What kind of dog was it that was worth my stepdaughter's life? And what're you doing in my home anyway?"

I jumped up and put my hands on my hips too, mimicking him, and glared at him and made sure he knew it was *down* I was glaring, not up.

"When I was in the navy, 'Chief Warrant Officer Thomas A. Wallace, United States Navy Retired,'" I said, dripping quotation marks around his title like snot, "landlocked on account of sexist meatheads like you, I had to take your crap. But I don't have to now."

His jaw fell open. "You were in the navy?" he asked, choosing to tackle the easy stuff first.

"Yes. You want to make something of it?"

"Too bad you didn't treat my daughter's—my

stepdaughter's—murderer the way you're treating me now," he whined.

"I treated him exactly the way I'm treating you," I said. "To me he was a jerk, neither more nor less, just like you. What're you going to do after you're through abusing me, go out and murder a woman who looks a little like me?"

"Get out of my home," he said, his voice low and menacing.

"It's my home too, Tom," his wife said calmly. "She'll stay until I want her to leave. Now both of you sit down and let's see if we can't be friends. Peggy's just trying to help."

We both stared at her, surprised. He started to say something, thought better of it, then marched out into the kitchen and noisily poured himself a cup of coffee. I sat back down on the edge of my chair.

"Bring the pot in here, please, dear," Mrs. Wallace said. "Peggy needs a refill."

I left my cup on the table. Didn't want to risk him pouring the coffee on my hand.

"What are you here for?" Wallace asked.

I explained it again, stressing my personal interest in Dana and the hope that maybe I could help the homicide cops figure out how, if it was true, Dana might have known who Jason was.

His close-set little eyes never blinked as he listened to me. Then he shrugged and said, "She could've met him anywhere. He could be a burger flipper at the local McDonald's."

"I don't think he's living on the street anymore either," I said. "I don't see how he could have dressed up the way he did for the memorial service if he was."

"So you think somebody's hiding him?"

"It's possible. It could even be somebody who

doesn't know what he's done." I turned to Mrs. Wallace. "You said Dana was going to have lunch with you on Friday, to talk about her future plans. What do you think they could have been?"

"I think Dana was going to leave here," she said, "and go back to Davis."

"Before the year was up?"

She nodded. "That's what she implied. I asked her if she was unhappy in the lab, and she said she'd tell me all about it at lunch."

I turned to her husband. "You said at the memorial service that she had her pick of the best veterinary schools in the country for postdoc work, but she decided to come here instead, even though she didn't think very highly of Doctor Atwood or her lab. Is that true?"

"It's true that's what she told us," he replied, still sulky.

"When Dana was at Davis," Mrs. Wallace said, "I once mentioned Doctor Atwood to her—she's such a big name here, you know—'Doctor J' and all that. Dana just laughed and said her fame is mostly a creation of the local media and anyway, she's no longer very highly thought of by other veterinary scientists. Dana's—was—a bit of a snob, I'm afraid."

"She said Julia Atwood's forgotten what veterinary medicine's all about," Tom Wallace added. "She's only interested in getting money from the government and the drug companies."

"But when Doctor Atwood offered Dana a postdoc here, she took it, and you don't have any idea why?"

"What I think," Barb Wallace said, "is that, deep down inside, she really wanted to come back home—to be near Tom and me. That's why she decided to come here."

"You'd like to think that," Wallace said roughly, "but that doesn't make it true." He stared out the window—or at his unfinished sailing ship. "I've always thought there was a man in California she was interested in—in love with, maybe. They broke up and she suddenly decided to burn her bridges and come back here—come home. Of course," he added sourly, "there could've been somebody here—she'd never tell us if there was."

"Tom's probably right," his wife said. "Once, a year or so ago, I called her long-distance and a man answered. There'd never been a man in her life before that I knew of, so I was quite surprised. I said, 'Is this Dana Michaels's apartment?' and he said, 'Yes, just a minute, I'll get her.' I didn't think to ask him his name, and when I asked Dana about it later—you know how mothers are—she just said he was a friend.

"After she moved back here I tried to pry a little. I asked her if there was anybody in her life. 'Not now,' she said. 'But there was somebody?' I asked. She looked at me for a long time with those eyes of hers she got from her dad, as though considering how much to tell me. Finally she said, 'Oh, yes, Mom, there was a man.' She clearly didn't want me to ask any more about him, but I did anyway. I couldn't help myself. 'Were you serious about him?'

"She laughed strangely and replied that she was as serious about him as she'd been about Beau and Heidi."

"You never told me that!" her husband exclaimed indignantly.

Beau and Heidi? "Who were Beau and Heidi?" I asked.

Mrs. Wallace looked at me and said, "Beau was her horse—a gift from her father when she was nine. Four or five years later Beau got sick, and we had to have him put down. Dana was too young to understand that; she tried to keep it from happening."

Tom Wallace grunted. "I had to take the horse in. Dana begged me not to—she carried on something awful—and when I came back home she called me a killer and wouldn't speak to me for weeks afterward. Not that she spoke much to me anyway."

He laughed humorlessly. "You'd think after she became a vet herself, she'd understand and forgive me—but I never saw any sign of it, if she did."

His wife took his hand and patted it. "Heidi was a dog she had later," she told me.

We talked for a while longer, and then Mrs. Wallace looked at her watch, got up suddenly, and went to the big window and stood there a moment, staring out at the gray rain-swept afternoon. Then she turned and looked at us, her eyes wide, and laughed unpleasantly.

"What's the matter, Barb?" her husband demanded.

"This time last week," she said softly, "Dana was alive. Just about now, she was walking back to the hospital and she met that man, that terrible man—and took his tape recorder away from him. If she hadn't done that, she'd still be alive. We would have had lunch on Friday . . . she was going to tell me her plans . . . for the future."

My skin started to crawl at her words, her tone of voice, her eyes staring at me, and across the room, Dana's eyes staring at the future off beyond the picture frame.

"Why did he have to pick her?" Mrs. Wallace cried with sudden shrillness. "Why couldn't it have been—?"

She realized what she was about to say, clamped a hand over her mouth, and stared at me as though appalled at herself. "You were just having second thoughts about not arresting him, weren't you," she said to me, "when you told Dana about him? You couldn't know you were setting her up to be murdered, could you?"

Tom Wallace got up quickly, went to her, and put his arm around her. He looked at me, his eyes empty. "You'd better go now," he said.

I went. I don't like crawling, so I walked out, chin up.

Fourteen

As I walked my beat that night I thought about how, one week earlier, while I'd been eating popcorn and watching *Gaslight* with Ginny, Dana was being killed. I wondered how Jason was celebrating the anniversary or if he was even aware of it. Had he left town? If so, I might have to live forever with the fear that someday he'd jump out at me from some dark place.

The dispatcher continued to find excuses to call me, of course, but I didn't mind. I met other cops more often than I usually did too. I didn't mind that either, especially since they signaled their arrival noisily—maybe because they knew they risked getting shot if they didn't.

Dana had invited her mother to lunch to talk about her future. What could she have meant by that? She'd originally decided to be a practicing vet, then had changed her mind and decided to become a professor of veterinary medicine, which was why she'd accepted the postdoc from the Atwood Lab— in spite of the fact that she'd once thought Doctor Atwood's reputation was overblown.

And I'd learned that Dana had had a boyfriend of some kind in California whom she'd loved the way she'd loved a horse her dad had given her when she was a child. Was he the man who'd stayed with her here back in early December—who might have been drunk and angry? If she planned to leave the Atwood Lab, was it for him? Or was it her office mate, Barry Russell, with whom she'd had a stormy relationship, but not so stormy that she hadn't told him about her encounter with Jason and that she thought she knew him from somewhere.

I biked over to the Ag Campus the next afternoon. I stood for a moment in front of the veterinary hospital and looked out over the lake and at the narrow opening in the bushes that marked the flight of steps down to it. It was a little after four, close to the time of day I'd first encountered Jason when I'd walked down to the lake to kill time while waiting for Rufus and Lillian. I glanced at my watch and realized that Lillian and Rufus, driven by their neighbor, Mr. Colby, were probably on their way here right now for Rufus's radiation treatment.

The Small Animal Clinic waiting room was empty, since it closed at four. I went back through the hospital to the radiation waiting room and then down the hall to the new wing of the hospital with its forbidding sign stencilled on the double doors: ATWOOD LABORATORY: AUTHORIZED PERSONNEL ONLY.

The last time I'd been in the office, only Lorraine Cullin, the secretary, and Millard Pyles, the director, had been there. This time several clerk-typists were still at their desks, though starting to clear them off for the night. Lorraine was alone in her office in back. It took her a moment to recognize me; then she gave me a startled look. I didn't suppose she ever expected to see me again.

I stood outside her open glass door and gave her my pleasantest smile and said hello. She asked what she could do for me, and I told her I wanted to talk to Dana Michaels's office mate, Barry Russell.

"Do you have an appointment?"

"I didn't think I'd need one." I hadn't called first because it's so much easier for people to say no to you over the phone than in person. Of course, you have to be able to get to those people, and sometimes you find secretaries like Lorraine Cullin standing between you and them, like the dragon who guards the gold even though she doesn't get to spend any of it herself.

She looked at a loss. "May I ask your reason for wanting to speak with Professor Russell?"

"I want to talk to him about Dana Michaels," I said. "I'm trying to help the city cops find Jason."

"You're an official part of the investigation?"

I never like that question because it gives me no room to maneuver. If I lied and said yes, I'd be in trouble if it ever got back to my superiors—and from what little I knew about Lorraine Cullen, I figured the chances were very good that it would.

"No," I said with a hint of contrition in my voice, "but since I feel somewhat responsible for her murder—because I didn't do more to apprehend Jason when I had the chance—I'd like to do what I can to help the police find him." I tried to sound humble, chastened, make shame work for me for a change.

She gave me a faintly sympathetic smile. "I think Doctor Atwood and Professor Pyles overreacted a little at the memorial service," she said. "But it was an emotional time for all of us who knew Dana. I'm sure you did what you thought was right at the time. From what you've said, this Jason didn't have 'killer' written all over his face, after all."

"No, he didn't," I said, pleased and a little surprised by her attempt at warmth.

"I'll see if he's in his office," she said. She picked up her phone and dialed, waited a few moments, then hung up and said, "He's not in." She glanced at a schedule on the wall next to her desk. "He's in his lab," she said.

"Where's that?"

She smiled regretfully. "I'm sorry, I can't let you back into the laboratory area without authorization. Perhaps you could leave him a note and a number where he could reach you?"

"I don't have any germs the animals or researchers back there need to be afraid of," I said with a smile. "Why not just let me drift back and talk to him personally?"

Her pale little eyes behind the sequined glasses hardened. "I'm afraid—" She broke off as somebody came into the office behind me.

"Oh, Millard," she said, "perhaps you can help. You remember Officer O'Neill, don't you? The campus policewoman who encountered the man who killed Dana. She wants to go back and talk to Doctor Russell in his lab."

Doctor Charlie, Doctor Atwood's gangly son, had come into the office too and was standing behind Millard Pyles, looking at me curiously over his head.

As I gave them both my winsomest smile, I wondered why some parents give their children first names that can only add to the burden of their last. Millard Pyles didn't return my smile, which put him one up on me; he just asked me why I wanted to talk to Russell.

I told them about my encounter with Jason at the church. "It wasn't a pleasant experience," I added.

"I don't suppose it was!" Pyles said, not sounding at all sympathetic.

"How awful!" Lorraine exclaimed.

"Let me see that," Doctor Charlie said, coming up and peering at the bandages on my neck. "So close to the jugular. You're a very lucky woman."

I nodded. "I don't want to live with the fear that he might come after me again."

"As I told you at the church," Pyles said, "I believe Jason was lying in wait for you when he encountered Dana. You should be very careful, Ms. O'Neill."

Pompous ass. "I'm being as careful as I can," I said dryly. "I'm trying to get to know Dana Michaels better. I've already talked to her parents; now I'd like to talk to her office mate."

"You're like a bloodhound, aren't you?" Doctor Charlie said with his slow smile. "Getting a whiff of something that belonged to the missing party." He looked a little like a bloodhound himself: sleepy and morose. "Although, of course, Barry Russell didn't belong to Dana." He looked around, perhaps to make sure he hadn't offended anybody.

"If anybody knows anything that could be helpful," Pyles said impatiently, "they would have spoken up last week, when the place was crawling with detectives. You had your chance to avert this murder, Miss O'Neill. Now let's leave it to the real police to clear it up."

Before I could say something I'd probably regret, Charlie intervened. "Really, Millard," he blurted, "you're sounding like Dana's stepfather at the church. I don't think Officer O'Neill has anything to blame herself for. I really don't."

I flashed him a grateful smile. Pyles looked taken aback at Charlie's sudden assertiveness.

"You're right, Charlie, of course," he said, as though soothing a child growing restless. "Believe me, Miss O'Neill, I don't blame you for how you handled the situation. I have a daughter myself, and I'm sure she would have done exactly what you did: tried to jolly the fellow along the best she could until she could escape. What I am saying is that you are letting your personal sense of responsibility interfere with your common sense. There's really nothing you can do that the police can't do better."

I fantasized about consulting one of those soldier-of-fortune magazines—Lieutenant Bixler subscribes to one—to see if I could rent or lease a flamethrower and turn it on Millard Pyles. He'd make an attractive pork rind.

Looking at Doctor Charlie, since the lab was his mother's, after all, and he ought to have something to say about who visited it, I said quietly, "Would it be too upsetting to the people in the labs if I went back and asked Doctor Russell if he could spare some time to talk to me?"

Charlie looked uncomfortable and started to say something, but Pyles jumped in first. He clearly didn't like my going, literally, over his head to Doctor Charlie. "We really can't permit that," he said stiffly. "Dana's—Doctor Michaels's—death has been a great shock to all of us, but now we must get our minds back on our work."

"Oh, come on, Millard," Charlie said. "If all she wants to do back there is talk to Russell, what's the harm in that? Don't be such a tyrant—you sound like Mother!"

Pyles gave him a startled look. "But Char—"

Sovereignly ignoring the man, Charlie turned to me. "I saw Russell going into his office as we came in here. Just go on down the hall and knock," he said grandly.

"But—" Lorraine looked quickly at Pyles. Pyles's little mouth turned into an outie sort of navel, and he turned on his heels and started to leave the room.

Before he could reach the door Doctor Julia Atwood herself filled it. She was wearing a white lab coat over a dowdy dress and carrying a clipboard. A young man sauntered in behind her.

"Give Kevin a time sheet," she told one of the clerk typists as her eyes moved slowly among her son, Pyles, and me. She gave no sign that she recognized me.

The young man she'd called Kevin took the time sheet and went over to an empty desk, giving me a quick up-and-down as he went by, then sat down and began filling it out. He was wearing old jeans that weren't very clean and a baseball cap on backward. He looked like I felt among these people, except it didn't seem to bother him.

"Julia," Pyles said, "you remember Officer O'Neill, don't you—you spoke with her at the memorial service for Dana. She says she's here because she wants to help the police try to find the man who murdered Doctor Michaels." He laughed nervously. "I don't think it's necessary for a would-be Miss Marple to upset the lab's routine again, myself, but Charlie disagrees. He's given her permission to speak to Barry Russell."

"Of course she can speak to Professor Russell," Doctor Atwood said, shuffling papers on Lorraine's desk. "She can speak to all forty-two people who work for us if she wants—forty-one, now that Dana's dead."

Then she looked up at her son. "But not on our time, Charlie. This is a research facility, not a school for detectives."

She turned slowly and raked me with her bulging gray eyes. "The laboratory is a temple, Miss O'Neill—as much a temple as a research hospital devoted to human health. I won't allow unauthorized people to wander in and out of the place for no good reason. I think Dana Michaels would agree with me on that. We thought very much alike."

Without waiting for me to respond, she turned to Kevin, just getting up from the desk. "Kevin," she said to him, "if you're finished with that, I'd like your help in my lab."

"Sure, Doctor Atwood," he said. "But would you sign this first?"

She scrawled her signature on his time sheet and handed it to Lorraine, then turned back to her son. "You can go home, Charlie," she said.

Paying no further attention to me, she went back out into the hall, with Kevin bringing up the rear: the high priestess returning to her temple, trailed by her acolyte. At the door, the acolyte turned, looked back at me, and winked.

Millard Pyles bent over Lorraine's shoulder and began telling her something he wanted her to take care of for him, jabbing with a plump finger at her computer screen. Charlie gave me a rueful smile and a shrug and shambled out the door, looking as though he'd been spanked.

As I walked back through the hospital, I thought about how the power had passed from Pyles to Charlie Atwood before Charlie's mother's sudden appearance. It was obvious that neither Pyles nor Lorraine had expected him to override Pyles's decision. But he'd wilted like an overcooked asparagus, and acquired a similar color, when his mother came in.

I stood outside a moment and debated how I was going to get to Barry Russell, deciding I'd have to do as Doctor Atwood had suggested: look Russell up in the phone book, call him, and see if he would agree to talk to me. My guess was, though, that someone—Doctor Atwood, Pyles, Lorraine— would warn him about me and advise him to tell me to mind my own business.

As I turned and started toward the parking lot, I saw Lillian coming toward me. Mr. Colby—Buzz— followed with Rufus in his carrier.

"What're you doing here, Peggy?" she asked. "Up to no good, I'll bet." She was wearing a cream-colored wool cape and a matching beret against the March wind.

I described how I'd been stonewalled by the people in the Atwood Lab. She listened, staring at the ground in front of her thanks to osteoporosis, her head shaking slightly thanks to age or sympathy with my plight or both.

She didn't say anything for a moment, then cocked her head up at me and, with mischief in her eyes, said, "Maybe you could bring Rufus in for his radiation treatment tomorrow, Peggy—Buzz needs a break, don't you Buzz?"

Without waiting for Mr. Colby's somewhat be-mused nod, she went on: "And I'm feeling a mite poorly myself"—these words are not part of Lillian's everyday vocabulary—"so you'll just have to come without me too. You'll have to accompany Rufus back to the radiation lab, of course—he doesn't like going alone."

Over her head, I saw Millard Pyles and Doctor Charlie come out one of the side doors of the hospital. Charlie's head was bent to Pyles and he was talking a mile a minute and gesturing with his long arms. Pyles's hands were clasped behind his back, and he was staring down at his tiny loafers, their tassels flapping. Then he looked up, spotted us staring at them, and turned and said something to Charlie, who gave me a startled look, as though I'd caught them talking about me. They strode past us without speaking. I thought Charlie looked embar-rassed.

"They look like suspicious characters, those two," Lillian said, scowling at them.

"The tall one's Doctor Atwood's son, Doctor

Charlie," I told her. "The other's the Atwood Lab's director, Millard Pyles."

"He must have done something dreadful in his previous life," she said, "to be saddled with a name like that in this one."

"I'm sorry to hear that you're feeling poorly," I deadpanned. "I'll be happy to bring Rufus in tomorrow, if he won't mind."

"He won't mind, will you, Rufus?"

Rufus lifted an indifferent ear and let it flop back down again.

I went to my car. To my annoyance, Mr. Colby followed me and stood next to me as I opened the back door and looked in. I wondered what he'd do if Jason jumped out at us—bash him over the head with Rufus's carrier?

It would serve Rufus right, I thought bitterly, since if it hadn't been for him, I never would have met Jason in the first place.

Fifteen

It was too late to call Al, my veterinarian ex-boyfriend, at his office that night. I didn't want to call him at home, of course, and risk having Dierdre, or Deirdre, answer the phone. She'd never forgiven me for stealing him from her at a party when she wasn't paying attention, although Al wasn't drunk or in a coma or anything at the time and she's apparently forgiven him sufficiently to marry him and have babies with him. So I waited until the next morning—the start of my three nights off—to call him. I gave his receptionist my name and waited a couple of minutes until he came on the line.

"Hello, Peggy," he said cautiously, as though he was afraid I might be intending to steal him away from Ms. Vowels again.

"Hi." I heard how strained my voice sounded and realized that this was going to be harder than I'd expected. "I want to help the homicide cops catch the man who killed Dana Michaels," I went on quickly, so there'd be no misunderstanding. "From what you heard Doctor Atwood say about me at the church, you can probably guess why."

"She wasn't very nice to you, was she," he said. "Just how do you think you're going to catch him?"

"He seems to know the University pretty well," I said, "which means he might've gone there or worked there, and Dana told her office mate she thought she'd seen him somewhere before, so he might have some connection with the veterinary hospital. I know the U pretty well too—a lot better than the city cops do."

"He'd have to be pretty stupid—or nuts—to still be hanging around there now, wouldn't he?"

I described how Jason had kidnapped me at knifepoint and ordered me to drive him to the Ag Campus, which meant he'd still been hanging around the place on Monday. "Yesterday," I went on, "I tried to get into the Atwood Lab to talk to Barry Russell, but Doctor Atwood and Millard Pyles more or less threw me out."

"I hope you're not going to ask me to help you get by them," Al said warily.

He would have, when we were together.

"No," I said, "but I'd like to talk to you anyway, to get some idea of what kind of place it is. You told me at the memorial service that you knew Dana Michaels—"

"Only slightly. We had coffee sometimes, when we met in the halls."

"That's better than nothing," I said. "Besides, you're my only contact in the veterinary medical school."

"I don't know how I can help you, Peggy. I'm only an adjunct professor, you know. I only teach one course a semester, and I don't have anything to do with the Atwood Lab, although I've known Julia Atwood for years and consider her a friend."

"You do?"

"Yes, but not a close one."

"C'mon, Al," I said, "lighten up." I'd had to urge him to do that sometimes when we were together too, so it rolled easily off the tongue. "How about lunch this afternoon at that little café with the funny name—Goode's Just Good Food—if it's still there?" I pronounced it the way Al and I used to when we were together, rhyming "food" with "good," and felt the sharp pang of loss, the way you do when you break up with somebody you love for reasons you think are outside your control, but you're not sure.

"I usually go home for lunch now," he said, "since Dierdre's staying home with the twins until they start school."

"Call her," I said. "Tell her I promise not to wash my hair or dress up. I'll even wear sandals with black socks. Tell her she can come too, if she wants. She can even bring the twins."

"You are desperate!" he said, laughing in spite of himself, the old familiar laugh. "All right, I'll meet you there at noon. It's a coffeehouse now, by the way—quiche, salads, soup, and rich pastries. But the espresso's good, so you'll like it."

Nothing stays the same, I thought. "Thanks, Al," I said.

From the outside it still looked like Goode's, but inside the booths along the walls with the high oak partitions that separated them and afforded some privacy were gone, replaced by little glass-topped tables scattered around the room, with uncomfortable chairs that looked as though they were made of wire. Plants hung from the ceiling here and there, posters advertised readings by obscure poets, and the lighting was dimmer.

I lied when I told Al I wouldn't dress up, but I didn't overdo it either. I wore wool slacks with a mohair sweater my Aunt Tess knit for me that sets off my green eyes and red hair. I tried on a scarf but took it off when I decided it looked too much like I was dressing for lunch with a former lover. I also passed on a pair of earrings Al once gave me and wore my usual gold posts instead.

I got there before him, chose a table in a corner,

and ordered a double *latte* with skim milk. "We call that a 'skinny *latte*,'" the waitress confided to me with a knowledgeable smirk.

"I'd feel silly, asking for something like that," I confided with a return smirk.

Al and I had broken up because he'd wanted me to move in with him and his teenage son, Josh, and I hadn't been ready for that kind of commitment. Now it occurred to me, not for the first time, that Josh must be about ready to graduate from high school, so my duties as stepmom would be almost over had I chosen to accept them.

I watched Al walk past the plate-glass window, pull open the door, and come in, as I'd seen him do a hundred times when we were together. He spotted me, grinned, and waved. I grinned and waved back. As he pulled up the chair across from me, I noticed he'd put on weight. When we were together, he struggled with the problem and spent a lot of time at the gym trying to work it off. He was apparently a little more relaxed about it now. Marriage does that, I suppose. Maybe if we'd gotten married, I would have quit the campus cops and had a kid or two myself and stayed home and made Al's lunch and lived happily and securely ever after—if people do that anymore.

We said awkward hellos and I asked him how Josh was.

"Great," he said enthusiastically, and told me about some of the colleges Josh was considering. "But when he's gone," Al went on, "we'll still have the twins, Ellen and Allen, to keep the house hopping. They're almost a year old."

I'd seen Al and Alphabet last summer, pushing a baby carriage that looked like it should be drawn by horses. Luckily the lake was crowded with people, and I vanished into them before they spotted me.

He asked me what I'd been up to lately.

"Not a whole lot," I answered with a shrug. "Still walk a beat, play racquetball, stuff like that."

"I thought by now you'd be married to that homicide cop friend of yours, Buck Hansen."

I shook my head. "Nobody marries Buck Hansen."

"You've even got that in common," he said.

"Yeah." All the smiling was taking a toll on the muscles around my mouth, so I grimaced instead. I started to tell him about Gary but thought that sounded too defensive, so I stopped.

Luckily the waitress came over then and I ordered a salad. "Don't usually see you here for lunch anymore, Al," she grumbled, her eyes bouncing from him to me. She disapproved of me, I could tell. He turned red and explained in a way that made it worse that we were old friends.

I let the sight of him as they talked stir up the memories. We'd done a lot together, Al and I. We'd spent a lot of our winter weekends cross-country skiing. Once we spent ten days skiing from lake to lake through the North Woods of Minnesota, sleeping in a tent and mummy bags we towed on a sled behind us along with food and water, in temperatures that at times dropped way below zero. We saw almost nobody the entire time. You get very close to somebody that way.

And once he'd saved my life when somebody had a pistol pointed at me with every intention of killing me. "I saved your bacon," he'd bragged afterward. Food was never far from Al's mind.

I was smiling at that memory as he turned from the waitress to me.

"What're you grinning at?"

"I wasn't grinning," I said, "I was smiling."

He chuckled.

"What're you laughing at?"

"I wasn't laughing," he said, "I was chuckling."

I decided it would be a good idea to get down to the business at hand, so I asked him to tell me about Dana Michaels.

"I don't know very much about her," he said. "As I told you on the phone, we mostly saw each other in the halls at the hospital and had coffee a few times in the lounge. We never talked about anything personal. She was mostly interested in what I had to tell her about being a vet in private practice. I got the impression she was considering dropping out of the lab and becoming a vet herself. I thought she was a loner. Not very good at small talk, or just not interested in it."

"Her mother and stepfather were surprised when she changed her mind about being a vet and came here to do research," I said. "Apparently she didn't think very highly of Doctor Atwood either."

Al nodded. "Yeah, I heard her stepfather say something about that at the memorial service. He wasn't very tactful, was he? To you either," he added.

I lied, said it didn't bother me. He glanced up and smiled knowingly.

"She must have concealed her opinion of Julia well," he said. "Julia doesn't have people in the lab who don't put up a good show of adoring her and who aren't a hundred percent committed to research."

"She spoke highly of Dana at the memorial service. Was that just being nice to Dana's family?"

"Oh, no. If Julia hadn't liked her, she wouldn't even have come to the service, much less spoken at it! She was very high on Dana—although it might not have been for purely scientific reasons."

"Meaning what?" I asked.

"Meaning Julia's ex-husband teaches at Davis, where Dana came from. Julia probably felt she'd stolen Dana away from him."

The waitress returned with our food. "From talking to her," Al continued when she'd gone away again, "I think Dana would have made a wonderful vet. She had a way with animals you don't see in everybody who goes into the field, unfortunately."

Al had a way with animals too. "Maybe she thought there'd be more money and prestige in research," I said.

He shrugged. "Whatever. But she must've been a good researcher. Julia Atwood has no patience with mediocrity."

"She doesn't seem to have much patience, period," I said, and told him about my encounter with her the day before in the Atwood Lab.

He nodded. "She runs the place like a cult," he said.

"A temple," I corrected him. "That's what she told me it was."

"Well, she has a right to call it what she wants, since it's her entire life—and she expects it to be the entire life of the people who work for her too."

"What's she like?" I asked, picking through my salad in search of something to eat. "I don't remember you ever mentioning her when we were together."

"But you wouldn't remember it even if I had, would you?" he pointed out correctly. "I got to know her years ago, back when she had her television program. She consulted me about the practical details of whatever the subject was that week: you know, how to keep cats from scratching the over-stuffed chairs and dogs from making a mess on the rug—stuff like that. She paid me for it too. Not much, but I was just starting out in my own practice, so I was glad to have the little extra income.

"Back then Julia—Doctor J, as she was known to her legions of pet-loving fans—came across as something between Saint Francis and Doctor Spock, and the program always ended with her holding an animal on her lap—anything from a poodle to a baby puma—with her son, known as little Doctor C, standing by to take them from her in case they bit, pooped, or peed."

I asked him why she'd given up the program.

"To devote more time to research. She'd just developed an adjuvant—"

"A what?"

"An adjuvant," he said. "In this case, it means something that allows all of a vaccine's components to live together in harmony, so you can immunize an animal against several diseases with one injection. Hers turned out to be the most effective on the market at the time, and the drug companies were dangling great sums of money in front of her to work on more of the same sorts of things. She became a big moneymaker for the U, which is why they added a wing to the hospital for her and named it after her. She's even got federal funding for one of her projects that shows promise for human innocu-lation as well."

"Does she have any kind of private life?"

"I don't have any idea. As I told you, her ex-husband's a professor at the veterinary school at Davis. Julia had been his student. They got married, had Charlie, and then she got the offer of a position here. She took it and they tried a 'commuter mar-riage,' but it didn't work. They had another child and got divorced a few years later. Julia ended up with the kids because Dodson—his name's Mark Dodson—didn't want them. The youngest son, Mark Junior, went out to live with his father when he was still a teenager. He died—drowned. Julia mentioned him at Dana's memorial service."

"I remember that," I said. In a very few words, Al had described a story big enough to be a Greek tragedy, a soap opera, or a modern novel. "I suppose I have to forgive her for being so hard on me—although it was unfair."

I thought of thanking Al for draping his arm around me while I was being attacked by Julia Atwood and Dana's stepdad but decided against it. He probably didn't remember doing it.

"She overreacted," he agreed, "probably because she's feeling guilty about neglecting her kids. They were raised by au pair girls she imported from Europe and by her secretary, Lorraine Cullin, when she was between au pair girls."

"Lorraine Cullin!" I exclaimed, appalled. "She doesn't look like the motherly type to me!"

"Not to me either," he said. "She's been with Julia from the start and will do anything for her. She's probably more loyal to the Atwood Lab than anybody in it except Julia herself—and has more power too."

"Being a surrogate mother to Doctor Atwood's kids seems to be taking loyalty a little far," I said.

Al smiled, a smile I'd once loved, marred now only by a small piece of lettuce stuck between his two front teeth. "I was at a Christmas party at Julia's once," he said. "She had too much to drink and got a little maudlin—and that's not like her at all. She gave a rambling lecture on ambitious people who neglect their children for their careers and don't realize it until it's too late. She admonished us not to make her mistake. We all knew she was thinking about Mark Junior."

"Charlie seems to have turned out okay," I said. "Socially a little awkward, and his mother treats him as though he's still a child. So, come to think of it, do Professor Pyles and Lorraine—but he seems nice enough. I suppose he owes his position to his mother."

"No doubt about it," Al said. "People laugh at him behind his back at the school. He's a good surgeon when his mother's not looking over his shoulder—I've seen him in action, so I know. But when she's anywhere around, he's all thumbs."

"Who's this Pyles character?" I asked. "Aside from being a pompous ass, I mean."

Al laughed. "All I know about him is he's in charge of the business side of the Lab. He keeps the wheels turning smoothly for Julia, although Lorraine probably does most of the work. Nobody's even sure he went to college, but he can put up a good front, so Julia got him the title of professor. That impresses the uninitiated, the business and government types they have to deal with over there."

Jim Gates had told me the same thing.

"Where would the U be without smoke and mirrors?" I said, shaking my head. "Speaking of which, a friend of mine told me there was a scandal of some kind a few years ago that involved the Atwood Lab."

Al buried his face in his coffee cup. "Yeah," he said. "But Julia wasn't involved—at least not directly. It was Charlie."

"So tell me about it."

He looked uncomfortable. "Charlie was accused of faking the results in a study he was doing for a drug company," he said finally. "It got in the papers, which forced the U to conduct an investigation. They found there'd been some carelessness in record keeping but no deliberate fraud." Al stared out over the coffee shop.

"You think that's all there was to it?"

"I wouldn't know," he said. "But everybody knows Charlie's heart isn't in research—he's only doing it because he can't say no to his mom. So it wouldn't surprise me if he made careless errors. I can't believe he'd do it deliberately."

"He was doing the study for a big drug company, wasn't he?" I said. "I don't suppose the fake research went against what the drug company wanted."

He shrugged, didn't say anything, stared off into the room behind me. I smiled to myself. I knew Al well enough to know when he was dragging his heels about something.

"Research never comes up with results that threaten the profits of whoever's paying for it, does it?" I said, pushing him a little.

"Don't be so cynical, Peggy."

"Where's the whistle-blower now?" I asked him. He hadn't mentioned him, but Gary had.

"The—? Oh, I have no idea."

Just because Al was an ex-lover didn't mean he could lie to me and get away with it. "Was he a friend of yours?" I asked.

Annoyed, he said, "It doesn't have anything to do with Dana Michaels, Peggy," in a tone that told me to drop it.

So I did. I asked him if he knew Barry Russell, Dana's office mate.

"I know what he looks like," he said, still a little huffy, "and I've heard the rumors you've obviously heard too. They dated for a while; then something happened between them and he wanted another office. Somebody overheard him calling her names or something."

"They were both competing for the same professorship and Russell was losing out, or thought he was."

"I hadn't heard that. I don't have your nose for gossip."

It's true. If you went by noses, you'd know I was a lot more into gossip than Al. His is kind of rounded and getting fleshy—but still very nice.

He looked at his watch; I looked at mine. We'd probably never done that before when we were together, unless we were synchronizing them for a later date.

We chatted about this and that for a few more minutes and then he reached for his wallet. I told him to put it away, reminding him that this was my treat.

When I'd paid the bill, we walked out into the late afternoon sunshine. Maybe it was my imagination, but I thought his eyes darted all around, as though afraid of being caught with me by his significant other. I thanked him for his help and we stood there, lingering—him too, I think.

Finally he said, "I'd be careful if I were you, Peggy. The Atwood Lab generates a lot of money for the U, and a lot of good publicity for it too. Animal lovers as well as the cattle raisers in the state benefit greatly from Julia Atwood's research. I wouldn't mess with her."

"What's she got to hide?"

"Probably nothing. But since the scandal involving Charlie, when a reporter was snooping around the lab trying to turn up dirt, they've all been quite paranoid about outsiders coming in and asking questions. Julia wouldn't hesitate to try to get you kicked off the police force if you annoyed her."

"I'm more worried about Jason than I am about losing my job," I said. "I want the creep off the streets. And the city cops aren't getting as close to him as he's gotten to me."

"I'm just saying, proceed with tact. Julia has a lot of clout."

"I'm always tactful, Al, you know that."

We both laughed, almost like old times. If What's-her-name had seen it, she'd probably have had a fit. I wanted to reach up and use a fingernail to remove the piece of lettuce from his teeth, but resisted the urge and told him about it instead.

It's an odd feeling, shaking a hand that once knew most of your body's secrets.

Sixteen

It was a little after one when I left Al, and I didn't have anything else to do until it was time to take Rufus to his radiation treatment, so I biked back home, called Buck, and asked him if he was making any progress in finding Jason.

"No," he said. He didn't sound like a happy man.

Gently prodded, he told me a clerk in a store that sold clerical garb thought he remembered somebody who looked like my description of Jason buying a clerical collar from him the day before Dana Michaels's memorial service. He paid cash.

"We haven't got a clue as to his whereabouts," Buck said. "It's as though he's vanished into thin air."

"It goes well with his nom-de-guerre, doesn't it?" I said. "Niemand."

"Maybe he's left town. Too bad we can't count on it."

I described how I'd been stonewalled trying to get into the Atwood Lab to talk to Barry Russell.

"What were you hoping to accomplish by talking to him?"

"I'm not sure," I said. "Maybe just to get more of a sense of who Dana Michaels was." I touched the Band-Aid on my neck absently. "I can't go on about my life hoping Jason isn't out there somewhere, planning to attack me again. I've got to do something or I'll go nuts. Besides, I think I owe it to Dana. Do you object to my trying to help, Buck?"

He sighed. We'd been through this before on a few other occasions. "No, Peggy. Do what you have to do, but be careful. You'd be better off doing it officially, as a detective, you know—and you had your chance at that. Doctor Atwood couldn't throw you out of her lab if you were on official business."

"Yeah, right!" The previous fall I'd accepted a temporary transfer to detective to see if I liked it. I didn't. I still think I made the right choice, but sometimes it would be nice to be able to flash your badge and watch doors open for you as if by magic.

The speed with which Buck had stopped trying to get me to mind my own business was a sign of how frustrated he was. He usually puts up a bigger fight.

I picked Rufus up at four and drove him over to the veterinary hospital. He'd been doing this for almost two weeks now, so he seemed to know the drill. I'd been involved with Jason for the same length of time; I envied the resigned way Rufus accepted his ordeal.

I paged through a copy of a magazine for cat owners and pretended to read until Jim Gates came out and led us down the hall to the radiation lab. Rufus wagged his tail in recognition and let Gates lift him out of his carrier.

Lillian told me she always watched the procedure. She said it made her feel better, even though Rufus, once he was sedated, wouldn't know the difference. So I stayed as Gates gave him his shot and carried him into the chamber. From the little control room outside, I watched on a television screen as Gates strapped Rufus down and positioned his head on what looked like foam blocks, so the area of his mouth to be treated would be in the right place under a machine that looked like a large overhead projector. Then he left the chamber and joined me in the control room.

I knew the treatment would take only a few minutes, but Gates wouldn't allow me to take Rufus home until he'd injected him with something to wake him up and then made sure he'd recovered consciousness properly. He was a good vet.

We both had our eyes on the television screen, watching the poodle, who lay there like an old mop head.

I asked Gates if he'd known Dana Michaels.

"Not really," he said. "I'm in the veterinary school and she was a member of the Atwood Lab. They don't associate much with us."

"I've heard that she was probably going to be offered a permanent position in the lab."

He shrugged, his eyes on the television screen.

"Wouldn't you be a candidate for the position too?"

He turned and looked at me strangely; then his eyes went back to the television screen. "Lord, no! You need a Ph.D. to be considered for a permanent position. I won't get mine for another year. Besides, I don't want to teach at a university."

"Why not?"

He lowered his voice, making a show of looking around. "Too much politicking, not enough animal care. Besides, I wouldn't want to work for Doctor Atwood. She's never heard of the forty-hour work week. When I finish up here, I'm going back out into private practice, where animal care comes first and where I can be my own boss."

"Doesn't animal care come first here?"

"Not anymore. It's almost all research now, since that's where the big bucks are. They're even thinking of doing away with the animal clinics—both the

small and the large—and with teaching too. I'd hate
to see that happen and wouldn't want to be here
when it does."

It's the same way in the rest of the University, I
thought. Educating kids lacks status and doesn't pay
very well anymore.

Keeping his voice neutral and low, Gates went
on: "Don't get me wrong. Doctor Atwood's an
outstanding scientist and we need them too, of
course. What I'm doing with Rufus didn't come
from practicing vets, it came from research." He
broke off. "C'mon, let's go get him."

I followed him into the radiation chamber and
watched as he removed the restraints. He carried the
sleeping poodle gently out and down to one of the
examining rooms, where he injected something
under his skin to wake him up. I asked Gates if he
would mind if I left Rufus with him while I went
down and talked to Barry Russell.

"Not at all," he said. "I have to be in here anyway,
doing some paperwork. Take your time."

I went back through the doors with the big black
ATWOOD LABORATORY: AUTHORIZED PERSONNEL ONLY
stencilled on them, my eyes itching, my nose starting to run. I'm mildly allergic to most things with
fur—poodles excepted, for a reason that was once
explained to me but I've forgotten—and being in a
building that was full of furry creatures wasn't
doing my nose any good. It was after five, but I was
prepared to walk quietly, so as not to alert Lorraine
if she was working late in the main office, which
she seemed to do fairly often. But the office door
was closed and the room dark behind the frosted
glass.

I wandered through the halls, looking at nameplates on doors, passed darkened labs and labs with people in them under bright lights. I spotted Doctor Atwood in one of them, but fortunately her broad back was turned to me. When I reached Russell's office, I noticed that Dana Michaels's name was still on the door, under his. I knocked and waited until he told me to come in.

He was leaning back in his swivel chair, his feet up on that little tray thing that pulls out from a desk, a laptop computer in his lap. He glanced up at me and said, "Peggy O'Neill, I believe! I've been waiting to hear from you, though I'm surprised to actually see you in the flesh." He was a pale, slight man with thinning blond hair, a wide mouth, and unusually red lips. His voice was mildly nasal, which made everything he said sound slightly ironic, which it may have been. "Everytime somebody phones," he went on, "I start guiltily and wonder if it's you, hard on my trail."

"I'm famous," I said, somewhat bemused. "I take it you've been warned not to talk to me."

"Indeed, we've all been. Julia—Doctor Atwood to you, my dear sleuth—is very protective of her sanctum sanctorum. She doesn't welcome visitors."

He gestured to the chair at a corner of his desk. Since he showed no signs of removing his feet, and since I didn't want to try to talk to him over them, I sat in the chair behind the desk on the other side of the room. He watched me, an amused smile playing on his lips. "That was Dana's desk. You're not afraid of ghosts, I see."

"No," I said, "I'm not."

"I suppose I should call the campus cops and have one of your colleagues come and haul you off to the poky, shouldn't I?"

"Why don't you?"

"You mean, why aren't I afraid of losing the position I killed Dana Michaels for by not having you tossed out on your ear?"

"That's a good way of putting it," I said.

He closed his laptop and put it aside. "Because I blew my chances to get that position when I lost my temper and called Dana names loudly enough for snoopy Lorraine to hear and report it to Julia, that's why. Only Julia gets to lose her temper and call people names around here."

"But now that Dana's dead," I pointed out, "aren't you back in the running?"

He shook his head. "You don't know Doctor Julia Atwood, I'm afraid. Once you're on her shit list, Peggy, dear, you never get off. If it weren't for the sinister and mysterious Mr. Jason, she'd probably think I killed Dana, either out of spite or because I thought it would help my chances to get the position. I owe the man that, at least."

I said, "Dana's death doesn't bother you much, does it, Doctor Russell?"

He pursed his thin red lips and thought about it. "That's not quite true," he said finally. "But I didn't really know her very well, and I confess I didn't much like her either. But it did come as a shock, her being killed like that."

"You say you didn't know her very well. But you dated her—"

"I didn't 'date' her," he said sharply. "We went out a few times, to funky little restaurants I've discovered since I got here that I thought she might enjoy—I was wrong about that, by the way, she didn't seem to even notice the food. We also went to a couple of flicks and a play. But they weren't dates. Dana—being very feminist—insisted on paying for herself right down to the penny. You wonder why I did this, since she was not exactly a party animal or a feast for the eyes?"

"Yes," I said. "Why did you?"

His voice became pious and he said, "I felt it was my Christian duty to try to make her feel at home."

I just looked at him.

He burst out laughing. "Something tells me you're not convinced. Okay, I confess—don't hit me again with that rubber hose, Officer! The real reason was that I was curious to know if she was after the position I thought I wanted and also to see if she was good enough to snatch it out from under my nose."

"And was she?"

He leaned back in his chair and stretched, his hands clasped behind his head, his feet still up on his desk, and stared at the ceiling.

"Yes and no. Or rather, no and yes." He glanced over at me to see what effect his coyness was having on me. I was sorry I didn't have a piece of rubber hose; I considered stapling his lips together with Dana's stapler.

"Yes, she was good enough for the position," he said after a moment, "though no better than I. But she was a woman, and Julia wanted more women in the lab."

"What's the 'no'? Didn't she want the position?"

"At first she did, I think," he said, frowning. "On our dates that weren't dates, I soon realized she was pumping me for information about the lab she could use to ingratiate herself with Julia and Charlie. She seemed overwhelmed by Julia's 'aura' and grateful to have the privilege of doing her postdoc work with her. She even seemed to find Charlie fascinating— and nobody, Peggy O'Neill, not even Dana, could find Charlie fascinating."

He gave a sour laugh, still staring at the ceiling. "That's when I got pissed at her. So I said something nasty about people who have to suck up to get promoted, and one thing led to another—she had a pretty quick temper herself, you know!—and I ended up calling her I forget what. A toady or something."

"'A calculating, two-faced ass-kisser,'" I said. Buck had had to read it to me from a piece of paper, but I have a distressing knack for remembering things like that.

Russell turned a delicate shade of pink. "Is that how Lorraine remembers it? Well, that's probably it, then. Sorry. It wasn't very creative, was it? Oh, well, we all have our off days."

He swung his shiny shoes off his desk, sat up, and smiled at me. "Ironic, isn't it? If I hadn't lost my temper, I'd probably be a shoo-in for the position now. Actually, I'd probably have been a shoo-in for the job even if Dana hadn't been killed."

"Oh? Why?"

"Because I think she changed her mind, decided she didn't really want it. Lately—the last month or so—she seemed to be just going through the motions. I think she was really cut out to be a hands-on vet, myself, who just got caught up in the academic mystique—whatever that is!—for a while. She spent a lot of time over in the Large Animal Clinic, helping out. She loved horses."

I asked him if he'd mind going over what he told the police about his encounter with Dana and Jason by the steps to the lake.

He got up and went over to one of the windows that looked out over the lake, stood there a moment, then turned back to me. "I was coming from my car," he said, "and I heard this guy—it was Jason, of course—hollering. I looked to see what it was all about and saw Dana coming up the steps with him hard on her heels. He called her a bitch and said she'd be sorry she'd ever met him. He also said he was going to kill her."

"You didn't go after him either!" I blurted, surprising myself.

"That's in your job description, Officer, not mine," he said, laughing at my confusion. "But don't blame yourself. He didn't look dangerous to me, and I didn't think he meant what he said—I thought it was just bluff. Dana thought so too, obviously, or she wouldn't have gone back out there and gotten herself killed, would she?"

"She told you she thought she recognized him."

"Yeah, after we'd got up here. I asked her who she thought he was, but she just shook her head and said she wasn't sure, she'd have to give it some more thought."

"Did you ask her about it later?"

He shook his head. "I don't like having to dig information out of people who play coy."

Different strokes: I kind of enjoy it, myself.

"Back at the time you and Dana were—not dating, did she ever mention a man who was staying at her house?"

"A man staying at Dana's house? Not very likely!" He laughed.

"Her neighbors heard a man's voice quarreling with her. They thought he'd been drinking."

Russell just shrugged, went back to his desk, and sat down. "That's not the Dana I knew," he said.

"Later that night she told you she was going home to try to beat the rain, right?"

He nodded. "I'd just come from the men's room and stopped to talk to Lorraine and Charlie in the hall. Dana came back from the lab and said she was going home early. Lorraine said she didn't think she should walk home in the dark and offered her a ride if she could wait half an hour. She had to put the finishing touches on something for the National Science Foundation people who were coming the next day. But Dana just laughed and said she wasn't afraid of Jason."

"Who besides you, Lorraine, and Charlie knew she was going home then?" I asked.

"You know," he said with a gentle smile, "a homicide detective—do you call them dicks?—sitting right where you're sitting now, Peggy, asked me the same question the day after Dana was killed. And my answer to him was the same as it is to you: how the hell should I know? There were other people in the labs that night, and the hospital's got people in it twenty-four hours a day. She could've told any of them. Why? You think Jason was in cahoots with somebody in the lab?"

I didn't bother to answer that, just got up to go.

"What're you going to do now?" I asked him.

He shrugged indifferently. "Once I got used to the idea that my future doesn't lie with the Atwoods, I put together my résumé and started sending it out. I have a couple of interviews lined up." He laughed, stretched. "Who knows? Davis might even take me back, just to spite Julia. There's no love lost between her and her ex, you know, who teaches there."

He called after me as I headed for the door: "Be careful going down the hall, Peggy. You don't want to meet Julia at the best of times, but today she's in a real snit."

"Why's that?"

"Lorraine called in sick, so she's had to postpone a meeting with the dean about next year's appropriations. Without Lorraine, Julia hasn't got a clue about where the money comes from that runs this place, so she can't talk to the dean alone. She's very annoyed. Maybe you should consider leaving by one of the back doors."

I would have, except I had to fetch Rufus.

Julia Atwood was coming out of the main office as I tried to slip past. She looked prepared to murder somebody even before she saw me.

She stopped dead in her tracks and looked me up and down. "What's the matter with your eyes?" she demanded. "Have you been crying?"

"No, I'm allergic to dog and cat fur," I said.

"You didn't think I meant it when I told you the hospital was off limits," she said, unaffected by my suffering.

"Well," I said, "I had to accompany my friend's dog, Rufus, to the radiation lab to keep him calm. His owner's orders," I added, hoping to appeal to the residual Doctor J in her, if there was any left. "Then I didn't see any point in just sitting out there waiting for him to wake up so I could take him home. Doctor Russell didn't mind talking to me for a few minutes." I was babbling, and I could see it was doing me no good—Doctor J had left the premises long ago.

"You seem to care a great deal for that dog," she said. "Two weeks ago you put his well-being above that of the women on campus, with tragic results."

"Why are you so opposed to my talking to Dana Michaels's office mate?" I said, my voice rising. "What difference does it make?"

"I'm opposed to you meddling in something that's none of your business," she snapped. "Amateurs, in my experience, always do more harm than good. My lab and I have been upset enough by Doctor Michaels's murder. I feel a great personal sense of loss over her death—a death I believe that you, had you been good at what you do, could have averted. We don't need you upsetting things even further now, trying to atone."

She plowed on before I could say anything. "I'm going to call your chief, whom I've met, and lodge a complaint against you, Officer O'Neill. I'll be very surprised if I ever see you in here again."

She turned on her heels and stalked back down the hall in the direction from which I'd just come— probably to read Barry Russell the riot act too.

I picked up Rufus, thanked Jim Gates for watching him, and left the hospital. Outside, I set down the carrier and stood there a moment, breathing in the clean, cold air. I took out my handkerchief and wiped my eyes and blew my nose. It didn't help, it just felt good, the way scratching an itch does.

I took the carrier to my car, checked to make sure nobody was in it, opened the door on the passenger side, and slid Rufus in.

"It's a temple," a man's voice behind me intoned.

Seventeen

I straightened up, banging my head on the door frame, and spun around.

It wasn't Jason.

"Dammit, you scared me!" I said, then recognized the student worker I'd seen in the Atwood Lab the day before who'd been filling out a time card.

"Sorry," he said. "I couldn't resist, but I didn't think you'd jump like that either. You okay?"

I grimaced, rubbed the top of my head, and said, "Thanks for asking."

He was a lanky kid with a bony face, still wearing dirty jeans and a baseball cap on backward over a mop of curly brown hair. I guessed his age to be somewhere between nineteen and nineteen and a half.

"She's a bitch, ain't she?" he said, tossing his head in the general direction of the hospital as he popped a cigarette into his mouth and lit it with a cheap lighter, cupping his hand around the flame against the wind.

"Who?" I asked, although I knew.

He just smiled down at me from the heights of adolescent cool. "Can't smoke anywhere in the hospital," he went on, "so I have to come out here. I gave some serious thought to quittin' in January, when I half froze my ass off. Now that spring's here, I don't have to decide right away." He looked me up and down. "My name's Kevin Wheatley. What's yours?"

When I told him, he nodded and said, "I sorta got the idea you're not a cop from the way Doc J was talkin' to you the other day. That's what a lot of us who work for her call her behind her back: Doc J. We'd be fired on the spot if she heard us call her that, of course, which is why we do it: puts a little zip in our lives, you know? So why're you interested in Dana?"

My interest in Kevin quickened: he'd called her Dana.

I told him I was a campus cop, trying to help find Jason. I briefly explained my various encounters with Jason. Kevin listened, then nodded solemnly and squinted critically at the damage Jason had done to my car. "I guess you might feel like helpin' put the creep behind bars, after all that." He didn't seem to see anything strange in what I was doing, which warmed me to him a little.

"You've seen the police sketch of him, right?"

He laughed. "Who hasn't?"

"I don't suppose you've ever seen anybody hanging around here who looked like that?"

"Yeah, right!" he said scornfully, rocking back and forth on his dirty tennis shoes. "And when the cops asked me about it, I just forgot to tell 'em."

"Sorry."

He shrugged. "They questioned everybody, of course, on account of they thought the creep could've been a student worker or maybe one of the guys works on the farm out there. He was livin' in one of those buildings; I guess you know that. But I never saw him before. Course, it's a big campus, the Ag Campus, so he might've hung around a while and none of us ever came across him. He's probably long gone now, though. I'll tell you what," he went on. "You catch Jason and turn him over to me, okay? I'd like just five minutes with him."

"It sounds like you liked Dana."

"I did."

"How'd you happen to know her?"

"Me?" He shrugged and looked out across the parking lot to the lake. "I saw her around a lot. I've been doin' work-study jobs at the hospital since I was a freshman, and I work all over the place." He gestured back at the hospital behind us. "I'm a business major but I come from off a farm, so I like bein' around animals—and I've gotta work to pay for tuition and stuff. Dana was working in ol' Atwood's lab, but she liked horses—she had one of her own when she was a kid, she told me, and she missed him. So sometimes she went down to the Large Animal Clinic and hung out with the horses. She even helped out sometimes when a horse was comin' out of surgery—try to calm it down, you know. That ain't the easiest thing in the world to do, 'cause the damn fools panic and kick and sometimes break their legs. Then you gotta put 'em down."

It was a vivid image: Dana trying to calm a horse so it wouldn't do anything that would get it "put down" the way her horse, Beau, had been.

"Did you talk to her much?" I asked.

Kevin shook his head, took a drag on his cigarette, and blew smoke that the wind snatched away before it could reach me. "Dana talked mostly with her hands—you know what I mean? The way she handled the animals, they responded to her. You see that a lot on a farm, people who can get through to animals with their hands—'cause they sure don't understand English!" He shrugged, squinting out across the lake. "If she hadn't been so much older'n me, I probably would've asked her out."

The ultimate compliment. "Did any of the less ageist students try?" I asked.

"I dunno," he said, taking no offense. "I doubt it, on account of Dana wasn't a real fox." He ran his eyes over me again, perhaps to see if he'd missed anything foxy the first time. "She wouldn't of rung most guys' bells," he went on, when he'd satisfied himself that I wouldn't either. "I liked her mostly on account of how she was with the animals. She didn't look like she'd be too much fun . . . at a party, or somethin'. Besides, there was somethin' about her that said, 'Back off!' " He looked at me closely. "You know what I mean? But not in an unfriendly way."

The difference between Jason and Kevin was that "Back off!" was offensive to Jason, and a challenge.

"I think she just cared more for animals than for people," Kevin went on, "and she was shy." He squinted through smoke in the steely-eyed way the tobacco companies had trained him to. "But she did have a boyfriend. Least, I think it was a boyfriend. They was fightin'."

"You saw Dana and a man fighting, so you thought he was her boyfriend? You don't think you listen to too much country music, do you?"

He grinned. "Well, it could've been a relative, I suppose. They fight too. But it wasn't her brother—I saw him at the memorial service. I was there."

"Fighting," I repeated. "Physically?"

"Naw! Though Dana looked like she'd liked to of killed 'im. They was fightin' with words. She was pissed off that he was up there." He tossed his head in the direction of the hospital. "She said he shouldn't't've come back here, and he said she shouldn't't've either. She sounded jittery. She didn't like him bein' there, and she told him to keep his voice down, which he mostly did. She said they'd talk about it again at her place when she got home that night."

"How do you know all this?" I asked. "They were quarreling in front of you?"

"Uh-uh. They thought they were alone. I was just takin' a little nap in one of the cattle pens in the Large Animal Clinic. I'd pulled an all-nighter, so I was pretty tired. Their arguin' woke me up. I just lay there and watched 'em through the slats. It's kind of interesting, watching and listening to people when they don't know you're there."

I knew. "When was this?"

He gave it some thought. "Middle of December, I guess."

The same time Dana's neighbors had thought they'd heard her quarreling with a drunken man in her house.

I asked him what the man had looked like.

"Nothin' like that picture of Jason, if that's what you're thinkin', or I'd of told the cops about it, wouldn't I?" He screwed up his eyes to help him remember. "What was she—about five-eight, five-nine? He was a lot bigger, maybe six foot. Heavyset, I think. Wearin' a jacket that wasn't warm enough for the weather. I remember noticin' that 'cause he looked cold and his teeth were chattering. And he was a lot older than Dana. I figure he was at least forty. He'd been drinkin' too."

"Drunk?"

"Gettin' there or been there, it sounded like." He gave me a kind of mournful look. "The guy was kind of a disappointment to me. I guess I figured she could do better'n that."

"Could you hear anything else they said?"

He shook his head. "Not much. I think he was tryin' to talk her out of doin' something, and she wasn't havin' any of it."

"Do you remember his words?"

"Somethin' like, 'It's none of your business, Dana,' and, 'It's water under the bridge, Dana, leave it alone, you'll just get hurt.' I couldn't hear what she answered to most of it, on account of she was speakin' real soft. She was probably afraid somebody would hear—and she was tellin' him to keep his voice down too. She was tryin' to get him out the door before anybody came in and saw him. I can't say I blame her. I don't suppose it would've gone over very big with Doc J or 'Hemorrhoids'—that's what we call Pyles—if they'd seen her arguin' with a drunk, would it? You heard what the doc said: this ain't your ordinary animal hospital, it's a temple. La-de-da!"

Kevin finished his cigarette, scraped it out on the bottom of one of his tennis shoes, and tossed the mangled corpse under my car where it wouldn't be found until I'd driven away. He squatted down on his haunches and stared at the sleeping Rufus in the backseat.

"Oh, and he promised her he'd stop drinkin' if she'd go back to California with 'im," he said. He laughed. "But y'gotta be stupid to believe a promise made by a drunk, and from the tone of her voice I could tell she thought so too. A guy who's drinkin' that early in the afternoon's nobody for a woman like Dana Michaels. But this guy didn't look like the killer type to me, if you're thinkin' he might've done it somehow and blamed it on Jason."

"You didn't hear her say his name, did you?" I asked.

"Not exactly *his* name," he said with a chuckle.

"Whose, then?"

"Her horse's: Beau. 'Wait for me at the house, Beau,' she said, and he said, 'Don't call me that!' his voice real sharp for once. 'Sorry,' she said, not soundin' real sorry. I can't say I blame the guy for getting mad, since Beau was the name of her horse when she was a kid. They had to put it down, she told me. Spelled b-e-a-u." He looked at me closely. "What's the matter?"

I shook my head. What was it Dana's mother had said? That she'd asked her daughter if there'd been a man at Davis and she'd said yes and implied she'd been as serious about him as she'd been about Beau and Heidi.

And now, apparently, he'd shown up here in December, begging her to return to California, promising to quit drinking if she did.

Who was this guy? Where was he now? And how was I going to find him?

I thanked Kevin for talking to me and slid into my car. Rufus was snoring softly in his carrier on the backseat.

"I hope you catch the creep," Kevin said, hanging on my car door. "And remember what I said: you do, you give me a few minutes with him, okay? I'll save the taxpayers money, big-time."

Eighteen

After I'd dropped Rufus off at Lillian's and driven home, I called Gary and told him I was too tired to have him over. I just wanted to get some sleep—I hadn't had any since three the previous afternoon. I ate a bowl of ramen noodles with vegetables, then channel surfed until I couldn't keep my eyes open any longer and dragged myself off to bed. That wasn't how I'd meant to spend Friday night.

The next night, Gary and I had dinner with Paula and Lawrence at Ernesto's, a Caribbean restaurant I like because it reminds me of the three years I spent in Puerto Rico in the navy, but without the lizards crawling on the walls and hanging from the ceiling above your head. The food's better too.

I don't see much of Paula and Lawrence since Paula quit the campus cops to go to law school. For a while during the winter the four of us were taking ballroom dancing lessons together, but we finally gave it up because the guys were enjoying it too much, stomping the beat, making the decisions about which way to go, flinging Paula and me out, and forcing us to twirl whenever the mood struck them. Ballroom dancing's pretty but a little too much like real life, which isn't.

We were in a booth in a candlelit alcove, our heads together over a big platter of callaloo—chicken over steaming rice, with chopped spinach and okra and a spicy sauce—and *tostones*, which is

plantain prepared like french fries. This is my idea
of comfort food. Lawrence was drinking beer; Paula
and Gary had some kind of Portuguese red wine; I
had an exotic nonalcoholic fruit drink. A band was
playing Caribbean music next to a small dance floor:
a marimba, bongos, guitars, and gourds.

Lawrence repeated what he'd told me earlier, that
I should ask for an indoor assignment until Jason
was safely locked away. "I would," he added, "if I
were in your shoes."

I said he'd have to if he were in my shoes, because
they'd pinch too much to walk in. Paula said that
maybe Jason had left town, in which case I had
nothing to worry about. "Trouble with that is," she
added glumly, "how would you know?"

After a while I said I didn't want to talk about
Jason any more that night.

When a sufficient number of people got up to
dance so we wouldn't be too noticeable, we did too.
Gary and I do a mean tango, believe it or not. It
helps that Gary, with his swarthy face, dark, deep-
set eyes, and sudden, beautiful smile, could pass for
Latin American. We can also do a convincing, if
somewhat overblown, samba, marred only by my
usually unsuccessful attempts not to giggle.

Paula and Lawrence make a striking couple.
Paula's tall, slender, and black, with a long neck and
a face that suggest that the African sculptors were
working from nature; Lawrence is tall, slender, and
blond, and a reasonably graceful dancer when he
remembers to count.

I was there the night he fell in love with her. Even
if somebody hadn't been murdered shortly afterward, I'd remember the occasion. I'm prepared to
swear under oath that a lightbulb went on above his
head and a choir began singing. It was intense just

watching. I can't imagine what it must have been like for Lawrence.

After we'd run through our repertoire of Latin American dances, we ordered dessert and espresso, and while waiting for it I excused myself and went to the ladies' room. The only thing I don't like about Ernesto's is that the smoking section is in front of the hall leading down to the rest rooms, which is appropriate, I guess—it used to be that's where the nonsmoking section was—but it means that anybody who wants to use them has to pass through the tobacco stench. A woman was sitting by herself at a small table, a cigarette in one hand, her head leaning into the palm of the other. She was staring abstractedly at a dish of crème brûlée, one of Ernesto's specialties, in front of her. She had shoulder-length curly blond hair and was dressed in a western-style jacket trimmed with black and glittering with rhinestones—quite a dramatic outfit if you were planning to line dance, I supposed. She didn't look up as I passed.

It was a small rest room with only two stalls. I'd just got comfortably seated when somebody came in, paused just inside the door for a moment, then came over and stood in front of my stall. I could see the points of scuffed western-style boots from where I sat.

"Olé, Peggy!"

Hands gripped the top of the stall door, and Jason's head rose slowly above it. In the garish light, his made-up face looked clownish under the curly blond wig.

"No, no!" he said in an admonishing voice. "Don't get up! This time I'm packin' iron. So just carry on as before, and we'll go on with the interview that got so rudely interrupted in your poor new car the other day. Sorry about that. Hope you're insured."

The strain of chinning himself was too much for him, and he dropped back down. "It's kind of disappointing," he went on, "you wearing a full skirt like that all bunched up on your thighs. Maybe if I promised not to shoot you, you'd let me see a little more?"

I didn't say anything, just stared at what I could see of him through the gap between the door and the stall.

"Peggy?"

"Is that a threat, Jason?" It annoyed me that my voice was trembling, but at least it was with disgust and anger, not fear.

He laughed. "Nah, just kidding. You've been busy lately, Peggy, haven't you? I've watched you going in and out of that old vet hospital the last few days—a very busy gal."

I just sat there, waiting.

"What's the matter, cat got your tongue?"

Waiting.

"You're still in there, aren't you?" he said. "Let's see what you're up to."

His head came up over the door again. I was standing now, ready for him, and I struck at his head with the palm of my hand. It glanced off his forehead as he fell away. I slid open the lock and started to pull the door toward me.

"Stop!" he said, breathless, angry, slightly panicked. I saw the pistol in his hand. "I'll shoot if you come out! And then I'll shoot anybody outside who tries to stop me from getting out of here—that'll probably be one of your friends, won't it?

"Lock it again," he ordered, and when I'd slid the lock back into place, he said, "Good. Now listen: if anybody comes in, do her a favor and don't give me away. Understand?''

"What do you want, Jason?"

He laughed. "You really do play hard to get, don't you? I just don't understand it—is it something I said? You've got some kind of thing going with all the old professors on campus—don't deny it—I saw the look on that old geezer's face the other night when he came out of Watts after you'd been in there a while. What'd you do for him, huh? And what's he got that I don't? Does your boyfriend know about him?''

I stared at the door, scratched and scarred with the comments on life and love of women who'd been there before me.

"What do you want, Jason?" I repeated. It felt as though I'd been asking him that question all my life.

"Now? Just to talk—'touch base,' as they say. If I don't leave town first, there'll be time for other things, you know? But why should I leave town if I don't want to? Your friend the homicide cop doesn't seem to be getting any closer to catching me. Speaking of which, what were you two doin' in his car for so long Monday night? Makin' out? Everybody but me, huh, Peggy? Well, we'll see. Every dog has his day: isn't that what they say up at the vet hospital?''

He paused, waiting for me to say something. I didn't.

"I'm not really a professional killer," he went on, more soberly, "just a situational one. Situational, as in ethics, you know what I mean? If it's good for you, go for it and feel bad for a few days afterward if somebody got hurt. If it don't feel good, don't do it and feel all warm and fuzzy on account of you didn't.''

"Is that how it is?" I asked. "You felt bad about

killing Dana for a couple of days, and that was it? Why don't I believe that?"

Now it was his turn to fall silent for a moment. "I didn't mean to kill Dana," he said quietly. "I just wanted my tape recorder back, and things got out of hand. It wasn't really murder, it was an accident."

"Tell me how you did it, Jason. Describe it to me."

"No. No, I don't think so, Peggy. I don't want to relive it."

"You mean you don't every day, every night?"

Silence again, from his side of the door.

And from mine: "How many times did you hit her, Jason?"

"Once, Peggy. I don't know if that's what killed her or if the fall did. I'll never forget the sound her head made, hitting the steps."

Dana had been hit at least twice after she fell; Bonnie Winkler was sure of that. One of those blows had killed her.

"What're you doing in there?" he asked suddenly. He laughed nervously. "It's a funny place to be interrogating a murderer, isn't it?"

He paused, waiting to hear from me. I stood there, waiting for—what? I wanted another woman to come in, to distract him. I *didn't* want another woman to come in and maybe get hurt.

"Well, enough banter," he said. "I gotta go before somebody else comes in. But we'll talk again soon. Isn't that what you want—to talk to me? And you know what I want from you, but this is no place for that. We need someplace where we won't be rushed—maybe your nice apartment. I happened to be passin' by a couple of days ago and glanced in. Nice! I like the blue wall-to-wall carpeting. Looked soft. You have anything you wanna say?" he almost shouted.

I didn't say anything.

"Well, okay." He sounded suddenly exhausted. "Now, give me a minute to make a dignified exit, will you? You'll need it anyway, to wash your hands. God, I hate people who don't wash their hands after going to the bathroom, don't you?"

I peered under the stall door to make sure he'd left, but I took my time following him out of the rest room. I washed my hands, stared down at them, and tried to stop them from trembling. They were shaking not with fear but with rage—outrage. *What do you want, Jason?*

Then I went out, paused, and looked around the dark restaurant. The musicians were still playing, people were dancing and laughing, eating, drinking, and smoking as though nothing out of the ordinary had taken place, and for them nothing had. Jason, of course, was gone. I glanced down at the table he'd been sitting at. There were a few crumpled dollar bills lying on it next to the cup of crème brûlée that he hadn't finished. Sticking out of the middle of it was his cigarette butt. There was also a purse dangling by its strap from the chair he'd been sitting on.

Paula watched me approach our table, saw my face, and got up. "What's the matter?"

"Jason," I said, "in drag. He followed me into the rest room. He's got a pistol." I described how he'd looked, said he'd probably gone out the back door.

"He did," Paula said. "I saw him."

Forgetting that she's no longer a cop, she got up and started for the door.

"Wait for me," Lawrence said, and got up and followed her.

I told Gary to go over and keep the busboys away from Jason's table, then went to the cashier, who was looking confused. I showed him my shield and told him the customer who'd just gone out the back was wanted by the police.

I called Buck's office, a number I know by heart, and when the call rolled over to another detective, I identified myself and described what had happened. He told me to stay where I was, there'd be cops all over the place in a few minutes.

Then I called Buck at home—I know that number by heart too—and told him about it.

"He left his purse," I added. "It didn't go with his outfit. I'll bet it belonged to Dana Michaels." I was beginning to think I knew Jason.

I went back to the table to wait for the cops. While I'd been talking to Buck, I'd felt only rage; I'd been too involved in the situation to feel what I began to feel now. I felt scorched, as though Jason's eyes, and his freedom with my private space, had been a physical violation. I wanted to go home, take a shower.

A minute later, cops began coming into the restaurant, and then Paula and Lawrence returned. They hadn't seen anything, but Ernesto's is in a fairly busy part of town and there'd been a lot of people on the streets.

Then two homicide detectives arrived, and while one of them was over at Jason's table, the other pulled up a chair and took down my story.

In the backseat of Paula and Lawrence's car, Gary turned to me, the muscles tight around his jaw, and asked if Jason had touched me.

He probably meant "How are you feeling?" but nobody's perfect, so I said, "No. And I'm fine, thanks."

The car was silent for a minute. Then I took pity on him and said, "He didn't do anything, just stared at me over the top of the stall. He got a good look at my knees."

Paula turned and stared at me, her lips compressed in disgust.

"I did manage to give him a hard palm to the forehead," I said, "but it didn't seem to hurt him very much."

"I wish it'd been me," she grated, her eyes blazing. She's got a black belt in tae kwon do.

"He gets off on tormenting women, on embarrassing them," Lawrence said. "That's what you told us he enjqyed doing with those other women. He'd lose interest in them if they gave him what he wanted. You've got to get off the dog watch now, Peggy."

"I've got another night before I have to make that decision," I said.

"There's nothing to decide!" he said angrily. Gary was wisely staying out of it.

"How would going off the dog watch have kept him from following me to Ernesto's tonight?" I flared. "He's keeping tabs on me. He knew I'd visited the veterinary hospital twice since Dana's murder. He's peered in my windows! Until he's caught, I won't have a life," I said, my voice rising dangerously. "He obviously doesn't want to kill me—not yet, anyway—because he could do that anytime, anyplace. So what does he want?"

I stayed at Gary's place that night. After he was asleep, I got up and went over to the window and stared out into the dark at the peacefully sleeping, moonlit street. I was wearing an old pair of Gary's pajamas. I hate flannel, but I didn't mind it that night. It was comforting somehow, like a lullaby and hot chocolate.

I wondered where Jason was and wondered what he was up to, what his plans were for me—for us—and what I could do about it.

I played over in my mind the episode in the women's rest room. There were things about it that puzzled me, not the least of which was why he'd gone to so much trouble to confront me like that. There'd been nothing salacious in his voice or look as his head came over the stall door, and there'd been no real passion in him as he'd spoken to me either. He'd shown no pleasure in having that power over me. What was the point? What did he want?

I have a friend, Sandra Carr. She's made a fortune writing thrillers about women in jeopardy: "femjeps," they're called. I like Sandra a lot in small doses, but I've read only one of her books, and I had to force myself to finish it. Characteristic of all of them, according to women I've talked to who read them avidly—my friend Ginny's one, I'm sorry to say—is that the heroines are strong, but some malign force outside themselves, usually in the form of a man, is threatening them, coming closer and closer. I don't want to live in such a world, or read about it for fun.

When I finally got to sleep, I dreamed that I was kneeling next to a horse lying on its side, trying to calm it. I was staring up at a man standing on the horse's other side, a surgical mask covering his mouth. "I'm Jason," he shouted down at me, blue in the face. "Don't you get it? Jason!"

I woke up with the name echoing in my head.

Nineteen

"You were right, Peggy," Buck told me on the phone the next morning. "It was Dana Michaels's purse. He left a note in it that says he doesn't need it any more—it doesn't go with any of his outfits."

"Funny man," I said. "I suppose you're wasting taxpayer dollars sending cops to every store in town that sells wigs." We have as many malls here as we have lakes—and that's a lot—and they all contain at least one store that sells wigs, for some inexplicable reason.

"We're covering the bases," he said without enthusiasm.

"The outfit he was wearing looked like it once belonged to a woman who'd tried country dancing and then come to her senses," I told him. "I've seen similar things hanging on the racks at clothing consignment stores." That's where I get most of my evening wear.

I also told him that when I asked Jason to describe how he'd killed Dana, he claimed he'd only hit her once and that it must've been the fall that killed her.

"You didn't tell him how many times she'd been struck, did you?"

"No."

"Good. Either he's lying to you or he doesn't remember how many times he hit her. But I want to hear it from him. In the meantime, I've called your chief, Captain DiPrima, and explained the situation to him. He agrees with me that—"

"Damn you, Buck, you had no right to do that! This is just—"

"I'd do the same if it were one of my officers—male or female," he said, unimpressed by my outrage. "There's no way you can protect yourself from a stalker if you're walking around the campus in the night—you know that as well as I do."

I was speechless with rage and angry at myself for feeling a great sense of relief, but I drew out the silence anyway, hoping to make him feel guilty.

"Well, it's probably a moot point anyway," I said finally. "I snuck into the Atwood Lab to talk to Barry Russell. Doctor J—everybody's favorite vet—caught me leaving and told me she was going to lodge a complaint with Captain DiPrima."

"You learn anything of interest from Russell?"

"Nothing your detectives didn't get," I said. "He agrees with Dana's mom that she was thinking of leaving the Atwood Lab and returning to California. He thought she'd lost interest in research." I also told him what I'd learned from Kevin Wheatley about the man he'd overheard quarreling with Dana in the Large Animal Clinic.

Buck listened without interrupting, then asked how that was going to help him find Jason.

"It probably isn't. It's just puzzling, that's all. What was she doing, getting involved with a shabby drunk and calling him by the name of a horse she'd loved? I don't like loose ends, Buck."

He laughed. He sounded tired too. "The lives of people who get murdered always have loose ends, Peggy. You heard what that old high school friend of hers said at the memorial service: Dana brought home strays. Beau was the name of a horse she couldn't save; she called a man she was involved with Beau because he was another animal she was trying to save.

"I've got to go now, Peggy," he went on. "I've got the kids of the victims of either a murder-suicide or a double murder coming in in a few minutes. I'll send a detective out to talk to your Mr. Wheatley, just in case he picked up something else while sleeping on the job he didn't tell us the first time around. In the meantime, be careful."

"What do you suggest I do, Buck? Leave town?"

"You have vacation time?"

"Not to use to go into hiding," I said, and hung up.

Sunday wasn't bad—Gary, Lillian, Rufus, and I went on a picnic in the arboretum in Nichols Park, and I stayed with Gary that night—but Monday I went back to my own place and it was awful: I had to force myself to go out shopping and I answered the phone reluctantly. I accused a telemarketer of being Jason, and when a young man came to collect money for a cause I believed in, I listened to his spiel through a crack in the door with the chain on and looked for Jason under his beard.

It was with a feeling of dread that I left my apartment that night to go to work, crossing the backyard to the garage with my hand on the waist pack where my pistol was concealed. The pack was designed for plain-clothes officers and I'd borrowed it from Ginny. My service revolver was fastened upside down on the inside of the flap, which was held in place by Velcro. You just tear the flap open and the pistol's right there by your hand, ready to draw.

It was a pleasant early-spring night, cold but no wind, and the sky was clear. Even though it was supposed to start raining after midnight and continue through the next morning, I would have ridden my bike to the University if it hadn't been for Jason. I liked the exercise it gave me, but riding a bike late at night is risky under the best of circumstances, which these weren't.

Lieutenant Bixler was waiting for me when I entered the squad room. We call him the Rooster because he struts and because his chest and belly make a perfect curve that ends right above his bandy legs. He took great pleasure in announcing that I would be staying in that night and cleaning up the property room.

"Also," he added in a voice everybody could hear, "the chief wants to see you in his office tomorrow at nine sharp. Doctor Julia Atwood of the Atwood Lab called and lodged a complaint. She wants to see your ass nailed to a wall."

"A curious desire," I muttered.

"What?"

"Nothing."

Cleaning up the property room is one of a number of indoor assignments given to pregnant or injured officers. One look told me what I already knew, that nobody had been either pregnant or injured in a long time. Sergeant Heller, whom I like a lot, was the shift sergeant that night, and he explained to me what I had to do: take every piece of property in the room—found, recovered stolen, held for pending court cases—and compare it with the case files in the computer. If a case had been completed, I had to put the property associated with it in a pile that somebody with authority could decide whether to destroy, try to return to its rightful owner, or auction off.

Noticing my lack of enthusiasm, Heller patted me

on the shoulder and assured me the task could be quite interesting. "A lot of memories in here," he added. He picked up a bicycle seat from a shelf, blew dust off it, and held it out in front of his face. "If only this seat could talk!" he sighed. "I remember the case, Peggy."

I burst out laughing. "Alas, poor seat!" I intoned. "I knew it, Sergeant Hiller—a seat of infinite jest, of most excellent fancy. It hath borne me on its back a thousand times. And now how abhorred in my imagination it is!"

Puzzled, he looked from the seat to me. "Huh?"

"Nothing," I said.

A little uncertainly, he put the seat back where he'd found it, patted me on the shoulder again, and quickly left the room. That's the trouble with a liberal arts education these days: nobody knows what you're talking about.

Hiller was wrong. Putting the property room in order was not just dusty and dirty, it was boring, and that was something else I held against Jason. But at least I could do it in one night and they'd have to find something else for me to do tomor—

"O'Neill!"

I woke up with a start.

It was Bixler. "You weren't asleep, were you?"

"No."

"Good, 'cause there's a lot of gals'd love having this job. So if you decide it's beneath you, let me know, okay?"

"Only gals?" I inquired sweetly.

He stood and glared doubtfully at me a moment longer, then turned and clomped back down the hall.

I picked up a manila envelope dated two years earlier and searched the computer for the corresponding case number. Exciting stuff, the way I imagine doing gravestone rubbings in a cemetery's exciting. I'd like to be able to say I stumbled across something that told me who Jason was or where I might look for him next, or solved some other crime that had been on the books a long time, but all I got was dirty fingers and a runny nose from the dust.

Ginny Raines came on duty at eight. She looked up in surprise when I strolled into her office with a cup of coffee.

"My God!" she exclaimed. "It's true what they say about vampires caught in daylight—they turn to dust!"

"Ha-ha," I enthused. "Captain DiPrima's going to nail my ass to a wall at Doctor Julia Atwood's request. You want to come watch?"

"The famous animal scientist?" She pursed her lips and thought about it a moment. "Sure, I'll come." She stretched an imaginary ass out in front of her and nailed it to an imaginary wall with an imaginary hammer, then studied the result, tilting her head this way and that. "What've you done to annoy Doctor J—stepped on a puppy dog's tail?"

When I'd finished explaining, she said, "You've got smudges around your eyes and on your sharp little nose. No, don't rub it off! It makes you look like a ragamuffin, and not even DiPrima would be so heartless as to nail a ragamuffin's ass to a wall."

She turned serious. "You're being stalked by a pervert who's already killed one woman, and yet you're trying to find him by upsetting people in the veterinary hospital. I'll bet if I ask nicely, you'll tell me how you reconcile these two things in your mind, won't you?"

"Dana Michaels told her office mate that she thought she knew Jason from somewhere," I recited. "That's one thing. Another is, I wanted to learn more about her life. In doing that, I've come up with more questions."

"Isn't that always the way!" Ginny sipped her diet cola and took a bite out of a rice cake. "But there's more to it than that, isn't there?" she added.

"What?" I asked, glaring at her.

"C'mon, Peggy, give!"

Before I could say anything to that, Bixler stuck his fat head in the door and said, "Now, O'Neill!"

The voice of the Rooster. I got up and followed him down to Captain DiPrima's office, trying not to imitate his splay-footed walk. I was in enough trouble already.

The campus police chief, Captain DiPrima—the chief gets to choose his own rank, so it could've been worse—is a trim, olive-complexioned man with close-set sunken eyes and dark hair starting to go gray. His hands are long and slender and he seems to know they're beautiful because he plays with pencils in front of his eyes so both you and he can watch them. He also looks good in a uniform and knows that too. He's not a bad guy, as administrators go, as long as you treat him with the respect his inflated salary makes him think he deserves. As a matter of principle, I try to keep my distance from him as I do from all administrators.

He didn't ask me to sit down. Bixler took up a position with his back against the office's single window, probably to make me squint whenever I had to look at him—a trick he learned from watching gestapo officers at work in old World War II movies.

"You've annoyed a powerful member of the University community," DiPrima began coldly.

There are few sins greater than annoying a powerful member of the University community.

"I know," I said. "But I'd like to point out that I wasn't on duty, Captain, I wasn't in uniform, and I didn't pretend to be on official business."

"Huh," Bixler grunted.

"I realize that," DiPrima said, flashing a smile. His smiles are all flashy because his teeth are so white they look fake, although they couldn't be: they're too irregular.

"There isn't a thing we can do to you for it, Officer O'Neill," he went on. "I explained that to Professor Pyles, the director of the Atwood Lab, who called to tell me how upset Doctor Atwood is."

"She wasn't upset," I said. "She was outraged that somebody—and an outsider, at that—would disobey her orders."

"Pyles thought you should be suspended, at the very least," DiPrima went on as if I hadn't spoken, "and was disappointed to learn the regulations don't allow for that. The best I could do for him was tell him he had the right to call the campus police and have them arrest any unauthorized person who refuses to leave voluntarily. He assured me that that's what he'll do the next time you try to go back into the lab areas."

"I don't understand why they're all so secretive," I said. "I'm only trying to help find whoever killed one of their postdocs. You'd think they'd be grateful."

Bixler shifted impatiently from foot to foot by the window.

"I can tell you why, if you really want to know," DiPrima said. "Some years ago, a worker in the Atwood Lab called the newspaper with a story about research irregularities. The newspaper sent a reporter to investigate, and the reporter crawled all over the lab looking for dirt. He or she picked up a lot of gossip, and some of it got in the papers. The so-called whistle-blower's charges turned out to be groundless and the fuss died down—but it left a bad taste in Atwood's mouth. She's run the place as a kind of walled fortress ever since."

"How do you know this?" I asked.

Bixler, anxious to see my posterior drying like jerky on a wall, was making impatient noises. DiPrima ignored him, played with his fingers in front of his face a moment, then looked up at me suddenly with his dark eyes.

"The call from Pyles was not the only one I received concerning you," he replied. "I also received a call from one of the regents, a man who lives comfortably in the pocket of the dairy farmers' lobby, which means he's a great supporter of the School of Veterinary Medicine."

"Talk about overkill!" I exclaimed.

DiPrima twitched a frosty smile and said, his voice soft, "We're making up our budget request for the next academic year, Officer O'Neill, and I have to submit it to the regents in a couple of weeks. I'd hate to have somebody like Doctor Atwood complaining to them about the behavior of one of my officers. I can understand your interest in the arrest of the man who killed the woman from the Atwood Lab, but I'm sure the city police, with their manpower and technology, are doing everything possible."

"I can't walk a beat until Jason's caught," I said, tempering my surliness since Captain DiPrima was being remarkably nice about the whole thing, "and there's not all that much left to do in cleaning up the property room. I can't make a career of it."

"I'm aware of that," he said. "I'm sure we can find something else to keep you busy until it's safe for you to work outside again. Lieutenant Bixler?"

"Somebody's gotta rewrite the *Field Training Officer's Manual*," Bixler said. "O'Neill thinks she's got a nice way with words. She's just what the doctor ordered—the vet, I mean," he added with heavy emphasis, to make sure we got it.

"That's an excellent idea, Lieutenant," DiPrima said, "although I don't suppose your motives are the worthiest."

My heart sank. The *FTO's Manual* is a thick book designed to acquaint rookies with the principles and procedures of the department. The only thing more boring than reading it would be having to update it.

DiPrima said, in a tone of voice that jarred horribly with the brilliant smile, "And please, Officer O'Neill, stay out of trouble, won't you—even on your own time? Because if you are caught where you're not supposed to be, and get arrested and convicted of trespassing, we'll be forced to reevaluate your fitness to be a police officer. I'd hate to have to do that, but there are others in the department who'd enjoy it a great deal."

I nodded and turned to go. As I did, he said, "Tell me something. Is Millard Pyles the pompous ass in person he is on the phone?"

"On the phone, at least, you couldn't know he wears loafers with tassels," I replied. DiPrima is a sharp dresser.

He nodded and turned to the papers on his desk.

"Don't go far, O'Neill," Bixler hollered after me as I started out the door. He was doing his best to conceal his disappointment at how easily I'd gotten off. "I got stacks of material you'll be wanting to go through. It's real exciting literature."

I went back to Ginny's office, sat where I could keep an eye out for Bixler, and summarized what DiPrima had told me.

"You got off easy," she said, "probably on account of DiPrima hates meatheaded civilians telling him what to do." She was snacking on carrot sticks and broccoli florets. "But you don't want to be walking a beat anyway, especially not at night. Now, before the Rooster so rudely interrupted us, we were analyzing you and your latest eccentric behavior."

"What's there to analyze?"

"Your reasons for snooping into the life of a dead woman. It's guilt, isn't it? You think you're to blame for her death."

"In a way, I guess," I admitted. "Maybe if I'd been nicer to Jason—when I first met him—he wouldn't have kept coming after me. I should have tried to explain to him why I didn't want to have coffee with him, or sit and talk with him."

"No explanations were necessary, Peggy," Ginny said.

"I know that! But still—"

"'But still,'" she repeated. "Poor Peggy. You drove him to kill. Before you came along, he was just a nice kid living out in one of the old buildings on the Ag Campus, minding his own business, tormenting the odd female student. After you, he smashes women over the head, kidnaps them, holds a knife to their throat—"

"Stop it, Ginny," I said wearily.

"Okay. So what have you found out about Dana that's so interesting?"

I smiled ruefully. "She wasn't very interesting," I said. "That's one thing I've found out. She seemed to love animals more than people. But she'd apparently had a relationship with a guy at Davis. When she got mad at him, she called him Beau, which was the name of a horse she loved too—who died. He came here in December and met her in the Large Animal Clinic barn. A guy I talked to overheard him begging her to go back to Davis. He said he thought she might get hurt if she stayed here."

"He didn't say she'd get hurt if she stayed in the Atwood Lab, did he?"

"I don't know. The guy who overheard them talking didn't hear everything they said. I want to know who the guy at Davis is," I added. "And I'm going to."

Ginny sighed noisily. "Right." Pushing her bag of veggies aside and staring into her computer screen, she added, "The rules for using the expandable baton have changed. You can't whack students on the knees with it anymore just because they banged into you on Rollerblades while talking to their friends on their cellular phones. Be sure to get that into the FTO's manual, Peggy. You know how bloodthirsty rookies are. Now beat it, I've got work to do."

I threw one of her carrot sticks at her.

Bixler had put together a tall stack of material for me to use in updating the manual, and he happily showed me to a windowless, airless cubicle where I could work on it without interruption.

"Because you'll need to do this during the day," he added, as he dropped the material on the gray steel desk with a dusty thump, "we'll have to rearrange your schedule. Be here tomorrow morning bright and early, O'Neill. Bright and early. It'll keep you out of trouble."

Twenty

It was raining when I got home, a steady drizzle. The red button on my answering machine was winking, and the counter said there was one message.

"Where were you last night, Peggy?" Jason's voice asked quietly. *"I saw you go into the police station at the usual time, but you didn't come out with the rest of the cops after roll call. I waited around for at least an hour—you know how faithful I am: commitment's my middle name. But I finally had to give up."*

He sighed. *"I noticed your car was in the parking lot all night, so you didn't go back home either. What's the problem? Lemme guess: the powers that be decided to keep you inside, right? It must be nice, workin' for people who are concerned about your safety.*

"I suppose you'll be going to bed now," he went on. *"I hope my call won't disturb your beauty rest. Do you sleep in pajamas? I think about that sometimes—I've built an entire 'Peggy O'Neill' around what I've seen of you: your red hair, your freckled face. I suppose the reality'll be a major disappointment—it usually is. But we'll see."*

The silence stretched out forever, but I waited to hear if he'd say anything more. In the kind of thrillers Sandra Carr writes, the heroine would have heard telltale noises in the background—the unmistakable sounds of a fortune-cookie factory, say—that would lead the police straight to the villain, but I couldn't hear anything at all.

"I was only kidding when I said you were to blame for Dana's death," Jason went on suddenly. "It was all my fault—even though she shouldn't've taken my tape recorder. But it wasn't my hitting her with the rock that killed her, it was her head hitting the cement that did it. It was an accident."

He was silent again for a few moments, then continued: "When I think about it, though, I think it was really Tolliver's fault. I've told you about Tolliver, haven't I? Well, I think Dana's death was his fault—or God's. But how could I convince the cops of that, not to speak of a judge and a jury? You know how simpleminded cops are, they'll just charge me with cold-blooded murder and lock me up and throw away the key. No thanks! Not that I think my life's so goddamned precious or anything: it ain't. It's just that I don't intend to spend it behind bars, no matter how worthless it is. So what I'll probably do is commit suicide someday—just as soon as I can find the right method. But it would be fun to sit down with you first and tell you why all this shit we're goin' through is either Tolliver's fault or God's. Maybe you could even help me figure out which. Well, I'll think about that, anyway. Good-night, Peggy."

He hung up. I wanted to destroy the machine. I wanted to throw myself down on the floor and cry. I wanted to get up and stalk around the room and scream and holler obscenities. Instead, I sat there and stared out at Lake Eleanor through my rain-streaked window and forced myself to take deep breaths until I was calm. Then I went into my bedroom, set my alarm for two hours later, when people would be starting work in California and I could do something to try to find a man Dana Michaels sometimes called Beau.

I slept badly, jerking awake at every creak the old house made. I was alone in it because my landlady, Mrs. Hammer, hadn't returned from spending the winter in Florida yet. I missed her; I liked falling asleep in the morning knowing she was puttering around upstairs. I thought of Jason peering in my windows.

When the alarm went off, I took a long shower, first hot and then cold, while a pot of strong coffee was brewing. Then I took the pot and a cup with me into my living room. It had stopped raining, but the sky was still overcast, though the clouds in the west seemed brighter than they had earlier.

First I called Gary at the newspaper. "Can I sleep over at your place again tonight?" I asked.

"Sure. But I thought you were working."

"I've been reassigned to pushing paper indoors," I told him, "which means I get to sleep when real people do. I'm kind of happy about it, actually, which tells you something."

"You okay?"

"I'm fine." I told him about the message Jason had left on my machine.

"I'll fix dinner tonight," he said after a moment. "Something you like."

I dialed long-distance information and got the number for the College of Veterinary Medicine at the University of California at Davis. I asked the woman who answered to transfer my call to Professor Mark Dodson, who'd been Dana Michaels's adviser. He was also Julia Atwood's ex-husband.

"Mark Dodson," a man's voice said.

I told him I was Gerri Mallory, that I was with the state crime lab, and that I wanted to talk to him about Dana Michaels.

"Haven't you caught the son of a bitch who killed her yet?" he shouted. "You probably never will now, if you haven't already. Don't they say that if you don't catch 'em within a day or two, you might as well give 'em a royal pardon and save the taxpayers money?"

"Something like that," I said, grimly official.

"There was a detective here right after Dana was murdered, asking questions about Barry Russell. I told him the truth—there wasn't anything between Barry and Dana as far as I could tell. Of course, nobody tells me anything, and I don't go around snooping into my students' underwear either. But Barry was a couple of years ahead of her and probably didn't even know she existed. Dana was nice, but Barry liked them a little friskier, if you get my drift," he added, contradicting something he'd said the moment before.

"I do," I said. "But there are some other things we're looking into—"

"Such as?" he demanded suspiciously. "Not Charlie, I hope."

"Charlie? You mean Charlie Atwood?"

"You wouldn't know it from his name, but last time I checked he was my son."

I told him we were concentrating our efforts on finding Jason, our strongest suspect, but until we could get our hands on him we weren't excluding other possibilities.

He laughed a little uneasily. "Charlie's not a possibility!"

"What makes you suppose we think he is?"

"I really put my foot in my mouth, didn't I? Or poor Charlie's foot." He laughed again. "I don't know, it's just that he's so—so goddamned clueless." He paused, perhaps to collect his thoughts. "With his luck, he'd have been found standing over poor Dana's body with a bloody ax or whatever it was. He wouldn't have committed the murder, of course; he'd have just happened to be passing the scene of the crime and picked up the ax to see what it was! Forget I ever brought up the subject."

"Okay," I said, "but I'm curious. His last name's Atwood—"

"And mine's Dodson. Right. My lovely ex-wife took the kids when she moved back there. I can't say I cared much, to be honest. I was working on whatever it was that was so important to me in those days—damned if I can recall what it was!—and I didn't have time to be a parent. So she took 'em with her. Next thing I know, she writes and tells me she's changing their names to Atwood—her name. What's in a name? I thought, so I didn't fight it. Besides, I had a son by my first wife, so the Dodson name was secure for another generation, for whatever that's worth." He barked a joyless laugh. "So what happens? Mark junior—the youngest boy—moves back here with me and petitions to have his name changed back to Dodson! Ironic, isn't it? Can you imagine how Julia must have felt when she heard?" He chuckled gleefully.

"Dana was a damn good doctor," he went on. "I couldn't understand why she decided to go into research. I figured she'd start her own practice somewhere. She was a real hands-on kind of vet, loved animals, even worked as a volunteer at the Humane Society here while carrying a heavy load of course work."

"One of the things we're curious about is why she decided to come here to do her postdoctoral work," I said.

"She had family there, didn't she? Parents?"

"Yes, but we don't think they were all that close. Could it have been because she wanted to work under your ex-wife?"

"I doubt it very much. Julia's still a big name out there, I suppose, but her best work's long behind her. She made her name with an adjuvant, if you know what that is." He waited for me to say I did before going on. "It's still one of the best in the business, of course, and she's come up with a bunch of other stuff that's nothing to sneeze at either—vaccines and such that've made a bundle for your university. But she hasn't come up with anything earthshaking in a while. I wouldn't call her burned-out, exactly. Let's be kind, just say she's slowing down."

I hadn't heard that. I guess it pays to get out of town once in a while—even if only by phone—to get some perspective on your own little world, where Julia Atwood was still held in awe. Of course, I had to consider the source. I wondered if Mark Dodson had done as well in his career as his former student and ex-wife had done in hers.

"Did you offer Dana a postdoc?" I asked. "That might've been the difference for her between staying there and coming here."

"No—she didn't apply to us for one! If she had, we would've matched or bettered whatever Julia gave her." He laughed. "Maybe Dana liked your climate!"

I tried to laugh at that one too, for friendship's sake. "Did you know her well enough to know if she had any close friends out there? We're considering the possibility that she came here to get away from an unhappy love affair."

He gave the chuckle of a man holding a pipe. "Well, that's always possible, of course," he said. "Still water sometimes, though not always, runs deep. But if Dana was involved in a love affair that

was so traumatic for her that she would flee back to
the Midwest to escape from it, she hid it well. You'd
suppose it would've shown on her face, or affected
the quality of her work, but it didn't—not as far as I
could see at any rate."

"How about somebody she called Beau?"

"Beau? Sounds like a character in a romance
novel set in the old South. I never heard that
name—not on a human being, anyway. My wife
and I had Dana over for dinner once or twice a
semester during the time she was here—with the
rest of my advisees, of course—but I don't recall her
ever bringing a man. I'd remember if she had."

"It could have been a female friend," I suggested.

He gave a nasty little laugh. "You criminal investigators think of everything, don't you? Sorry—I
can't help you with her personal life. But I can't see
a woman stalking another woman all the way from
here to there and then bashing her over the head.
Do women do that now?"

"Now that we've taken off our halos, wings, and
Mona Lisa smiles, we do anything humans do," I
assured him.

"That's too bad," he said. "I suppose my dear ex-
wife is taking Dana's murder as a personal affront."

I told him that Doctor Atwood seemed quite
moved by Dana's death at the memorial service—
she'd even mentioned the loss of her own son.

"Did she!" he said with a snort. "What an old
hypocrite she is! Now that Mark's dead and just
a memory to her, she can afford to take some time
off from her work to shed a maternal tear! Did
she insinuate that she was a wonderful mother
too?"

"She didn't say anything about that," I said.

"Good! Because it was that dry stick of a secretary

of hers, what's-her-name, who raised the boys, and au pair girls who didn't speak English—until Mark got tired of it and moved back out here.''

And drowned, according to Al. I wondered what kind of a parent Mark Senior had been.

Twenty-one

After asking Dodson a few more questions he didn't seem able to answer, I thanked him, hung up, and stared glumly out my window at a thin line of cold blue sky, but all it illuminated for me was another dead end. I padded out to my kitchen, dumped the cold coffee out of my cup, poured in some fresh coffee, took it back to the living room, and sat and watched it get cold too.

Now what?

I went over the notes I'd scribbled during my talk with Dodson. Again I'd found somebody who was puzzled that Dana Michaels had come to the U to do postdoctoral work at the Atwood Lab. Like Dana's mother, Dodson thought Dana was a hands-on vet, not a researcher. She'd even worked as a volunteer at the local Humane Society while in school at Davis.

The Humane Society.

Since I was with the crime lab and had unlimited access to the taxpayers' dollars, I picked up the phone again, called Davis information, asked for the number of the Humane Society, and dialed it. The woman who answered said her name was Erin and asked me how she could help me. Dogs were barking in the background.

I gave her the same story I'd given Dodson and asked her if she'd ever had a Dana Michaels working there.

"Why, yes," she said, "she was a volunteer until June, but she's no longer here. Why?"

I told her Dana was dead and that we were trying to get in touch with people who'd known her during her Davis days.

"Oh, dear!" she said. "Well, we all knew her a little, but I don't think any of us was what you'd call a real friend, except—oh dear!"

" 'Oh, dear,' what?"

"Well, Pete—" She stopped, obviously confused.

"Pete?"

"Watson," she said, "Peter Watson, a veterinary technician who works for us. Was—was Dana a victim of foul play?"

"I'm afraid so."

"When?" There was a strange note in her voice.

"March sixth."

"What time?"

Wondering what this was all about, I gave her the police estimate.

"Just a minute, I gotta check something." Above the noise of the dogs I could hear her rummaging through papers. After a moment I heard her laugh, and then she came back on the phone. "Pete couldn't have done it," she announced firmly.

"I'm glad to hear it," I said. "Why not?"

"March sixth was a Wednesday, right? Well, Pete was here until at least five that day, and if push comes to shove I can prove it, 'cause I have his schedule for the whole month of March right here in front of me, and he didn't miss a day that week." She caught her breath and rushed on. "I don't see how he could've left here after five and caught a plane and flown all the way there in time to kill Dana when you said she was killed—do you?— especially since it's later there than here, right?" she added triumphantly. She sounded like a defense attorney grilling a prosecution witness.

I agreed that it seemed unlikely and asked her why Pete might want to kill Dana Michaels, now that we were sure he hadn't.

"Because they were friends," she said. I wondered if the constant barking had scrambled her brains, or if she just listened to the same country music Kevin Wheatley listened to. She must have heard something odd in her answer too because she added, "But they broke up."

"Then they were more than friends?"

"Yes—for a while anyway. I really don't feel comfortable talking about Pete like this," she added, a bit late in the game.

That was disappointing. I would have liked to get all the gossip I could about him before talking to him personally. I asked her if I could speak to him.

"Oh, dear!" she said. "You can't."

"Why can't I?"

"He's not here."

"Well, perhaps you can tell me when he'll be in, or give me his home phone number."

"I don't know when he'll be in," she wailed, "and I don't think he's home!"

I put on my best therapist's voice. "Perhaps you'd like to tell me about it."

"I'm not sure I should."

"Please."

"Well." She thought about it and then plunged in. "Pete hasn't been in since Thursday."

"Has he ever just not shown up for a few days like this before?"

She was silent for a few moments. "Yes—but not this long—three whole days—at least, not since he and Dana broke up."

"When was that?"

"Lemme think." She thought. "About a year and a half ago, it must've been."

"And he took a few days off then?"

Pause. "More than a couple of days," she said. "More like a week."

"Was he drunk?"

"How'd you guess?"

"And I'll bet they broke up over his drinking, didn't they?"

"That's what we all think." She sighed noisily. "Pete's drinking has cost him so much. He's a vet— a veterinarian, I mean, of course. Or was. We don't know if he lost his license to practice or if he just quit. Mr. Wilkinson's warned him about going off on toots several times. Mr. Wilkinson's our director." She lowered her voice. "But he wasn't about to fire him unless his drinking got much worse— Pete's too useful around here. But this time Mr. Wilkinson's very angry about his just up and leaving without giving us some warning or even letting us know, so I'm not sure he'll let him come back. He was our only full-time vet tech and we've been really shorthanded since he left."

She paused to catch her breath. "My opinion is," she went on, lowering her voice, "that Mr. Wilkinson'll probably let him keep his job if he comes back soon—he's only been gone three workdays, after all. We're on a very tight budget here, you know, so Pete's a godsend—a vet we're only paying a vet tech's salary."

"How long has he worked for you?"

"He was here before I came, so I don't know for sure. I've been here almost four years."

"Tell me about Dana Michaels," I said.

"There's not really a whole lot to say about her.

She was nice—the quiet type. She was a student at Davis, which is just down the highway, and she worked for us as a volunteer. Most of the people who work here are volunteers. We were really sorry when she got her Ph.D. and left."

"You say they broke up about a year and a half ago. But Dana didn't graduate until June, so they must've been working here together for a few months after they broke up."

"Oh, sure—they stayed friends. Dana cared a lot about Pete, she just didn't want to marry him."

"But he wanted her to."

"That's what we think," Erin said. "People heard them talking, you know. We weren't eavesdropping or anything, but sometimes we'd hear little snatches of their conversation. And you could see it on his face, the way he looked at her. She went on mothering him, the way wives do their husbands sometimes, right up until the day she left."

"Mothered him, huh?"

"Oh, yeah, she always mothered him, even though he was older than her—we all mother Pete. Dana covered for him too a couple of times when we knew he was out on a toot, or too hungover to come to work—she always said he had the flu, but we knew what that meant. That stopped after they'd been together for a while because he stopped drinking mostly—she was a real good influence on him—but he still slipped sometimes." A thought seemed to strike her. "How come you want to know so much about Pete? You weren't just kidding about the time when Dana was murdered, were you?"

When I assured her I wouldn't stoop to anything so low, she went on: "Good, 'cause he's a very nice guy, just messed up. But he wouldn't hurt a fly. If he'd just do something about his drinking, he could still make something of himself. He's real good-looking and a charmer when he's not drunk or hungover. We think of him as a kind of mystery man. You know, a man with a tragic past. I mean, why does somebody with so much going for him drink so much?"

My father was a real charmer too when he wasn't drunk or hungover. It's amazing how tolerant people are of such charming drunks, until they've lived with them a while.

"Didn't he ever tell you anything about himself?"

"Uh-uh. He dated one of the other gals for a few months until he got a little too weird even for her— drinking too much, I mean—and so she dropped him. After that, he just came in and did his job and left, always with a kind of thunder cloud over his head, you know? Then Dana came along and he got better for a while, but he just couldn't keep it up."

"She called him Beau sometimes too, didn't she?"

"Oh dear!" she exclaimed, drawing again on her rich store of profanity. "How'd you know? She only called him that when she was p.o.'d at him, 'cause it always made him mad. But not violent," she went on quickly. "He's not the violent type. He'd just get annoyed with her, tell her not to do it."

"He also took a vacation in December, didn't he?"

She checked the records. "That's right. He was gone a week."

During which time he'd come here to try to talk Dana into returning to California and they'd quarreled.

"It's going to really break the poor guy up when he finds out she's dead," Erin said. Then a thought seemed to strike her. "Or do you think that's why he's gone off now, on account of he heard she'd been murdered? Golly, wouldn't that be funny—I mean, in a sick kind of way—if he was there somewhere doing the same thing you are, trying to find the guy who killed her? I'll tell you one thing, I wouldn't like to be the killer if Pete gets his hands on him. Pete's a quiet guy, but you know what they say about still water."

I knew, yes.

I thanked her for her help, then sat back in my chair and wondered what her help meant. Watson was a drunk in love with Dana, who collected strays, both the four- and the two-footed variety. She'd apparently tried to reform Watson and when she failed, she'd found it difficult to break off with him: he'd followed her here and tried to talk her into going back to California. But why had she decided to do research, instead of start a veterinary practice? Why had she come here in the first place—especially since she didn't respect Julia Atwood? And why had she changed her mind and decided to give up research—if her mother and Barry Russell were right about that?

What was it Kevin Wheatley thought Watson had said to her? That something was none of her business, it was water under the bridge. "Leave it alone," he said, "or you'll get hurt."

Leave what alone?

Did Jason just happen along and kill her before whatever she was doing could get her hurt, or were the two things connected?

Buck, up to his ears in a murder-suicide or double murder, among other equally awful crimes, didn't have the time to obsess over one murder, especially with all the evidence pointing to Jason and no evidence pointing anywhere else. But I had the time, just because Jason was obsessing over me.

I looked out my window at patches of sunlight sparkling on Lake Eleanor through broken clouds and wondered where Peter Watson was now. He'd failed to show up for work on Friday and hadn't been in since. Did Dana's murder have anything to do with it, or was he just off on one of his periodic toots, as Erin called them? And if his disappearance was connected to Dana's murder, how had he discovered it?

A "mystery man," Erin had called him. He'd once been a vet himself, but either no longer was or chose not to practice, working instead as a veterinary technician, which I gathered was a fairly low-paying job.

It was a long shot, but I got out my copy of the University's student-staff directory, looked up the School of Veterinary Medicine, and dialed the number. In as official a voice as I could muster, I told the woman who answered that I was with the Internal Revenue Service and was looking for an address for a former veterinary student named Peter Watson. "We owe him some money," I added.

"That must be a first," she said dryly. "Hold on a sec, I'll see what I have in the computer." I held my breath as I listened to her clack away on her keyboard.

"Nope," she said, and my already weary heart started to sink even further until she added, "No forwarding address. Sorry."

"You mean he was there?"

"I thought you said you knew that. He left in ninety."

I asked her for his address back then.

"It's nice to know you're as eager to give money back as you are to take it," she said. "Just kidding," she added quickly. She clacked her keys some more and read off an address that was about a mile southeast of the Old Campus, near the freeway. Until a few years ago, I knew, that area had been inexpensive student housing. Now it was block after block of upscale high-rise condos, no help at all to me since anybody living there then would be long gone now.

I asked her if he was married.

"That's what it says here," she answered. "Why? Isn't he anymore?"

"No, but maybe we can locate him through his ex-wife. Do you have her name?"

"No, sorry, it's not on the computer. You could try his adviser, of course. He might know what happened to Watson."

"Who was his adviser?"

"Doctor Charles Atwood. You want the address?"

Twenty-two

Just to be thorough, I dialed Peter Watson's six-year-old phone number. A man answered whose sleepy voice trembled with anger as he assured me he'd never heard of anybody with that name. I thanked him and hung up. Why is it when you dial a wrong number during the day, you always get somebody who works nights? That's why I have an answering machine.

It was a little after two. I decided I needed to talk to Charlie Atwood about his former advisee. Five hours earlier, Captain DiPrima had warned me not to trespass at the Atwood Lab or I'd lose my job, but I didn't want to talk to Charlie on the phone. You learn so much more when you can actually see the person you're talking to, and besides, I needed cold air and exercise to keep me awake.

I biked over to the Ag Campus, hoping I'd meet Jason on the way, since I was wearing Ginny's waist pack with my revolver inside, loaded and ready. Twenty-five minutes later I was pedaling down the road through the experimental farmland with its dark, wet soil almost ready for spring planting. At the far end of the field, I could see the storage buildings where Jason had been holed up for a time and where he'd wanted to take me after the memorial service for Dana.

When I got to the hospital, I walked down to the Atwood Lab and into the main office just as if I belonged there. Lorraine Cullin looked up, and the already perfunctory smile withered even further when she recognized me.

"You look like you've recovered," I said brightly. Because Lorraine had been ill on Friday, Doctor Atwood had had to change her plans to see the dean, which had probably made her angrier at me than she might otherwise have been.

"It was just a bug I always get in the spring. My, you're certainly the foolhardy one, Miss O'Neill— or else you don't value your job as a campus policewoman!" She gave me one of her papery smiles. "Doctor Atwood has warned you not to come back here again. I also believe she received a firm promise from your chief that you wouldn't."

"My chief can only promise you won't see me when I'm on duty," I said pleasantly, "and Doctor Atwood said I wasn't to come back here without authorization. But as you can see, I'm wearing civilian clothes, not a uniform, and if Doctor Charles Atwood invites me to visit him in his office, then it should be okay, shouldn't it—or do you have to run it past his mother first?" I'd come within a hair's breadth of saying "mommy."

She raised her little chin indignantly and started to say something, thought better of it, picked up her phone, and jabbed at a button on it instead. After a few moments, she said, "Charles? That campus policewoman your mother lodged a complaint against is here and she wants to speak to you." She listened a moment, then looked up at me and said, "What about?"

"A former student of his."

She waited for me to say the student's name. When I didn't, she spoke into the receiver again, repeating my words.

"The student's name?" she asked me after a moment, a faint gleam of triumph in her eyes.

"Peter Watson."

She gaped at me, then quickly lowered her eyes to the mouthpiece again and repeated Watson's name into the phone. "Are you sure, Charles?" she said after a moment. "Your mother—" She listened again, her lips pursing slightly, then hung up.

"He says he'll see you," she said grimly. "His office is down the hall, the second door on the left."

"You don't have to tell his mother I'm here, do you?" I said with a smile.

"You're very lucky," she replied. "She's at a meeting this morning. I will, however, notify Professor Pyles, who trusts me to keep him informed of what goes on in the laboratory."

"Who's Peter Watson?" I asked.

"If Professor Pyles gives me permission to talk to you, Miss O'Neill, I'll be happy to," she replied, flustered. "But not otherwise."

"It's quite a hush-hush operation you have here, isn't it?" I said.

She didn't reply, just continued to glare at me and wait for me to leave. I went back out into the corridor and down to Charlie's office, knocked, and went in.

He sat behind a big executive-style desk that was remarkably free of paper. As I'd seen at the memorial service, he was a big man in his mid-thirties, with his mother's large, round head, prominent eyes, and heavy features but none of the ruthlessness I'd seen in her face. A strand of his thick graying hair kept falling down over one eye, and he kept swiping at it with one of his big hands as though it were a pesky mosquito.

He looked at me curiously, gave me a rather

doggy smile. "What's your interest in Peter Watson?" he asked.

"He was a friend of Dana Michaels," I said, "when she was at Davis."

"He was? Really? I didn't know that. What about it?"

"He's a loose end," I said, "and I don't like them. I want to know how he fits into her life—and her death too, if he does."

He laughed good-naturedly. "You don't like loose ends, do you? Really!"

I smiled, waiting politely for him to go on.

"How could Watson fit into her death?" he asked. "It was that psychopath—Jason—who killed her. What evidence do you have—?"

"None. It's just that I don't know how Jason fits in either. If he killed Dana Michaels, why's he still here? Why hasn't he put as many miles as he can between himself and us?"

"He's crazy, that's why. It's really quite simple, Ms. O'Neill!"

"Maybe. I'm wondering if he's one of those people who confess to crimes they didn't commit, and is hanging around to enjoy the excitement."

Charlie shook his head, giving me what he may have thought was a pitying look. "Barry Russell heard him threaten to kill Dana, a passerby saw him at the scene of the crime, and he had a motive! He's going to have a difficult time proving he didn't kill her, if he didn't—assuming he's ever caught, that is."

"That's another thing," I said. "Why can't they catch him? Somebody has to be hiding him."

His eyes stared into mine, then darted away again, looking for something to focus on. "So where do you think Watson fits in?" he asked. "You don't think *he* killed Dana?"

I didn't, not if Erin at the Humane Society was right about when he got off work the night Dana was killed, but to Charlie I said, "It's possible. They'd been lovers. And in December he stayed with her here for a while. He even came up here to the hospital and talked to her. Somebody spotted them."

"He met her here!" Charlie repeated. "You mean, here in the lab?"

"No, on the other side of the building, in the Large Animal Clinic. She apparently didn't want anybody to see them together. He was probably drunk."

"Oh. Why did he come here?" He picked up a paper clip and began straightening it out with his big fingers.

"To talk her into going back to California," I said. "And to beg her to leave something alone she was involved in—he was worried she might get hurt."

Doctor Charlie shook his head, looking baffled. "Hurt? How? Why?"

"I don't know yet," I said. "But she did get hurt, didn't she? He was right about that."

"And with no evidence, you still don't think that was just a coincidence?"

"Maybe it was. I just want to be sure, that's all. I'd also like to find out why Watson's name seems to elicit such a strong reaction from you, and from Lorraine too—as though it was something you ate that doesn't agree with you."

He stared out his window for a minute, as though wishing he were outside, far away. Then he exhaled noisily and his eyes came back to me. "I guess that's a pretty good description of how we feel about it," he said. "You're pretty observant, aren't you?" He appeared to make up his mind about something. "All right, Ms. O'Neill," he said finally. "I really doubt that this is going to be of any help to you in solving Dana's murder, but I might as well come clean."

I waited, a patient smile on my face, for him to decide how to begin doing that.

"We invested a lot of time and money in Peter," he said. "I called him Peter," he added sadly. "I thought of him not just as someone working under my direction but as a friend. He was here on a postdoc fellowship, just as Dana was later. Fellowships don't grow on trees, you know, Ms. O'Neill, and the competition is always stiff. If we hadn't given it to him, we could have given it to somebody else, somebody who wouldn't have had Peter's problems and could have put it to good use."

He looked at me with large eyes that asked for my understanding. "So you see, when you bring up Peter's name, it brings back some bitter memories for me. My mother was opposed to giving him the fellowship. She thought there was something a little 'off' about him." There was a hint of bitterness in his laugh. "But I insisted—I wanted to give him a chance. He was desperate for it, I could see that.

"I don't go against Mother very often," he went on with a little self-deprecatory smile. "Nobody does. And I don't win very many arguments with her either—as I'm sure you can imagine. But I won that one!" He paused dramatically, then lowered his eyes to his desktop. "And Peter proved my mother right. Peter betrayed my trust."

And the cock crowed, I thought irreverently.

I asked him what Peter had done that was so awful.

"Some of it was personality. Peter was a bright young man, but not as bright as he thought he was. He didn't think we gave him enough credit for the work he did, and he clashed with Mother about that. That's a no-no."

He absently contemplated the destruction of the paper clip in his big hands for a moment, then tossed the pieces into a wastepaper basket beside his desk, where they landed with a tinny rattle. "I'm not surprised to hear you say he was drunk when he was here talking to Dana," he went on. "He had a drinking problem then too—although at first I didn't think it was serious. But quite a few people, I among them, smelled alcohol on his breath during working hours sometimes. I cautioned him about it. Once I even called him into my office—in the old lab, of course, before this one was built—and warned him in no uncertain terms that scientists can't drink on the job."

He sighed noisily. "I think he tried to control his drinking, I really do. But he was an alcoholic, and they can't help themselves, you see. His work became sloppier and sloppier, and he even began to fail to show up at the lab."

He shook his head. "Peter was very nice, Miss O'Neill, when he was sober—a lovely man, and I'm sure everybody who knew of his problem was rooting for him. Some people in the lab—myself included—even tried to cover for him at first, but in the long run it was useless and we had to let him go. It was a very unpleasant situation, let me tell you."

He gave me a brave smile. "Especially for me because I wanted him to succeed, since I'd insisted on bringing him here in the first place. As I mentioned, I don't stand up to my mother very often."

"You say you were his adviser and mentor in the department," I said. "But after you let him go, you never heard from him again?"

He shook his head, found another paper clip on

his desk, and began destroying it. I watched his hands. They were large and clumsy looking, but I remembered that Al had told me he was a fine surgeon—when his mother wasn't watching over his shoulder.

"No," he said. "And quite frankly, I don't want to hear from him again either. He'd been such a painful and embarrassing disappointment to me."

"He was married back then, I think. Did you know his wife?"

"Oh yes," he said. "She was a lovely woman, although I don't remember her name—Dede or Debbie, something like that. I don't know what became of her. I may have heard that they got divorced around the time he left us. Why?"

Why wouldn't he remember the name of a once favorite advisee's wife? Why was he protesting too much that he didn't remember her name? Or was I imagining things? Had Jason taken me over the edge with him?

"Watson hasn't shown up for work in Davis since Thursday," I said. "I wonder if he might be here and, if so, if his ex-wife knows where I could find him. He hasn't tried to contact you in the past few days, has he?"

"Peter?" He laughed harshly. "No! Why would he? He'd be ashamed to face me again. He knew how much pain and embarrassment he caused me."

"Do you know why he moved back to California?"

He threw out his arms. "I didn't know he had!" he cried. "To be honest, Miss O'Neill, I didn't care where he went; I was just glad he left, glad to get the whole sordid mess over and done with. I suppose he moved back there because he did his graduate work at Davis before coming to us."

"Really? So your father must have known him too," I said.

He blinked at me. "You know my father teaches at Davis? Have you spoken to him?"

"Yes."

"About Peter?"

"No. Should I?" I hadn't known about Peter when I'd talked to Mark Dodson. Either Dodson hadn't known about Dana's relationship with Peter or else he'd decided it wasn't any of my business. I recalled that he had worried that I might think Charlie was involved in Dana's murder.

"Dad probably wouldn't even remember him," Charlie said with a wave of his hand. "Peter was a student there so many years ago, long before Dana's time. That's why it's such a surprise to me that he and Dana knew each other." He straightened the edges of some papers, glanced at his watch, looked up at me, then laughed nervously. "One of Dana's friends at the memorial service said something about how she picked up 'strays.' I don't know how she found Peter—if she in fact did—but he would certainly qualify as a stray."

"Do you remember Dana's stepfather saying he was surprised she'd come here," I asked, "because she didn't really respect your mother and the work she was doing?"

"Yes," he said, shaking his big head sadly. "Mother was hurt when he told her that, but she doesn't believe it—none of us does. Dana gave *no* indication she was unhappy here. Her work was outstanding and she was always pleasant and respectful to Mother—to all of us. In fact, we were giving strong consideration to offering her a permanent position in the lab, and she gave us every reason to think she would accept."

I couldn't think of anything else to ask him, so I got up. He came around his desk quickly and opened his door for me. As he accompanied me back down the corridor to the main office, he said, "If you're right that Peter—Watson—was trying to get her to go back to California, it's really too bad she didn't go, isn't it? She would probably still be alive."

He entered the main office before me. "Lorraine!" he barked. "Did you know that Peter Watson was a friend of Dana Michaels?"

"Of course not," she said. Millard Pyles was perched on her desk, just as he'd been the first time I'd met him and Lorraine—and Dana Michaels. This time, however, his face was livid with anger, which I found to be an improvement.

"Lorraine tells me you're now trying to find Peter Watson," he said, his voice icy. "Hasn't your friend Jason been enough of a challenge for you, Officer O'Neill?" Without waiting for an answer, he went on: "What's your interest in Watson?"

"According to Ms. O'Neill here, he was here sometime last winter," Charlie said. "He was trying to talk her into returning to California. Isn't that strange?"

"So what?" Pyles asked me, not bothering to look at Charlie.

"I'm interested in Dana's life," I said, "so any friend of hers is a potential friend of mine. Watson was worried about her last December—he was afraid she was going to get hurt."

"Watson was a drunk, pure and simple," Pyles said. "I saw no sign that Dana was concerned about anything except the outcome of the research she was doing—which I understand was going very well."

"She was using radioactive isotopes, of course,"

Charlie stuck in, "and they can be dangerous. Maybe that's what Watson was concerned about."

Maybe that was all it was, I thought. I hadn't been with Kevin Wheatley, eavesdropping on Dana and Watson, so I didn't know what they'd been talking about. And maybe these people were upset with me only because I dared to ask questions in their "temple" without a degree in veterinary medicine.

I asked Lorraine if Watson had called in the past week. Without looking up from her screen, she said, "No, he has not! Why on earth would he?"

"Do you remember his wife's name?" I asked her.

She gave me an exasperated look. "I do not!" she snapped.

"She was a stockbroker on the fast track," Pyles stuck in. "I couldn't understand what she was doing married to a lush like Watson. He left here under a cloud, as I'm sure Charlie has told you. I find it hard to believe that a woman like Dana would have anything to do with a man like that. She was a winner; Watson was a drunk."

Charlie turned to the clerk-typists in the room and asked if any of them remembered getting a call from somebody asking for Dana since her death. They all said no.

"Are you going through all of Dana's friends," Pyles asked me, his voice incredulous, "expecting you'll find Jason hiding out with one of them?"

"Jason's not the only aspect of Dana Michaels's life I'm interested in," I said.

"Well," he said, "you'll probably find Watson under a railroad bridge with a bottle in a paper bag. Maybe you'll find your friend Jason down there with him," he added viciously.

Twenty-three

I debated whether or not to go back home and call Dana's mother and stepfather but decided to bike over to their condominium instead. I'd spent too much time on the phone already that day, and it was only about five miles from the U. If I went back home, I'd probably fall asleep—if I managed to get to sleep at all—and wake up in the middle of the night and be a complete wreck for my new and exciting day job.

Nobody followed me, and nobody was lurking outside the Wallaces' condominium.

I dialed their apartment number, and a few moments later the retired warrant officer barked hello. I identified myself and asked to speak to his wife.

"What about?"

"Your stepdaughter's murder, of course," I said. It wasn't any of his business, but I didn't think it would further my cause to tell him that.

"You any closer to getting your hands on the son of a bitch who killed her than you were last week?"

"No," I said, "I'm just following some leads of my own."

"What leads?" he demanded.

"How about letting me come up? I'm tired of talking on phones."

"Barb's not home."

"You expect her back soon?"

"She's out at one of the malls with a friend. I expect her home any time—but you never know with a woman who's shopping, do you?" He seemed to expect a reaction to that, so I didn't say anything, just waited him out.

When the buzzer sounded, I dragged my bike into the foyer and took the elevator up to the Wallaces' apartment. Tom Wallace met me at the door, a tall glass of something dark and with ice in his hand.

"Iced tea," he said, as if reading my mind, "southern style, brewed with sugar. You ever stationed in Norfolk?"

I told him I'd spent my last year in the navy there.

"Then you know what it is. Want some?"

"Sure." It wasn't the season for iced tea here, but in the South they drank it all year round.

He seemed self-conscious, uneasy at having me—or was it a woman?—alone with him in the apartment.

"You still looking in all the wrong places for the guy who killed Dana, are you?" he said, as he handed me my glass.

"Probably. Jason's been harassing me regularly since the murder. If he just wanted to kill me, he could have done it easily by now. Apparently he gets off on tormenting women, and I'm his choice for March."

I went over to the window. The sailing ship was in the same state of incompleteness it had been in the last time I was there. "It's a Yankee clipper, isn't it?" I said. I saw a lot of those when I was stationed in the Caribbean.

He nodded. "It was a present from Dana for my birthday. She had to give me something," he added with a rueful smile. "Her mother probably picked it out. Paid for it too, I'll bet." He shrugged and took a swallow of tea. "I never had kids of my own, y'know. I didn't want Dana either at first, to be honest, but she came with the package, so I decided to make an effort." He smiled faintly. "Turned out she already had a father, a dead one, so I was about as useful to her as tits on a boar."

He laughed, I wasn't sure at what. "So I took it as a challenge to see if I could get her to love me. Waste of time—like making model sailing vessels. She had pictures of her dad all over her room. I hate to lose," he added brusquely.

"You probably didn't come off to her as needy enough," I said. "And you were still alive."

He gave me a grateful smile. "Yeah, that's probably it. So," he said, changing the subject abruptly, "you're mad you didn't get to go to sea, huh? Well, you didn't miss much."

"I'd like to have found that out for myself."

"Guys would've made it hell for you."

"Why?"

"'Cause you're a woman, of course." He looked at me as though I didn't have the brains I'd been born with. That was as southern as tea brewed with sugar too.

"I know I'm a woman. What's that got to do with guys making it hell for me if I went to sea?"

"They'd always be hitting on you. It might even get dangerous. It's just human nature. Guys are guys."

"You think people are slaves to their biology?" I asked. "Like ducks," I added, remembering an afternoon on a lake a couple of weeks earlier.

His eyes shifted away from me, came back, shifted away again. A little eerie, but I was probably a little eerie to him too. "It's just asking too much of guys—being on a ship with women for months at a time and no other outlet for their—"

"But you'd have the same outlets you had before women were allowed to go to sea, wouldn't you?"

It was pleasant, watching him turn crimson. He started to say something, thought better of it, took a large gulp of tea, and choked on it. Mercifully, I heard the elevator door open and close outside the apartment door, and a moment later Barb Wallace came in. She was carrying a shopping bag. Her eyes jumped back and forth between us as she took off her coat and hung it in a small closet.

"Hello," she said to me, looking slightly embarrassed, remembering perhaps how we'd parted the last time, and then, "Would you excuse me for a few minutes?"

Neither her husband nor I spoke a word while she was gone, just sipped our tea and rattled our ice cubes at each other. She came back a few minutes later, stopping in the kitchen to fix herself some tea.

"You're still trying to find this man, Jason?" she asked me. "The police, with all their resources, don't seem to be able to catch him."

"I'm not sure anymore that Jason killed your daughter," I said to her. That was the first time I'd said it aloud.

Tom Wallace's eyes opened wide in disbelief. Then he shook his head as if to clear it and made a disgusted noise. "What's he up to then, harassing you? Huh?"

"I don't know. Maybe he's just piggybacking on Dana's murder—pretending he killed her to make himself seem more terrifying to me. After all, I rejected him."

Wallace stared at me, then looked over at the big picture window at his sailing ship. "If Jason didn't do it, who did?" he demanded.

"I don't know yet," I replied. I wanted to ask him

where he was the night Dana'd been killed but decided that would get me thrown out on my ear and tell me nothing at all. He worked nights at the bar he owned with his brother. I wondered if Buck had checked his alibi before Jason became the sole focus of his investigation. I'd have to ask him.

"The homicide cops working along that line too?" Wallace asked.

"I don't know." I didn't think Buck was, but I didn't want to tell Wallace that. "Another thought's occurred to me too," I said.

"Oh?" he said.

"That Jason's covering for somebody. He's trying to draw the police's attention away from the real killer."

"You have any reason for thinking so?"

"No. It's just that Jason doesn't seem like a killer to me. He seems more like somebody who's watched too much television and is pretending to be one."

"For God's sake," Wallace exploded. "The man's as good as confessed he didn't mean to kill Dana— he just wanted to get his goddamned tape recorder back!"

Again I almost let it out that Dana had been hit several more times after she was down. But Buck didn't want that information made public—and I certainly couldn't take it upon myself to add to Barb Wallace's grief.

"That's true," I agreed. "But the two things don't add up in my mind—his accidentally killing Dana and then stalking me in such a puerile way. If it was an accident and he didn't really mean to kill her, I don't think he'd be stalking me: he'd be putting as much distance between himself and this place as he could. Or he'd kill himself, I think, after the realization of what he'd done had really sunk in." I hadn't

thought of that before, but it seemed right to me
now.

"And if he'd meant to kill her," I went on, "he'd
be more convincing as a stalker, and I'd probably be
dead now too."

"What are you," Wallace cried, "a connoisseur of
perverts?"

"No more than any other woman," I said.

"We got a call that might interest you, Peggy,"
Barb Wallace put in quickly. "Thursday night—the
day after you were here. It was from a friend of
Dana's in California."

I laughed, annoyed. "Peter Watson, right?"

"Yes. How'd you know?"

"I've spent half the day chasing after him! What'd
he want?"

"He was trying to get in touch with Dana," she
said. "He didn't know she'd been—that she was
dead."

"Said he'd been trying her house off and on for
two weeks," Tom Wallace stuck in gruffly. "Never
got an answer. Even called her in the middle of the
night a couple of times, he said. So he finally called
us."

"He'd tried to get hold of her through the Atwood
Lab first," Barb Wallace went on, "but they wouldn't
tell him anything."

So either Lorraine had lied to me when she'd told
me he hadn't called the lab, or somebody else had
taken Watson's call who hadn't told me the truth
either: Charlie or Pyles or one of the clerk-typists. It
could have been Doctor Atwood herself, I supposed,
but I doubted it, since she probably didn't answer
her own phone.

I asked Mrs. Wallace if Watson had said anything
about his relationship with Dana.

"Just that they'd been friends in Davis. He said

they'd worked together at the Humane Society out there, and they talked on the phone sometimes."

I told them about Dana and Peter's relationship at Davis and the Humane Society and how it ended, and about him coming here in December.

"I thought it was a little strange, him getting all worked up because she didn't answer her phone if they were just friends," Wallace said. "I figured it had to be something like that."

"She must have cared for him a great deal," Barb Wallace said, "if she called him Beau."

I asked her how Watson had taken it when she'd told him Dana had been murdered.

"He was shocked, of course," she answered. "He wanted to know everything. I told him about Jason and that the police hadn't caught him yet."

"How'd he react to that?"

"He said the police were wasting their time, and hung up."

We talked about other things for a while longer and then I had to leave before it got too dark to bike home. Also, Gary was picking me up at my place later.

"I haven't even thought about cleaning out her house yet," Barb Wallace said. "I just haven't been able to face going through her things. Tom's offered to do it, but . . ." She shrugged, letting the words trail off.

I biked home cautiously, then fixed myself a double espresso to try to stay awake until Gary arrived. I was too tired to spend any more time that day thinking about Dana Michaels and Peter Watson. Something was nagging at my mind, something I'd overlooked, but whenever I tried to focus on it, it slid away. Jason had screwed up my work schedule, my sleep schedule, my life, and my head, and I just wanted to forget about everything for a while.

I picked up a book and began to read—then woke up with a start when somebody pounded on my door, and before I could get out of my chair, a key turned in the lock.

It was Gary, of course.

"Sorry," he said, seeing the look on my face. "I rang the doorbell twice and you didn't answer. You okay?"

I got my coat and a change of clothes for the next day and we drove over to his place. He made dinner while I watched people desperate to fill television airtime do and say things that didn't make any sense to me, but their teeth were magnificent.

After dinner we went downstairs to Lillian's and played ridiculous board games, with Rufus snoring gently in Lillian's lap, oblivious to the mess he'd gotten me into. According to Doctor Gates he was coming along well. Only a few more days remained of his ordeal. I envied him that. When I fell asleep while the cards were being dealt, Gary led me upstairs to bed.

"So how'd you spend your day?" he asked, as I brushed my teeth.

"Scouring the country for somebody named Peter Watson via telephone," I mumbled, splattering foam on the mirror. "I racked up quite a long-distance bill."

"Peter Watson?" Gary repeated. "Who's he?"

I rinsed and padded back to the bedroom, climbed into bed, picked through Gary's selection of pillows to find the one I like, plumped it, put my head down, and sank gratefully into it. "A friend of Dana Michaels," I mumbled. "He got kicked out of the Atwood Lab—Oh, my God!"

"What?"

"Dumb!" I shouted, suddenly wide awake. "Dumb, dumb, dumb!"

"You're going to suffer brain damage," Gary said, "smacking your forehead like that."

"Remember you telling me about the scandal in the Atwood Lab and the whistle-blower who got fired?"

"Yeah?"

"Do you remember his name?"

"No, but I could call Max—it's still early. She was the reporter who had the story."

"I don't think that'll be necessary," I said grimly, as things suddenly began falling into place. No longer tired, I jumped out of bed, dug out Gary's phone book, and looked up Al's number.

"Who're you calling?" Gary asked.

"An old lover." On Friday at lunch, I'd asked Al about the scandal, and he'd been strangely elusive about the whistle-blower. He'd made it clear he didn't want to talk about him. Al had known Julia Atwood too; he'd even been invited to her parties.

Dierdre answered the phone. I told her who I was and asked if I could talk to Al. There was a pause and then, quickly—for Dierdre never wants to appear at a loss by anything—she said, "Of course, Peggy. I'll get him. He was reading Ellen and Little Allen to sleep, but I think he's fallen asleep himself." She chuckled domestically.

Two minutes later: "Yes?" Al, cautious, housebroken. I could imagine his tousled hair, the sleepy look in his eyes mixed with wariness.

"Sorry to bother you at home," I said, "but I need to know the name of the whistle-blower we talked about last week—the one in the Atwood Lab."

Long pause. In the background, the peculiar stillness of a home with sleeping children.

"Why?"

"It's Peter Watson, isn't it?" I said impatiently.

"Yes. Why?"

"I'm trying to get hold of him. I think he's connected with Dana Michaels's murder."

"What about this man Jason?"

"I don't know." *C'mon Al*, I said to myself, *let's move along here now. You're holding out on me, I know you are.*

"What do you want from me?" he asked slowly.

"I'd like to talk to his ex-wife," I replied, "if she's still around. You said you were in the vet school back then and knew the Atwoods. I thought you might know her name and what became of her."

"Dierdre," he said.

"What?" I thought he was calling her.

"Dierdre was Peter's wife," he said.

Twenty-four

I asked him if Dana had known that.

"Probably not. I certainly didn't tell her."

"Did she ever mention him?"

"Not that I recall. She did ask me once if I'd heard the story about the scandal in the Atwood Lab six years ago—she'd heard some rumors, she said. I didn't tell her anything, of course, and she dropped the subject."

I got Dierdre back on the phone and asked her if we could get together to talk about Peter. After many questions, she consulted with Al and then, with what I thought was an unseemly lack of enthusiasm, agreed that I could come over the next evening at seven.

Bright and early the next morning I slouched into the police station. It seemed unnatural. Normally I would have been going home at that hour, not coming in to work. I exchanged banter with a couple of cops going off duty as I poured myself a cup of coffee, the usual vampire jokes. "I thought you were supposed to be in a coffin by now," one of them said.

"That's where I'm heading," I snarled.

I spent the day crouched over the computer screen, staring at the updates of the *Field Training Officer's Manual*. I'm a decent typist, but I'd never used a word processor, so I had to wade through the manual for that too, trying to figure out how to delete and add text and perform other tasks that Mr. and Mrs. O'Neill's daughter was not put on the planet for.

Ginny stuck her head in once and asked me how things were going.

I told her I was getting carpal tunnel syndrome.

"Medically impossible in half a day," she said.

Since she was wearing her windbreaker, I asked her where she was going.

"Off to ask a secretary in geology about some plane tickets she ordered for a faculty member who went to a conference in Las Vegas last week."

"Why?"

"There was no geology conference in Las Vegas last week," she replied, "and no faculty member was out of town either. But I'm told the secretary's boyfriend lives there."

"You sniff skulduggery."

"Yeah. If I'm back in time, you want to have lunch?"

"Sure, if I can get up out of this chair. I think my spine's fused."

The day passed slowly in the stuffy windowless cubicle, interrupted only when other cops came in and taunted me good-naturedly and Bixler came in to dump more work on my desk—a man who hasn't done an honest day's work in his life.

I drove to my place after work, showered, and changed into clothes appropriate for a visit with an ex-lover's wife, then went over to Gary's for dinner. After dinner I drove to Al and Dierdre's.

They lived in a Tudor-style house in a nice neighborhood with lots of colorful plastic kids toys littering the yards and sidewalks. I liked the house—didn't even mind the neighborhood—but the landscaping depressed me: compulsively trimmed little hedges framed flower beds that looked manicured, and pure white gravel covered all visible soil as though dirt in a garden were something to be ashamed of. That wasn't the Al I remembered. Could I have saved him from this, I wondered, if I'd been willing to marry him and be a mom to his kid, and have a few of my own?

He opened the door for me, smiling self-consciously. Dierdre stood in the living room behind him, a toddler in each arm, perhaps to ward off evil.

"Hi, Peggy," she said brightly. "This is Peggy," she told her children. "An old pal of your dad's."

They were picking their noses, apparently to the same beat—they were twins, after all—and so vigorously that they were pulling their upper lips up off their milk teeth.

"Stop that," Al told them proudly. "You don't want to gross Peggy out, do you?"

Too late.

"You have a nice home," I said. It wasn't the taste of the Al I'd known, which had run to old and battered furniture you could get lost in. This was all heavy, uncomfortable-looking stuff in a style I didn't recognize: late Inquisition, possibly. I spotted a watercolor tucked away in a dark corner that Al had done when we were together, a view of Lake Eleanor in the summer, with sailboats. I studied it a moment, remembering what we'd done while he was waiting for it to dry. I turned to him and smiled and said, "Nice!"

He turned pink and quickly grabbed the kids from Dierdre and said he'd give them their bath. Be sure to get their index fingers, I thought.

"I've made coffee," Dierdre said. "Al says you're quite the coffee connoisseur."

"It's my only vice now," I said, feeling suddenly very old.

Her eyes flicked up at me, then away, and then she told me to make myself at home. I chose a white leather chair as far away from a couple of sleeping Persian cats as I could get. Al had been more of a dog than a cat person in my day. Maybe he still had a couple rooting up the backyard, or maybe the twins were enough for him now. The noises of small animals being bathed could be heard in another part of the house: the growl of an adult male, children's laughter echoing off tile.

Even from the living room, I could smell that it was coffee disguised as something else: hazelnuts, I supposed, from previous bad experience with scented coffee.

Dierdre and I had met only a couple of times before, years ago, at parties we'd been invited to by mutual acquaintances. She'd brought Al. At one of them, something clicked between Al and me and we'd left in midparty without telling Dierdre, who was off in a corner flirting with a judge. Al assumed, probably correctly, that she was hoping to trade up from a veterinarian to a jurist. That was the last time I'd spoken with Dierdre until now. Given our brief history, I had to feel grateful that she'd agreed to meet with me to talk about her ex-husband.

After she'd poured our coffee from a silver coffee service, she sat back in a chair, smoothed her expensive skirt down over long, trim legs, and said crisply, "What do you want to know about Peter?" She had chestnut hair, thick and shoulder length like a mane, and a slightly horsey face—just right for a vet's wife.

"Could you start by telling me about the scandal in the Atwood Lab?" I asked.

"I never dreamed I'd have to live through all that

again," she said with a bleak smile. "Especially with you!"

She saw that I didn't know what to say to that, so she waved it aside. "It seems like a lifetime ago, but it was only six years. Peter had been so thrilled to be a part of the Atwood Lab and working with the legendary Doctor Julia Atwood herself. And then the legend turned around and destroyed him."

"How'd she do that?"

"Oh, Peter helped, of course," she said angrily. "He was involved in some of the dirty work too, so when he'd finally had enough and tried to blow the whistle on them, they were able to put most of the blame on him. They claimed he knew he was about to be exposed and tried to get his shot in first."

"Maybe you could start at the beginning?" I suggested.

"All right," she sighed. "Peter was working with Charles Atwood—Doctor Charlie they called him—on a project. It was some kind of follow-up study on one of the vaccines Julia Atwood had developed, some kind of multivaccine for cats or dogs—I don't remember. According to Peter, it wasn't as effective as they'd expected. Nearly as many animals were getting the diseases who'd been given the Atwood vaccine as some of the competitors'. Furthermore, Charlie was giving some of the test animals both the Atwood vaccine and other drugs, which made the test results completely invalid, of course."

"You said Peter was also involved in the false research."

She nodded. "He'd signed off on some of the studies with the false data in them, knowing it was false. When he told me about it later, he said Charlie and the administrative head—Pyles, I think his name was—had ordered him to, and he'd done it because he was afraid they'd ruin him if he didn't."

She gave a quiet laugh. "And then a terrible thing happened."

"What?"

"Peter's conscience started bothering him. I'd suspected something was wrong for quite a while— he was silent a lot more than usual; he brooded a lot and got angry easily. Frankly, I was worried that he'd started drinking again, or was about to. Peter called himself an alcoholic, you see, and sometimes attended AA meetings. And he'd been through treatment—before we'd gotten together, of course," she added fastidiously. "Your coffee's getting cold. Shall I pour it out and get you some more?"

"Thanks, no."

"Anyway, he finally broke down and told me what he'd been involved in. Now that he was in over his head," she added bitterly, "he wanted me to tell him what to do!"

She looked around her living room uneasily; then her eyes came back to me. "I didn't know what to tell him. It was clear he'd been part of something both illegal and unethical. But it was also clear—to me, at least—that if he reported it, the chances were good he'd be finished at the University—at any university. All universities claim they encourage whistle-blowers, since it's just about the only way to catch research fraud. But in practice they treat them the way the Mafia treats stool pigeons."

"Peter was a vet, though," I said. "He could have gone into private practice, couldn't he?"

"Sure, but that wasn't what he wanted. He wanted to be a professor, a scientific researcher. That's all he'd ever wanted to be!"

She stared through me, back into the past, while

in the present a child began crying and soon after another took up the refrain.

"Finally he decided to take his chances with Doctor Atwood—the good 'Doctor J,'" she said sardonically. "He didn't think she knew what her son was up to, and he thought she'd thank Peter for letting her know.

"I remember how he looked when he came home after talking to her," she continued, her voice hardening. "Haunted. He said he'd never seen eyes as cold as Julia Atwood's when she listened to him tell her what her son was up to."

"Did he think she was involved?"

"He wasn't sure. But her reputation was, and the lab's. If it got out that something fishy was going on, she'd risk losing some of the big drug company contracts, and maybe the lab too. The next week, Peter found himself reassigned to another project, almost a make-work project, off in some dark corner of the lab. He complained about it and was told that he wasn't needed on the old project anymore; it was mostly completed anyway. He knew that wasn't true, but there wasn't anything he could do about it. He also found that his colleagues were no longer as friendly towards him as they'd been and seemed to be avoiding him. He was being shunned, in other words, the way they do in some of those strange religious sects. He was starting to feel like a nonperson, a nobody."

Niemand, I thought, perhaps inconsequentially. "Then what did he do?"

"He didn't do anything until he learned his postdoc wasn't going to be renewed. That was tantamount to a death sentence, of course, and he knew it. So he asked why and was told his performance wasn't satisfactory. Up until he'd gone to

Julia Atwood, he'd gotten outstanding evaluations. Now, suddenly, they were negative.

"So he went to the dean of the School of Veterinary Medicine and told him the whole story. The dean was very sympathetic and promised to look into it—and didn't. Why should he? Doctor Atwood was bringing in a lot of money to the school, really putting the place on the map. They were building her a lab. Why would they want to rock the boat?

"So Peter went to the newspaper." She shrugged. "Why not, since he had nothing to lose anymore. He knew his only chance to get out of it with his future intact was if he could prove Charlie's misconduct. He talked to one of the editors, who assigned a young reporter, a woman, to check into it."

Dierdre got up suddenly and glared down at me as though it were my fault. "You should have heard the drawbridges going up all over the Ag Campus then! They stonewalled her! She talked to some of Peter's colleagues in the lab, to try to get them to confirm what he said. They all denied knowing anything about it. That made the reporter suspicious, so she really started looking into the lab's operation, and she found out enough so that the newspaper demanded the University investigate."

At least now I could understand why the people in the Atwood Lab were so paranoid about having outsiders come in and ask questions.

"The first thing that happened was," she continued, "the University president announced that a 'blue ribbon' committee of outside experts had been called in to conduct a thorough investigation of the lab's operation, and he also announced that he had full confidence that 'Doctor J'—one of the University's 'points of light,' he called her—would be completely vindicated. The second thing that happened 'was that a University attorney called the reporter in and showed her Peter's job performance ratings during the year and a half he'd been in the lab, as well as a letter Charlie had put in Watson's file concerning his drinking during working hours. The reporter confronted Peter with all this and asked for his reaction."

She looked down into her coffee cup. I waited for her to go on. She looked back up at me and said dryly, "Unfortunately, she caught Peter at a bad time."

"He was drunk."

She gave me a melancholy smile. "Not drunk, no. Not drunk but getting there. Under the pressure of being ostracized—turned into something that no longer existed—and knowing his dream was dead, he started drinking again."

She threw up a hand. "Oh, I know what you're going to say, Peggy," she added quickly, "that people drink because they're alcoholics, and their problems are just excuses!" Apparently Al had told her something about me and my thoughts on alcoholism.

"But you have no idea what it's like to go up against the University," she went on. "The people who run it, and who identify their own careers with 'the good of the U,' have all the power, and they don't hesitate to use it against anybody who dares criticize them or anybody who's connected with them—and Doctor Atwood was and is a powerful figure in the University community. Of course, it's really no worse than any other huge corporation that exists mainly to protect the people who profit from it," she added with a shrug, "but it just seems so much worse, because that's not what a university is *supposed* to be, is it?"

"But what about Peter's charges against the lab? What did the outside investigators find?"

She smiled. "Things must've been pretty bad, considering that the outside committee was made up of friends and colleagues of Julia Atwood, because they actually found that one of the projects, the one supervised by Charlie, was, in fact, seriously flawed. But they blamed it on his inexperience as a supervisor and—get this!—on his having relied too heavily on one of his assistants, who'd signed off on a number of the studies! They recommended that Doctor Atwood herself take a more active role in supervising the work done by the people under her. They meant Charlie, of course, although they didn't say so."

"The assistant was Peter," I said.

"Of course," she said. "Charlie got off with a slap on the wrist; Peter lost everything. It's possible the newspaper would have gone on with its investigation—Peter thought there was a lot more illegal activity going on in the lab—but just then one of Julia Atwood's kids died—drowned in the Pacific, his body never recovered." She shuddered, then listened for a moment to the happy noises of small children being stuffed into pajamas in the background.

"Tragic," she went on, giving me a sardonic smile, "but it couldn't have happened at a better time for the Atwoods! The newspaper ran a photograph of Julia at the boy's memorial service. She was staring mournfully into the camera as if asking us to please not kick her anymore—she was only working for the good of animals. The hypocrite!"

"That was what her ex-husband called her too," I said, "when I told him she'd mentioned her dead son at Dana Michaels's memorial service."

"He wasn't any better," Dierdre snapped. "According to the gossip, both Atwoods were too career-oriented to be interested in their children. He dumped both of them on her and she turned them over to her secretary—a woman named Lorraine something—who pretty much raised them, together with au pair girls she imported from Europe."

She laughed. "The rumor was that whenever the au pairs learned enough English to realize how Atwood was exploiting them, Lorraine would pack 'em off back where they came from and send for new ones. Al tells me she's still the secretary and still mothers Charlie, who still needs it. Nothing much changes around that place, does it?"

"You said the youngest boy drowned in the Pacific?" I asked. "I'd heard that he went out to live with his dad in Davis. That's not on the ocean."

"According to the stories we heard," she said, "he was vacationing in Mexico when he drowned. His sailboat capsized."

"And so the scandal died."

Dierdre nodded, staring down into her coffee cup.

"You said Peter knew about other illegal things going on in the Atwood lab. What other things?"

"He suspected they were doing something illegal with federal money," she went on. "I don't remember the details, but he thought the secretary was involved too. She'd have to be, I suppose, since she kept the books. Lorraine had more power in the lab than anyone but Julia Atwood, and if she didn't like you, look out! You could come in some morning and find your office had been moved to a broom closet."

I asked her what finally happened to Peter.

She didn't say anything for a minute, just sat there and chewed absently on a fingernail.

"He knew he had no future in academia, so he wanted us to return to California, where he intended to start over as a vet. But I could see that he was totally defeated, and I didn't believe he could just walk away from his lifelong dream. He wasn't the man I'd married anymore. Besides, I didn't want to have to go someplace where I had no contacts, friends, or family and start over."

"So you divorced him and haven't heard from him since?"

"Until you called," she said, "I assumed the University had buried him someplace, probably on one of the experimental farms where his body would never be found. They'd killed him, after all— wasn't it their responsibility to give him a proper burial?"

Twenty-five

Al brought in the children then, their hair damp, wearing pink and blue pajamas with clowns and balloons—sleepers, we called them when I was a child—to say good-night. I got up quickly, suddenly feeling like an outsider—a nobody like Jason, like Watson—and went over and stooped down and shook the hands of the little mammals before they could get their fingers up their noses again. Then I smiled at Al and followed Dierdre to the door and thanked her for her time.

"You're welcome," she said, but I could see her mind was no longer on me or Peter Watson or murder, it was on the three people waiting for her behind us. Outside, I scanned the brightly lit street for cars with Jason in them and when I got to my car I checked to be sure it was empty before getting in. Dierdre watched from her door until I drove off. I was able to resist the urge to honk: beep, beep.

Bixler came in the next morning with two fat manuals and dropped them on my desk, jarring me out of my reverie. One was labeled "Procedures," the other was the state's statute book.

"When you're through with the rookie manual, O'Neill," he said, "you can bring the procedures manual up-to-date. The legislature's made lots of changes this session, so it'll keep you busy and out of trouble for a while." Trailing chuckles like cigar fumes, he marched away down the hall.

As soon as he was out of earshot I called Buck and told him what I'd learned about Peter Watson and his connection with Dana and the Atwood Lab.

"Dana had no respect for Doctor Atwood or her research," I went on. "Furthermore, she wasn't really interested in research—everybody I've spoken to says she was a great hands-on sort of vet. Yet after breaking up with Watson, she accepted a postdoc from Atwood and came here, presumably to start an academic career. Why?"

"Do you think she came here to do what Watson wasn't able to do?" he asked. "Expose the Atwood Lab and destroy the Atwoods?"

"Yes!" I said eagerly. "Maybe she thought she could save Watson that way—she has a history of trying to save 'strays,' remember. Or if not save him, then revenge him. They ruined him, after all."

"You only have his ex-wife's word for that," Buck reminded me. "Dierdre."

"Dierdre's okay," I said. "Just a little equine and she serves perfumed coffee. But listen, Buck: according to Barry Russell, Dana was pumping him for information about the lab and the Atwoods—he thought it was because she wanted the job they had open. She was also sucking up to Charlie, something Russell found hard to understand. Charlie had been Peter Watson's adviser before her."

"Six years before her," Buck reminded me. "And you only have Barry Russell's word for what Dana was doing while they were going out together. Whatever happened to him as your favorite suspect, by the way?"

Without waiting for me to reply, he droned on: "Besides, Peggy, ambitious people often have to suck up to their superiors to get anywhere—you wouldn't know anything about that, of course. And it seems to have been working for Michaels, since Professor Atwood was planning to offer her a permanent position."

"That's what she said at the memorial service anyway," I objected. "But how do you know she was telling the truth? Dana's mother also told me Dana wanted to have lunch with her to discuss her future plans. Her mother thought she was going to leave the lab even before the year was over."

"That's pure speculation," Buck said. "I'm sure you're right that the man who was with her in December was Watson. You may even be right that Dana Michaels was here to complete the job he couldn't. But how are we going to prove it, Peggy? And even if we could, how'll we get any evidence that anybody at the lab knew she was spying on them? And even if we could do that, it still doesn't mean anybody there killed her. After all, the University has other ways of disposing of whistle-blowers—as I'm sure Peter Watson will tell you when you locate him.

"And you're also forgetting Jason. How does he fit in, if he didn't kill Michaels? He's just a guy who happened to amble by, found the body, and decided to take credit for her murder—maybe to try to get a date with you?"

"Don't joke about that, please! I don't know how he fits in, but I don't believe in coincidences that big. Right after Dana's murder, you told me nobody connected with the Atwood Lab has an ironclad alibi, right?"

"That's right. Charles—Doctor Charlie—Millard Pyles, and Lorraine Cullin were all working on their presentations to the National Science Foundation inspectors who were coming in the next day. Julia

Atwood claims she was at home, and since she lives alone, it would be hard to prove she wasn't. Cullin and Charlie, as well as Russell, were all there when Dana told them she was going to try to beat the storm home."

"Odd that Doctor Atwood herself wasn't there," I said, "slaving away with all the rest of them."

Buck must not have found that worth responding to: he didn't say anything.

"If Dana had evidence there was illegal activity going on in the lab," I went on, "then she might've been planning to show it to the foundation people—and someone might've killed her to keep her from doing it."

"Right. 'If' and 'might've,' Peggy. Now all we have to do is prove it. Any suggestions?"

"Find Peter Watson," I said. "He knows what Dana was doing here, and he shouldn't be too hard to find. Unlike Jason, he doesn't have any reason to hide."

"Why haven't you talked to him?" he asked.

"Because he's disappeared!" I'd forgotten I hadn't mentioned that to Buck. I explained what Erin, the woman I'd talked to at the Humane Society, had told me.

Buck's impatience boiled over. "You know I can't authorize a search for him," he said, "especially one in California. The man's a drunk! When he heard that Dana Michaels was dead, he did what drunks do, went on a bender. Dammit, Peggy, I can't even find Jason, who almost certainly did kill Dana Michaels, and you're telling me I should be looking for a man who's probably in a bar somewhere in California! You haven't been getting enough sleep. You're not thinking clearly."

"I know it. I'll get to bed early tonight. But I'm worried about him. He's known about Dana's murder since Thursday. Where is he and what's he up to? I just think he should be here, spilling his guts to you."

Buck sighed. "Only because you think he's got something to spill," he said. "All right, Peggy, I'll do some discreet asking around—but he hasn't been gone long enough to be a missing person yet, especially if nobody's reported him missing."

And we hung up on that note and I went back to my computer screen and manuals.

Twenty-six

Concentrating on something called "Procedures Manual" would have been hard at the best of times, which these weren't. I kept playing over in my head what I'd learned about Peter Watson and what I knew about Jason. Watson had learned of Dana's murder Thursday night and hadn't shown up for work since. Where was he?

It was quiet in the stuffy little cubicle, the muffled noises of people talking, phones ringing, and keyboards clacking threatening to put me to sleep. I hadn't heard Bixler's bull-moose voice in a while: he was either out checking on the beat cops to make sure they weren't goofing off or holed up in his office with one of his hunting or girlie magazines.

When I couldn't take it any longer, I sneaked down the hall to Ginny's office, slid in, and closed the door behind me.

"I want to use your phone," I told her, "to make a long-distance call." Her phone had long-distance access, mine didn't.

"You can't," she said, shoving the phone at me. "It's against regulations."

I called the Humane Society in Davis and Erin answered, which saved time. When I'd identified myself, I asked her if they'd heard from Watson.

"No," she said sadly, "and now we probably never will."

"Why?"

"I can't see Pete crawling back here with his tail between his legs," she said, "begging Mr. Wilkinson to let him have his job back, can you? Well, you don't know Pete, so how would you know? Mr. Wilkinson warned him the last time in no uncertain terms that there'd be no more second chances. Mr. Wilkinson's a Mormon, you know, and they don't approve of drinking. Heck, we even had to fight to get a Coke machine in, so you know how he must've felt when Pete didn't show up for work on account of he was off on a toot."

She laughed. "Of course, Mormons are frugal, so Mr. Wilkinson was probably balancing his religious beliefs against having a man of Pete's veterinary skills working for next to nothing. But even Mormons have limits, I suppose."

I asked her if she had tried Pete's apartment again.

"Oh, sure. I called again right after I talked to you, but he didn't answer. I called yesterday too, even though I knew it was probably too late to save his job. I haven't called today, though. You want to do it? You've got a long-distance phone budget, don't you?"

"Of course," I said, feeling Ginny's exasperated eyes on me. In her annoyance, she was unwrapping a chocolate bar noisily. I grabbed a pad of paper, wrote down Watson's phone number. "You don't have the caretaker's number by any chance too, do you?"

"Uh-uh. Why? You think Pete might be in his apartment, too sick to answer his phone—or dead?"

"It's possible. Things like that don't just happen to strangers. Oh, and what's his address?"

She gave it to me. "It's a little U-shaped court," she added. "I've dropped Pete off there after work a

few times over the years 'cause he doesn't own a car.
Like I told you before, we can't pay him enough so
he can live someplace really nice. Not that my pay's
all that good either—the Humane Society runs on a
pretty thin margin. Maybe I should think of becoming a detective like you. I'll bet it pays better. You
like it?''

"It's okay," I said. "And we've got barking dogs
here too, so you'd feel right at home."

"Yeah?" She sounded interested. "Police dogs?"

"In a manner of speaking."

Before Ginny could say anything, I dialed Watson's number. I let it ring a long time, but there was
no answer. Now what?

I turned to Ginny, slid the address over to her,
told her it was an apartment house in Davis, California. "I want to talk to the caretaker. You can make it
happen, can't you?"

"What do I get in return?" she asked, speaking
with her mouth full.

"You get to pick the movie next time. Anything
you want."

"The Sound of Music?"

I hesitated, then agreed. "You are desperate!" she
said, giving me a grin filled with chocolate and nuts,
then called Davis Information and asked for the city
rental licensing office. After a moment she said,
"Yes, I'd like the phone number of the manag-
ing company or owner of the rental property at
three forty-three East Verdugo in Davis. . . . Sure,
thanks."

Using her shoulder to hold the phone to her ear
while she waited, she asked me if I expected to find
Jason in Davis. I only had time to say "Who
knows?" before the clerk was back on the line.

Ginny scribbled, said thanks again, and hung up.

"Edna Lovejoy," she said, sliding the pad over to me. "She owns the place."

I took the phone from her and dialed the number. "Edna," a woman's voice shouted over loud television voices. I identified myself as Peggy Watson, Pete Watson's sister, from Minneapolis, Minnesota.

"Yeah?" she hollered.

"Pete Watson," I repeated. "Apartment C."

"Oh, Pete. Sure. What about him?"

"I've been trying to get hold of him for two days," I said loudly, hoping Bixler wasn't anywhere nearby, since the walls are thin. "He was supposed to be coming to visit us—to see his niece and nephew, Ellen and Little Allen. Twins," I added, because I always think extraneous detail adds credibility to a lie. "But he hasn't shown up and doesn't answer his phone."

"Hasn't shown up, huh?" Edna Lovejoy said over the voice of a popular talk show host—the sincere one, I can't remember her name. Mercifully, she turned down the sound on her TV.

"I'm really worried about him," I continued. "It's so unlike Pete not to show up when he says he will. We even went out to the airport and waited for him."

"I don't know what to tell you," she said, in a voice that didn't do a very good job of concealing the fact that she could tell me a lot.

"I really do think there must be something wrong," I said. "He may be sick—or worse. Would you mind knocking on his door, maybe even going in and checking to see if he's there?"

Ginny put her head down on the desk, covered her ears. "I can't believe this," she said in a muffled voice.

Another pause. "You know your brother has a

drinking problem, don't you?" Edna Lovejoy said bluntly.

I sighed. "Yes, but I thought he'd finally got it under control."

"He did, for a while there. But he slipped sometimes. I can always spot the signs—I'm AA myself."

"I think it had something to do with a woman he was dating," I said.

"Yeah, love that turns sour always makes a good excuse to fall off the wagon. Hell, some people screw up their love lives just to have an excuse to drink again!"

"I know," I said. "Our dad was an alcoholic too. That's why I'm so worried about Pete. Could you please check his apartment for me, see if he's there, or if there's any indication of where he could be?"

A sigh, another pause. "I suppose I could do that," she said. "But you stay on the line! I'm takin' the phone with me, so if he's in there and gets mad, I'm handing it to him. Okay?"

"That's fine," I said.

A chair squeaked noisily and I heard her rummaging around. "Looking for my slippers," she muttered. "Here they are."

"What's going on?" Ginny whispered.

"She's putting on her slippers," I told her.

A door opened and closed in sunny Davis, California, and I was suddenly outside and crossing a lawn that separated the two sides of the court. I'd grown up in Southern California and lived in a neighborhood of such places. I imagined that this one was white stucco with a Spanish tile roof, maybe roses in bloom, avocado and lemon trees, and camellias.

"You hear me okay?" Edna hollered.

"Fine," I said. "A little static, not much."

"'Fine, a little static, not much,'" Ginny echoed in a parody of me.

"It's a cheap cordless, but it's good," Edna said. "I hang it on my belt when I'm out mowing the lawn, that way I don't have to keep—here we are. Doorbell has kind of an empty sound to it. I always think they sound different if somebody's home than if they aren't."

I did too.

"C'mon, Peter, open up," she said, knocking loudly. "Hi, Loretta. You haven't seen Pete lately, have you?"

There was a brief conversation I couldn't hear, then: "That was Mrs. Patterson, Pete's neighbor in B. Says she hasn't seen him since Friday night, but she thinks he had a visitor Saturday morning 'cause she heard the doorbell ring and Pete opened up.

"Well, he's not home—or not answering, anyway. But I'll take a look inside, if you want, just in case. But it'll be on your head."

Sounds of metal scratching metal. *"Sweet Holy Jesus!* Something stinks—" Loud static, then, faintly: "Oh, my God! Oh, my God! Excuse me, I'm sorry—I'm gonna be sick! No, Loretta—you can't go in—"

Ginny's door burst open and Bixler stormed in, his little stoat's eyes glittering with indignation and pleasure. "Caught you goofing off again, didn't I, O'Neill?" he blustered.

"I found Peter Watson."

"Where?" Buck asked.

I told him. "I called you as soon as we hung up," I added. "I figured it would save time if you explained to the cops there how I happened to get his landlady to go in by pretending to be his sister."

"I'm not sure I can," he said dryly, "but I'll try.

They're going to want to talk to you too sooner or later. You going to be there a while?"

"Until three. I'll bet it wasn't a natural death," I added.

"Let's wait and see."

The Davis cops hadn't called by the time I left work at three, but Buck did. A hypodermic had been found next to Watson's body, and a puncture wound on his arm. The remains of the liquid in the hypodermic was the color of bubble gum, which suggested to the medical examiner—considering that Watson was a veterinarian—a drug with the pretty name Beauthanasia, used to put animals to sleep.

"They haven't excluded suicide," Buck said.

"They found a note?"

"Not yet. But the apartment's a mess—beer cans scattered all over it, a couple of empty bottles of cheap whiskey, dirty clothes. Maybe one's in there somewhere."

"Could the place have been searched?"

"Too soon to say, but it sounded to me more like Watson had been on a long binge. Where are you going to be tonight? I told them who you were and what you'd told me about Watson, but they're going to want to talk to you too."

I told him I'd be at Gary's again, and we hung up.

As I put on my jacket and started out of my cubicle, it occurred to me to call my house to see if I'd got any messages—I was thinking of Jason, of course, and he didn't disappoint me.

"Hey, Peggy, where are you? You can't stay away forever, can you? C'mon home. All your doors and windows are locked, and I probably wouldn't be able to come down your chimney like Santa—although I'm skinny enough now, since I'm pining away for love of you. I miss you so much I'll probably drop by

tonight, just to press my nose against your window. Will you have that man with you I saw you dancing with at the restaurant Saturday night? He's not good enough for you, Peggy, believe me, or he wouldn't of stepped on your toes so much." He laughed.

Then his voice roughened. *"You can't hide from me forever, you know. Not unless you leave town and change your name, maybe get into the witness protection program. I'm Nobody, Peggy—how can the cops catch Nobody?"* He hung up.

I stood there, staring down at the phone. And then I made up my mind to go home and wait for his next call.

Twenty-seven

Gary called from work, wanting to know if I was going to spend the night at his place. I told him no, I needed to be alone. He wanted to know why, but I said I was expecting an important phone call, and I'd tell him later.

I made myself a cup of coffee and tried to read but found it hard to concentrate. I wasn't sure Jason was going to call that night; I was just sure he was going to call sometime soon and I wanted to be there when he did. I planned to try to talk him into meeting me someplace.

He called at six. He had a different plan.

"Guess what I've got?" he began.

"What, Jason?"

"An old dog, Peggy—a poodle, a far cry from Heinrich, the loyal German shepherd of my youth—but still, a dog. And every boy needs a dog, I think. Of course, I have to share him with his owner, Mrs. Przynski, and a gentleman named, believe it or not, Buzz Colby. Say hello to Peggy, Mrs. Przynski."

My heart missed a beat and my knuckles turned white on the phone. Why hadn't I expected something like this?

"Oh, Peggy," Lillian said, "I'm sorry! We were driving away from the hospital when—"

"This isn't the time or place for long stories, Mrs. P.," Jason broke in. "You can tell Peggy all about it over cookies and milk someday. Peggy, you still still there? I've got a deal for you if you want to hear it."

"Yes," I said, "I do."

He laughed. "I thought you might. I'm leaving town and I want to say good-bye—in person. We haven't talked in person since Ernesto's ladies' room. Remember?"

"Yes."

"So here's the deal: you got a cordless phone?"

"I'm speaking on it."

"That's good. You come out on your front porch—now, fast, and keep talkin'."

I did as he said, stepped out onto the porch, the phone at my ear. "You want me to come out onto the stoop too?" I asked.

"Yeah. But don't say anything to raise the suspicions of those good people coming by with their dog. Just smile and wave."

A couple strolled past with a dog on a leash as I stepped onto the stoop. They waved as they passed. I waved back.

"That's nice, Peggy," Jason said. "You look real neighborly."

I glanced up and down the street. It was almost dark, but I spotted Buzz's old green Chevy down to my right. I could see figures in the front seat.

"Okay," Jason said. "Now c'mon down the steps nice 'n easy and cross the street. Look like you do this every day."

"Tell me the plan first," I said.

"It's simple. I trade them for you."

"That is simple," I agreed. "How do you want to do it?"

"You come up to the car on the driver's side. They get out. You get behind the wheel. We drive away.

Any sudden change in plans, somebody gets hurt. I'm armed."

"All right," I said. As I approached the car, I heard Jason say, "Okay, folks, you can get out now. Sorry to have been such a bother—and don't worry about Peggy. She's gonna be okay."

Both the driver's and passenger's door opened and Buzz and Lillian got out. "Don't forget the pooch," Jason said from the backseat. I could hear him now both on the phone and in person.

Buzz bent and picked up the carrier. Rufus was standing in it with his legs braced, looking out, worried. Lillian, on the curb, whispered loudly, "Run, Peggy! He's got a gun!"

"It's okay," I told her with a smile. "Everything's going to be fine. I've got Jason just where I want him."

"Oh, Peggy!"

I heard Jason's laugh in the backseat. "Will you hurry up?" he said. "I can't stand these long good-byes."

I slid behind the wheel, turned, and said, "Where to?"

He directed me to the Ag Campus. He was strangely silent on the way, sunk back in his seat, his eyes hooded and staring straight ahead, as though all the energy had gone out of him. A pistol lay on his lap, his hands folded on top of it.

"We're going to one of those storage buildings?" I asked as we came up to the road that cuts through the experimental farm.

"Wrong," he said. "Your cop friend might figure we'd come this way. Keep goin', I'll tell you when to turn."

After another minute he ordered me to turn right. We drove a ways and then he directed me through a

neighborhood of old homes and finally down a cul-
de-sac that ended on a slight rise just before the
lake. I could see some of the Ag Campus buildings
as darker silhouettes against the night sky on the
other side of the lake, and the lights of the veterinary hospital on the hill above it.

"Stop in front of that dark house," he said,
leaning forward and pointing. "We'll walk the rest
of the way."

I parked, turned off the engine and the lights, and
got out when he told me to. Nobody was on the
sidewalk. It was the dinner hour.

"We're going to Dana Michaels's house, aren't
we?" I said. Jason was walking a couple of steps
behind me, his hands buried in his windbreaker.

"You got it," he answered.

He wasn't afraid of ghosts, either, I thought,
remembering what Barry Russell had told me when
I'd sat behind Dana's desk in his office.

"Have you been hiding out here the whole time?"

"Yeah. We gotta get past her neighbors without
makin' any noise. You attract their attention, I might
have to shoot them too. Okay?"

"Just tell me what to do," I said.

Dana's was the end house in a row of three
connected houses, each with its own tiny yard
hidden behind a tall redwood privacy fence. Beyond
it was a landscaped hill that fell steeply to the lake
and the path going around it.

Jason made me unlatch the gate in the fence at
Dana's house, and he latched it again after me. A
quarter-moon threw the jagged shadow of a still-
leafless mountain ash across the yard. He handed
me a key and I opened the front door and went in,
with him right behind me. I didn't know where his
pistol was, in his hand or in his pocket.

The house was small, with the living room to my

left, the dining room to my right, a little open kitchen in back. Stairs led up to the second floor. Even in the dim light, I could see that the furniture was too heavy, too large for this small space, and it struck me as sad that Dana Michaels, the navy brat who'd loved animals and taken in strays, loved a drunk and tried to do what he'd failed to do, had been killed coming home to this: a house that wasn't even her own.

I asked Jason how long he'd been living here.

"About a week," he said. "I figured the cops wouldn't be coming back. I made a copy of the key before returning Dana's purse to you. You're actin' pretty calm about this, aren't you?"

I didn't say anything to that, just asked him if I could sit down.

"This won't take that long," he replied.

I smiled at that, crossed the room to an over-stuffed chair, and sat down.

I took my time looking at him standing in the middle of the shadowy room, holding the pistol loosely at his side, as if he didn't know what it was for. Except for when he'd been in drag in the ladies' room at Ernesto's, I hadn't seen him since Dana's memorial service, when he'd been disguised as a pastor, his hair and beard darkened. His hair was blond again, as I'd seen it on the shore two weeks before, but short and neatly trimmed now, and his face was clean-shaven.

"You know why we're here, Peggy, don't you?" he said.

"You tell me," I said.

"I'm leaving," he said, "but before I go, I want to see you with your clothes off." His voice was flat, listless, like a bad actor reading lines for the first time.

"Why not?" I said. "I've always looked good by

moonlight. But you have to do something for me first."

"What?"

"Tell me the whole story. How we've ended up here in Dana Michaels's rented house, you and I." I leaned back in my chair, crossed my legs, and shifted the waist pack to one side. It would take me about three seconds, I guessed, to draw my pistol. Time enough.

"Uh-uh," he said. "No deal."

"Then you'll have to shoot me, won't you—or do you think you could get my clothes off by force?"

"Not without makin' too much noise," he blustered.

"You're right about the noise."

"I tell you the story and then you'll take off your clothes?"

I nodded solemnly. "And frankly, I expect to get the better part of the deal. Sit down, why don't you? Get comfortable."

He looked at me a long time, suspicious, then sat down on the edge of the couch, a coffee table between us, and a gun.

"It's like this," he began.

Twenty-eight

"I told you I used to live here, when I was a kid. Right?"

"Right."

He nodded. "I just came back on account of I didn't have anything better I wanted to do. So while I was hangin' out at my old man's, I thought maybe I'd try to write a book—about my life, you know? I'd thought about it before, but never had the time. But I've been a lot of places and seen and done a lot of interesting stuff—more than most people, probably—so I figured it would be easy. Except it wasn't. When I finally got down to it, I didn't even know where to start."

He laughed, aggravated. "So I kind of dropped that idea for a while. Then I got the idea of writing a mystery—a murder mystery. I figured they'd be easy to write on account of they start when somebody gets murdered and then somebody else tries to figure out who done it and why and when he does, you're done. And I figured I could put in a lot of the stuff I'd done and heard about in my life, to make it longer and more interesting. It sounded like an easy way to pick up a few bucks. You know what I was gonna call it, Peggy?"

"What?"

His crooked teeth flickered briefly in the shadowy room. *"Nobody Done It.* Get it? Nobody?"

I told him I got it and asked him what it was going to be about.

"A guy who can't find anything to do with his life that wouldn't be stupid. See, he starts out thinking that's not what life's supposed to be—stupid, I mean—on account of if it is, what's the point?" He paused a moment, as if waiting for my answer. When I didn't say anything, he added, "Anyway, that's what the dumb jerk starts out thinking. Hey, you want a Coke? Dana left Coke in the fridge." He was holding the pistol in his lap, absently fiddling with it.

"You go ahead," I said. "I'm fine."

He stared at me uncertainly again, then got up and went into the kitchen, never taking his eyes off me, and got himself a Coke from the refrigerator.

"This is weird, you know," he said with a nervous laugh when he returned, "talking to you like this."

I said I thought so too.

He popped the can and took a big swallow. "Anyway, I was gonna make Nobody the murderer. See, he kills somebody—sort of by accident the way I killed Dana. And then this other guy tries to catch him, some kind of real uptight guy who maybe doesn't believe in truth and justice, he's just doing his job, okay?"

"Or maybe Nobody's conscience starts to eat away at him until he finally turns himself in," I suggested.

"Oh, yeah," Jason said with a little smile, "I read *Crime and Punishment* too. Miss Stevens, my twelfth-grade English teacher, conned the class into trying to read it by claiming it was a good detective story. It didn't take anybody very long to figure out she was lyin'. I even figured out she hadn't read it herself. I read it, though, and as I was reading it, I was thinking: Jeez, all this fuss over the murder of one old lady! Cartoons I was watchin' Sunday mornings had more murders in 'em than that!''

He took another quick slug of Coke. "Anyhow, I couldn't think of a reason why Nobody would kill anybody. I thought that maybe, if I made the victim a rich businessman, he could've screwed Nobody in a deal or something, but I didn't know enough about business and I didn't want to waste a lot of time learning about it either. Besides, if the businessman had screwed Nobody some way, Nobody wouldn't care, really. Nobody didn't care that much about anything.''

"But you said he killed somebody by accident," I reminded him. "So he didn't really need a motive."

"Yeah, but *why?*" Jason asked, looking as though he wanted to tear his hair. "I mean, you've gotta have a reason for killin' somebody even by accident, don't you? Unless it's a hit 'n run, and who'd pay money to read a book about a hit 'n run accident? Nobody didn't want nothin' bad enough to even *quarrel* over, much less kill 'em for! Maybe he could kill somebody in a fight—like, they were drunk in a bar or something—but then I had to think of the situation of the detective who was going to try to find him. Why would he bother? Why would he waste time trying to figure out who killed somebody in a bar fight?''

"Maybe your detective felt he was somehow responsible for the victim's murder," I suggested.

He glanced at me and smiled. "Guilt, you mean? What's that?"

"Well, then how about personal responsibility?"

"Yeah, right! That's all we got left, ain't it? 'Random acts of kindness.' That's the scariest thought of all!''

He drained the can of pop, put it down on the coffee table between us, wiped his mouth. "I told you about Tolliver," he went on, "a guy I knew in Mexico, right?".

"I remember," I said. "You told me Dana's murder was his fault. Or God's."

Jason didn't look as though he'd heard me. "You didn't want to mess with Tolliver, especially when he was drinkin'. But sometimes you just couldn't get out of his way. And if he decided it was your turn to be his buddy, look out! 'Cause no matter how hard you tried, sooner or later you were going to piss him off, either by agreeing with him too slow or too fast.

"He told me he once killed a guy just 'cause he didn't like the way the guy always smiled when Tolliver frowned at him. I believed him—I saw Tolliver almost kill a couple of guys, in fights. He never knew when to stop, once he got goin'.

"I pissed him off one time and before I knew it he had his knife at my throat. Right here—on my Adam's apple, the point digging in. I could feel the blood dribbling down onto my T-shirt and I looked into his eyes and I knew he was gonna kill me. I smiled a huge shit-eating smile and I screamed, 'Don't, Tolliver!' and then I remembered how he'd killed a guy for smiling like that. You know what happened next, Peggy?"

He waited until I'd asked him what happened next.

"What happened next was, he didn't kill me!" Jason laughed, shaking his head in disbelief. "He just wiped his knife off on my shirt and he said, 'Your blood's on it anyway, so I might as well use it instead of ruinin' mine too.' That's where I got the line I used on you in your car, remember?" His eyes narrowed suddenly. "How come you're lookin' so comfortable?"

"I enjoy listening to stories," I said.

"Yeah, well, anyway, another time Tolliver made

me go out with him in a sailboat, a catamaran, and we're out there in the ocean and he's steerin' and I'm hikin' out—you know, leaning way out for balance—but I'm not too good at it and the goddamn boat flips over. All of a sudden we're treading water. He shouts that it's my fault and he's gonna drown me, and he starts swimming towards me. I start swimming to shore as hard as I can, but I know I don't stand a chance 'cause Tolliver's a good swimmer—he's the best! So I know I'm dead.

"But somehow I make it to shore anyway. I'm winded and I got no strength left; I know I'm dead and I'm cryin' about it—bawlin' like a baby! I look back, expectin' to see ol' Tolliver right there behind me—you know the way you look back in a nightmare and you can't run?"

Jason stared at me, his eyes wide and glowing in the moonlit room. He looked as though he was hearing the story for the first time himself or reliving it.

"Tolliver ain't there, Peggy," he whispered. "The ocean's empty except for the cat way out. I can just see one of the pontoons and a piece of the sail—but no Tolliver. No Tolliver. He drowned, Peggy. Got a cramp, I guess, and drowned. He would've killed me for sure if he hadn't drowned."

He looked at me, waited for me to say something.

"It was a miracle, right?" he asked, when I didn't. "Another random act of kindness on God's part. Right?"

Keeping his eyes on me, he went to the refrigerator again, got another Coke, and returned to the couch.

"I went back to the place we was stayin' at," he went on, "and took Tolliver's stuff—his driver's license and his money too—and left my own stuff in its place. We looked sort of alike, me and Tolliver, which was why he liked me. We had the same color eyes and hair and we both had beards. I never really thought I'd get away with it, but so what? I just thought it would be fun to be dead for a while—but not really, you know?"

He swallowed some Coke, glanced sharply at me, then shrugged and sank back into the couch. "So you can see, Peggy, it was Tolliver who's to blame for Dana's death, even though by the time I met her he was lyin' on the ocean floor, the meat cleaned off his bones by hungry fishes. If he'd killed me like he was supposed to—twice—she'd be alive and workin' across the lake in the Atwood Lab, or here where we are now, safe and sound." He glanced around Dana's living room as if to make sure she really wasn't there. "It was either Tolliver's fault or God's," he concluded. "You can take your pick."

"There's a third way of looking at it," I said. "Tolliver—or God—only made it possible for you to meet Dana. What you did then was up to you."

Jason started to get angry, the way some people do when you bring up personal responsibility—which isn't the same as "random acts of kindness" at all—but before he could open his mouth to say anything, I said, "You were telling me about your struggle to write a mystery."

"Yeah, right." He seemed glad to change the subject. He took a deep breath and began again: "So anyway, I was gonna write this murder mystery and have Nobody kill somebody. I never did figure out why, but I figured when I got to the end and then let it sit a while, the reason would come to me." He laughed, exasperated. "I mean, here's this dead body—there's gotta be a reason for it, right?"

I nodded encouragingly. "You said you were having trouble choosing a victim."

"Yeah, I kept goin' round and round about that. At first I thought I'd make it a kid, on account of I figured if it was a kid got murdered, readers would think it was a serious book and not just for fun. But I couldn't do it; I wasn't ready to kill a kid my first time out.

"So then I thought I'd play it safe and make it somebody boring the reader wouldn't care about—a dentist, maybe. But I couldn't care about somebody like that either, so how could I make my detective care? And if the detective did care, I wouldn't have enough respect for him to write the book!"

"And if the victim was sympathetic or interesting, you didn't want to kill him at all, is that right, Jason?" I asked.

"Yeah, that's right." He shook his head, reliving his creative struggles. "So then I decided the victim should be a woman. You can care a lot more about a woman than about a dentist, but not the same way you care about a kid."

"You could make a dentist interesting if you tried," I said.

"I suppose. But what would the motive for killin' him be? He stole the killer's girl? Is that a reason to kill anybody? I couldn't get interested in hunting down a guy who'd kill somebody because he stole his girl!

"And that was what stopped me when I tried to make the victim a woman too: it was her boyfriend did it on account of she dumped him. But you don't kill a woman because she dumps you; you send her flowers!"

He stopped and looked me in the eye. "The thing

is, Peggy," he went on, "I couldn't find any reason why anybody I'd respect would kill anybody, unless maybe it was to save an innocent person's life. But then it wouldn't really be murder, would it? And the reader wouldn't want the detective to catch the killer in that case either."

"So what did you do?"

"Gave up." He stared down at the Coke can in his hand for a few seconds, then slowly began to squeeze it out of shape. "I even screwed up tryin' to write a mystery," he added, shaking his head in dismay.

I started laughing.

He glanced up, startled. "What's so funny?"

"You, Jason! You can't think of a good reason why anybody would want to commit murder, and yet you want me to think you've done it!"

"I never said I was a murderer! Dana's death was an accident."

"No, it was murder—cold-blooded murder."

"You just said—"

"I said *you* didn't kill Dana."

"That's bullshit. I did."

"Prove it! How'd you do it?"

He looked pained, shook his head. "I don't want to live it all over again, Peggy. It's too horrible. I'll never forget—"

"You don't want to live it all over again because you can't. You didn't do it."

"The hell I—"

"I said prove it!"

"All right! Like I told you before, Dana pissed me off. You'd told her about me, so she was ready for me and she laughed at me, told me to beat it. I didn't, so she took my tape recorder—just snatched it away from me! So I had to stand out there in the cold and wait for her—and it seemed like forever!

But then she came back out and I went up to her—
we were at the top of the steps—and I asked her
nicely to *please* give me back my tape recorder. She
shoved me out of her way, Peggy, like I was
invisible—nobody! So I went after her and hit her."

"With what?"

"I told you before, with a rock from the lake."

"Then what?"

"That's it. Like I told you, she fell. I didn't mean
to hit her that hard, but I was mad."

"Describe it for me, Jason. Exactly how you did
it."

"She shoved me out of her way and started down
the steps," he said, speaking with exaggerated slowness, as if to a child, "so I reached into my pocket
and took out the rock and hit her and she just went
down headfirst and landed on her face. She didn't
even say anything. I don't think she knew what hit
her, Peggy. I was really scared, but I grabbed her
purse, thinkin' the tape recorder was in it, and ran
away. I didn't know she was dead!"

"You had the rock in your pocket? Why?"

"I dunno," he said, shrugging. "I just picked it up
on the shore somewhere, I don't know why."

I shook my head. "Dana was hit at least twice,
Jason, once the way you describe it and once or
twice more after she'd fallen. It's possible you could
have hit her the first time, although I don't think
you did: you're not the type. You've admitted it
yourself—you don't want anything badly enough.
You didn't give that much of a damn about the tape
recorder, which you probably stole anyway. But
even if you'd hit her the first time, you didn't hit her
again. I could see it on your face when I told you,
Jason: you didn't know she was hit more than
once."

"You're lying! You're just tryin' to trick me."

"Look at me, Jason. Do I look like I'm lying?"

"Okay, so maybe I did hit her again after I knocked her down. I guess I did. I was seein' red and I sort of blanked out and—"

"Stop it! Who was waiting for her on the steps with the rock, ready to kill her when she came out of the hospital? Who, Jason?"

His shoulders sagged. "I don't know. I don't know, Peggy. She was dead when I got to her. I'd been waiting for her—I'd seen her coming and going before, so I knew she lived on the lake somewhere and had to come down those steps sooner or later to go home. Then I had to take a leak, so I went into the bushes and when I came back to the steps, I heard her voice and somebody else's—a guy's. They were arguin' and then Dana starts to scream and—"

"Who killed her, damn you?"

"I'm tellin' the truth, Peggy! Honest!"

"No, you're not. If a stranger had killed her, you wouldn't have played jokes with her death the way you've been playing jokes with Dana's for over two weeks. You're not that cruel, Jason. You've been tormenting me to mislead the police. You're protecting somebody. Why, I don't know. But you've failed at that too, because you're just not nasty enough!"

Something flickered in his eyes. "I told you," he repeated, "I don't know who killed her. I didn't recognize him."

"Him?"

"Yeah, him. I didn't recognize him."

I shook my head. "You'd have run up to the hospital and called the police. I know you, Jason; I know that's what you'd have done!"

He tried to laugh. "You kidding, Peggy? With my record of harassing women? They would've arrested *me* for her murder. I could see she was dead. Her eyes were open and she didn't blink when I put my hand in front of 'em. So I took her purse, thinkin' the tape recorder was in it, and ran."

"If you'd gotten close enough to see her eyes and take her purse," I said, "you'd also have seen what somebody did to her head with a rock."

His mouth opened; he tried to say something, couldn't.

"You would have called the police," I went on. "You could have done that anonymously. You wouldn't have left her lying in the rain like that, not unless you were protecting somebody. I know you, Jason," I said again. "*I know you!*"

"No, you don't! Stop sayin' that! You don't know who I am at all—nobody does!" He sat there a moment, his eyes jumping around the room as though searching for something else to say to convince me that one of his stories was true. Then he got up suddenly. I got up too.

"Stay where you are," he said, edging toward the front door, the pistol pointed at me. "I'm leaving now. I've told you the truth. I don't know who killed Dana."

"You're going?" I said. "Aren't you forgetting something?"

"What?"

"I haven't taken off my clothes for you yet, Jason. Don't you see how soft the moonlight is in Dana's house now?"

"I'm not in the mood anymore," he said. "I like it better when a woman puts up a fight."

"You're not going anywhere," I said, and took a step toward him.

He backed toward the door, tried to steady the gun. "Stay there, dammit! I don't want to shoot you, Peggy."

I took another step toward him and he took

another step back. His high forehead was shiny with sweat.

"I'll shoot you in the kneecap," he said.

"No, you won't. That would cripple me for life and hurt like hell besides. Your conscience won't let you do a thing like that. Jason, listen to me: I'm sorry, but you're not capable of cold-blooded murder."

I took another step, hoping I knew what I was talking about, but stopped when I saw his knuckle turning white on the trigger. We were too close now for him to miss if the gun went off.

"But someone you know isn't like you," I went on, feeling the sweat start to trickle down my sides, "someone who killed Dana Michaels in cold blood and has killed somebody else too—in California. Did you know that, Jason?"

"In California?" He looked frightened. "Who?"

"A man named Peter Watson, whose only crime was that he once caught Charlie Atwood cheating on his research and tried to get Charlie's mother to do something about it. He was a friend of Dana's. Did you know you were protecting a double murderer?"

He was staring at me, through me, at something terrible he was seeing that I couldn't see yet.

"Who, Jason? Was it Barry Russell, Dana's office mate?" I watched his eyes. They didn't react to that.

"Millard Pyles?"

"Stop," he said. He'd reached the door and was groping behind him for the knob.

"How about Doctor Charlie—the sainted Doctor J's son?"

"*I said stop!*"

And then I got it.

He knew I'd got it too, could see it in my

expression. His sweaty face contorted in agony and he screamed, "Don't say it! Don't say it, Peggy!"

But I said it anyway. "Jason," I said. "Doctor J's son."

"Oh, shit, oh, shit! Why'd you say it? I'm gonna *have* to kill you now!"

"To protect somebody who's murdered two people in cold blood?"

He stared at me wild-eyed for a moment. Then the pistol steadied and the two of us stood there a long time, our lives balanced on the gun between us. Then he said "Oh, shit!" again and let the arm holding the pistol fall to his side. "I'm a fuckup at this too."

A soft voice behind me said, "You're a very clever woman, Miss O'Neill."

Twenty-nine

"Aunt Lorraine!" Jason cried. What're you doing here?"

"Making sure everything went the way I told you it had to, Mark."

"You said you didn't mean to kill Dana. You said it was an accident."

"I had to kill her," she said, as she came down the stairs from the second floor. "I didn't know what else to do. She was going to destroy your family— your mother, your brother—and everything they'd built together. I had to do it—and I had to do it when I did it. It was Dana Michaels's own fault."

"Peggy says you killed somebody else too, some-body—"

"I heard what she said, but she's lying. Nobody connected with *us* was killed in California, Mark. She's trying to get you off your guard so she can take your gun away and put you in jail. She just wants to be a hero."

"Ask her where she was on Friday, Jason," I said, "the day Peter Watson was killed."

He looked puzzled. "She was at work," he said. "Weren't you, Aunt Lorraine?"

"Of course I was, Mark."

"Your mother was upset about Lorraine being away from the office on Friday," I said. "She called in sick, then flew out to California and killed Watson." I didn't know this for sure, of course, but it seemed plausible—and it got Jason's attention. Mark Junior would always be Jason to me. "You could easily check it, Jason," I added. "Call your mother or your brother."

"I can't do that," he said. "They think I'm dead—they have to go on thinking I'm dead."

"And Jason's alive."

"Yes!"

I looked at Lorraine. "But the police know about Watson now, and they know about his connection to Dana. How are you going to blame his murder on Jason?"

"Peter Watson's death was a suicide," she said calmly. "He killed himself with one of the drugs they use to dispose of animals. When you're found here, dead, with 'Jason's' fingerprints all over the murder weapon, the police'll think he finally got you."

I turned to Jason. "Nobody but Watson's killer—and maybe the police in Davis by now—could know how Watson died."

He turned slowly to Lorraine. "You can't kill Peggy, Aunt Lorraine," he said.

"Don't be silly," she said. "I have to. But you don't need to stay, Mark; you've done your part. I can take care of the rest myself. You just go back to the house and wait for me."

"No!"

"Mark!" she said. "We can't let this prying woman live. If she does, she'll destroy your mother and your brother, just as Dana Michaels was going to do."

"Is that true, Peggy?"

"Your mother and brother haven't killed any-body," I told him. "The only person who'll be destroyed is Lorraine, who's committed two murders in cold blood and wants you to be her accomplice in a third.''

"I only killed them for your *family*, Mark!" she said.

He looked from her to me, then back at her. "But did you ask them first, Aunt Lorraine? Maybe they wouldn't have *wanted* you to kill them."

She stared at him for a long moment, and I thought I saw a trace of bleak amusement on her face. "Go home, Mark," she said sternly. "Now."

"No! You can't kill Peggy—I won't let you!" He gave her a big smile. "C'mon, now, Aunt Lorraine, we'll think of some—" He started toward her, the pistol he was holding at his side.

She shot him as I dived over the couch. She fired again and the wall where I'd been standing exploded, showering me with plaster as I hit the floor. I rolled onto my back, up against the back of the couch, ripped open Ginny's waist pack and yanked out my service revolver.

Lorraine's gun went off again and a bullet tore through the couch above my head. I screamed. A few seconds went by. I lay there holding my breath, staring up at the ceiling and waiting for another shot, knowing that I might not hear it if she aimed any lower than the last time. The only sounds in the room were Jason's labored breathing.

Then I felt more than heard Lorraine kneel on the couch. I lay there, staring up, waiting. After a moment, her head came into view over the back, and as it did, I put the mouth of my pistol against her throat, sat up, and told her not to move.

The glare she gave me through her sequined glasses was terrible to look at, but she did as I said.

Thirty

Everybody was mad at me.

"You risked your life for an old *dog!*" Lillian said, cradling the animal in question in her arms while averting her face to avoid his breath. "If Rufus could speak, he'd be mad at you too!"

"I never would've met Jason if I hadn't been helping to save that miserable animal's life!" I protested indignantly. "How could I just stand by and let Jason kill him after all the trouble he caused me?"

Gary didn't think that was funny. "You never thought the dog was in any danger, Peggy—or your life either," he said. "You thought you knew Jason."

"Turned out I did," I said defensively.

"You could've been wrong." He stomped away.

Ginny Raines, when she heard about it, blamed it on *Gaslight*, the movie we'd seen the night Dana Michaels was killed. "But in the movie," she pointed out, "the killer was tied to a chair when Bergman asked to be alone with him, you damned fool!"

"Jason wasn't a killer," I pointed out.

"You couldn't know that!"

A week later, Buck invited me to dinner at the outrageously expensive restaurant he currently favors, which meant I got to wear the emerald green dress I'd found at a consignment shop. It goes with the gold necklace and earrings my Aunt Tess brought back for me from Italy last year. I like to dress up sometimes.

It was Buck's treat, which was a good thing, since I wouldn't shell out that much money for so little food, although it was beautifully arranged on the plate. Buck refuses to talk about murder during dinner, but after we'd finished, as he sniffed cognac, he said, "Scheherazade told stories to postpone her death. You conned a man you had every reason to think was a killer into telling *you* a story."

"And now it's your turn," I said, stirring my cappuccino with a finger to offend him.

"Well," he began, "as you guessed, Dana came here to destroy the Atwood Lab, either to avenge Peter Watson, whom she'd loved, or because he'd told her how Charles Atwood had been faking the results of the lab's research to the detriment of animals."

"Or both," I said. "I don't think Dana made fine distinctions between the people she loved and animals."

"If you say so, Peggy. In any case, what she found was a misuse of federal money on a grand scale that was a far more serious crime than what she'd come looking for."

"The Atwoods were embezzling money?"

"That's not how they'd put it," he said. "You see, Peggy, Julia Atwood had been one of the giants in her field, but nobody stays on top forever. As a scientist, she probably knew that, but apparently she didn't think the laws of nature applied to her. She didn't think most laws applied to her," he added.

He stared down into his cognac bowl for a moment before going on. "She wanted one more triumph, and she did what she thought she had to do to achieve it. She believed she could develop a vaccine against HIV in animals that would set the veterinary medical community on its ear, but nobody—not the University, the federal government, or the drug companies—believed in her strongly enough to give her the financial support she needed to pursue it. So she simply plundered another federal grant she had and used the money for her personal project. That's a crime, one that Millard Pyles and Lorraine Cullin were her accomplices in. She couldn't have done it without their knowledge and help."

"How'd they think they could get away with it?"

He shrugged. "Because they'd got away with it before, according to Pyles, who's spilling his guts. Taking from one project to pay for another happens all the time in scientific research. I mean, if you order an expensive computer, say, for one project you're working on that doesn't require an expensive computer, and use it for another project, who'll ever find out? Or if you pay a research assistant from funds earmarked for one project but use her or him for another project, who'll ever know? The federal government can't afford to send experts around the country checking to make sure all the money it gives away is being used appropriately."

"That's what they need whistle-blowers for," I said.

"Right. But who's going to blow the whistle after seeing what happens to the careers of men like Peter Watson?"

"Doctor Atwood would probably have gotten away with it," I said, "if Dana Michaels hadn't come looking for dirt and, thanks to Watson, known where to look. How much money are we talking about?"

"It's too early to say," Buck replied, "but the

University auditors, with federal regulators breathing down their necks to make sure they don't overlook anything—''

''Or sweep it under a rug.''

''—think that over the past four or five years the Atwoods have misused at least a million and a half dollars in federal money.''

''I wonder if they would have murdered Dana to keep it from coming out,'' I said, ''or stopped Lorraine from murdering her if she'd given them the chance.''

''She wouldn't have given them the chance, of course,'' Buck said, ''since she killed Dana Michaels to save her own skin, not theirs.''

She'd started a dummy company that she called Veterinary Consultants, Inc., through which she stole money from the Atwood Lab. Dana, while going through the lab's files late at night looking for evidence of misuse of funds, came across records of money billed to Veterinary Consultants for services she knew that she or other researchers had done as a regular part of their duties. Her suspicions must have been further aroused when she couldn't find Veterinary Consultants in the phone book. So she decided to play detective.

''She called the University's Accounts Payable Office,'' Buck said, ''and told the clerk who answered that an officer from Veterinary Consultants had complained that they hadn't been paid for something they'd done. She asked the clerk to verify that a check had been issued. The clerk looked it up and told Dana that a check had been issued and had cleared the University's bank four days later. Dana asked her to send her a copy of the check.''

''Let me guess,'' I said. ''The check was endorsed by Lorraine.''

"Right."

"How'd she find out Dana was on to her?"

"The day she killed Dana, Lorraine had to call Accounts Payable herself, and the clerk—being the helpful type—asked her if she'd resolved the dispute with Veterinary Consultants. That must have given Lorraine the shock of her life, of course, since she *was* Veterinary Consultants. But she recovered sufficiently to ask the clerk where she'd sent the copy of the check. The clerk gave her Dana's name and office address."

"And that was Dana's death warrant."

"Yes. Lorraine didn't know Dana was out to destroy the lab itself; she only knew she had evidence that would destroy her. And she had nobody to talk to about it either, of course. She couldn't go to Doctor Atwood and tell her, since Atwood would hardly look with sympathy on her embezzling from the lab."

"'The temple,'" I muttered.

"So when she heard that Dana was leaving to go home early that night, she slipped out one of the hospital's back exits, waited for her on the steps, and killed her. She couldn't think of any other way to avoid a long prison term."

"She couldn't afford the kind of lawyers the Atwoods have," I said. "Given her popularity in the state, it's unlikely Doctor J will spend any time in jail, although she'll probably lose her job at the U." The University had already begun the process of stripping both Atwoods of tenure and firing them to prove how capable it was of policing itself.

"I suppose Jason," I went on, "off somewhere taking a leak, as he told me, heard the noise of Dana being killed and went up the steps to investigate. He found his dear Aunt Lorraine standing over her body. It must have been quite a recognition scene. Did she have any idea that my Jason was her Mark Dodson Jr.?"

Buck shook his head. "None. He'd been hanging around the Ag Campus for about a week, pestering women, living in one of those storage buildings, and trying to decide if he wanted to let his mother and brother know he was alive. When he told her who he was, Lorraine said she'd killed Dana by accident and promised to explain it to him at her place later that night. Then she used Dana's keys to get into her house and look for anything else of an incriminating nature against her.

"What she found instead was the evidence Dana had collected to use against Julia Atwood. It was right out in the open, since Dana had seen no reason to hide it. Lorraine collected it all and showed it to Jason later. Since he didn't know Lorraine was involved in anything criminal herself, he let her convince him she'd killed Dana solely to save his family.

"Lorraine's next shock," Buck went on, "came when Peter Watson called to find out why he hadn't heard from Dana. Lorraine had no idea they'd been friends. Afraid of what he'd do once he found out about Dana's death, and afraid Dana might have told him some of the things she'd found, she flew out to Davis and killed him, using one of the poisons available in the Atwood Lab. Watson didn't put up any struggle: he was drunk. Lorraine doesn't think he even recognized her."

I sat back in my chair and looked around the restaurant at the elegantly clad people, their heads bent reverently over their food, and wondered what they'd make of the story I'd just heard.

Jason's story of Tolliver and the catamaran seemed to be true, as far as Buck had been able to find out. Tolliver was a kid pretty much like Jason, from someplace in Utah.

"After Tolliver drowned," Buck said, "and we'll probably never know if it was an accident—"

"It was, Buck," I said. "Jason's no killer."

He just smiled. "As I say, after Tolliver drowned, Jason switched identities with him and spent the next six years bumming around Mexico and this country. He returned here and hung around the University for a few days, not sure what he wanted to do—make contact with his mother and brother again or not."

"And so Jason the reprobate finally found a purpose in life," I said, "to save his family and Aunt Lorraine, his dear surrogate mom, by convincing you he was Dana's killer. Well, why not? He thought he was a complete loser anyway. He'd even failed at trying to write a murder mystery!"

Buck swirled cognac, sniffed fumes. After a minute, he glanced up at me and said quietly, "But he did succeed at something, Peggy."

"Yeah," I said. "Making my life hell for a couple of weeks."

"That too. But he also kept you alive."

"He did what?" I said, shocked.

My reaction pleased Buck. He thinks I'm too smug. "Lorraine tried to talk him into killing you," he said. "She thought it would add authenticity to the theory that Jason was the man we were looking for. He refused, said he'd do it his way, by tormenting you and then leaving town."

"He told you this?"

He nodded, smiling sadly. "And Lorraine confirmed it. She's proud of him. It was the first time she ever remembered him standing up for himself."

I just shook my head, remembering how calmly she'd shot him in Dana's house.

Buck called for the check and paid it with a piece of plastic that glittered, and then we walked out into the crisp early April night. As we were waiting for a uniformed valet to fetch his car, Buck said, "It's ironic, isn't it? You decided you might be able to help us find Jason because Dana told her office mate she thought she knew him from somewhere. If it hadn't been for that, you wouldn't have gotten involved."

"Probably not," I agreed, grinning because I had a small surprise for him too, and if he hadn't brought the subject up, I would have.

"But she was mistaken, wasn't she?" he went on. "She didn't know him at all."

"That bothered me," I said. "You know how I hate loose ends. Yesterday, it finally occurred to me to call Jason's father in Davis and ask him if he had photographs of his long-lost son in his home or office—somewhere where Dana might have seen them."

"I should have thought of that!" Buck said, annoyed with himself.

I smiled smugly. "He had a couple of snapshots in frames in his office, where Dana would have seen them many times. I asked him why he kept them there, and he said he'd be damned if he knew, since the kid had never been anything but trouble."

"I wonder what Jason would make of that," Buck said, as his car pulled up. "Tolliver, or God?"

I shrugged indifferently, got into the car on the passenger side as Buck tipped the valet.

"I suppose you could ask him," he said, as we drove away from the restaurant.

"Ask Jason?"

"He wants you to visit him at the hospital.

He thinks you owe it to him, since he didn't kill you.''

Staring out into the night, I thought about it for a few seconds, then shook my head. ''People shouldn't expect rewards for not killing you,'' I said, and changed the subject.

Meet Peggy O'Neill
A Campus Cop With a Ph.D. in Murder

"A 'Must Read' for fans of Sue Grafton"
Alfred Hitchcock Mystery Magazine

Exciting Mysteries by M.D. Lake

ONCE UPON A CRIME 77520-4/$5.50 US/$7.50 Can

AMENDS FOR MURDER 75865-2/$4.99 US/$6.99 Can

COLD COMFORT 76032-0/$4.99 US/ $6.99 Can

POISONED IVY 76573-X/$5.50 US/$7.50 Can

A GIFT FOR MURDER 76855-0/$4.50 US/$5.50 Can

MURDER BY MAIL 76856-9/$4.99 US/$5.99 Can

GRAVE CHOICES 77521-2/$4.99 US/$6.99 Can

Explore Uncharted Terrains of Mystery with *Anna Pigeon, Parks Ranger* by

NEVADA BARR

TRACK OF THE CAT

72164-3/$4.99 US/$5.99 Can

National parks ranger Anna Pigeon must hunt down the killer of a fellow ranger in the Southwestern wilderness—and it looks as if the trail might lead her to a two-legged beast.

A SUPERIOR DEATH

72362-X/$4.99 US/$6.99 Can

Anna must leave the serene backcountry to investigate a fresh corpse found on a submerged shipwreck at the bottom of Lake Superior—how did it get there, and, more important, who put it there?

ILL WIND

72363-8/$5.99 US/$7.99 Can

An overwhelming number of medical emergencies and two unexplained deaths transforms Colorado's Mesa Verde National Park into a murderous puzzle Anna must quickly solve.

⇒JILL CHURCHILL⇐

"JANE JEFFREY IS IRRESISTIBLE!"
Alfred Hitchcock's Mystery Magazine

Delightful Mysteries Featuring
Suburban Mom Jane Jeffry

GRIME AND PUNISHMENT
76400-8/$4.99 US/$6.99 CAN

A FAREWELL TO YARNS
76399-0/$5.50 US/$7.50 CAN

A QUICHE BEFORE DYING
76932-8/$4.99 US/$6.99 CAN

THE CLASS MENAGERIE
77380-5/$4.99 US/$5.99 CAN

A KNIFE TO REMEMBER
77381-3/$5.99 US/$7.99 CAN

FROM HERE TO PATERNITY
77715-0/$5.99 US/$7.99 CAN

Coming Soon
SILENCE OF THE HAMS
77716-9/$5.99 US/$7.99 CAN